THE
IRONIES
of LIFE

To Terri

R. Pauli

11-16-2023

THE
IRONIES
of LIFE

Richard Paullin

TATE PUBLISHING
AND ENTERPRISES, LLC

Published by Tate Publishing & Enterprises, LLC
127 E. Trade Center Terrace | Mustang, Oklahoma 73064 USA
1.888.361.9473 | www.tatepublishing.com

Tate Publishing is committed to excellence in the publishing industry. The company reflects the philosophy established by the founders, based on Psalm 68:11,
"The Lord gave the word and great was the company of those who published it."

Published in the United States of America

ISBN: 978-1-62746-640-0
1. Fiction / General
2. Fiction / Coming Of Age
13.10.23

Though we travel the world over
To find the beautiful
We must carry it with us
Or we will not find it

—Ralph Waldo Emerson

We each give more to others than we ever know.

—Richard Paullin

CHAPTER 1

At the age of twenty-eight, Jane decided it was time she found out what was on the other side of the Hudson River. She packed her suitcases, loaded them in her red Subaru Outback she had christened Subie, and headed out to see America. She saw many interesting sights during her month-long travels, but besides seeing America, she wanted America to see her, namely its men, a species with whom she had never gained acceptance in New York City or its immediate environs.

She hoped a change of scenery would help her meet a man—someone she could care about, someone she could love. She didn't care what he looked like. She expected him to be bald and short, with not too big a potbelly. She'd given up on Prince Charming years ago.

She had no illusions about herself. She knew she was plain. She had a broad forehead, eyes a bit too close, a hawkish nose, thin lips, and a smallish mouth. She'd heard plain Jane jokes for as long as she could remember. She'd been hurt by cruel jokes and felt the sting of the opposite sex's rejection so many times she had lost count.

She referred to this as her desperation trip. If she didn't meet a man west of the Hudson, she'd remain a virgin the rest of her life. She would devote her energy to teaching special education students who had given her much happiness and fulfillment for the last three years. That would be her life, helping those who needed it most.

Men had approached her during her travels, but she realized all they wanted to know was why she had driven so far alone. The main attraction seemed to be her New York license plate. They couldn't take their eyes from it as they asked questions about New York—the gruesome murders, the mafia, the drug gangs, but not a single question about her. They glanced in her direction several times as they asked questions, then with western politeness say, "Nice talkin' to ya, ma'am," touch the brim of their hat with their right index finger and walk away. Jane was convinced she would die a virgin.

Her trip was nearing its end. Her last stop was Roswell, New Mexico. She had heard about the museums that had indisputable evidence flying saucers existed along with the remains of aliens from some other planet. She didn't believe in flying saucers or extraterrestrials, but she was curious to have a look-see at the museums that insisted on their existence.

She arrived in Roswell before noon, parked Subie in a lot, and started down the main drag. The honky-tonk atmosphere of the town destroyed the credibility of the flying saucer theory in her estimation, but she knew her students would be fascinated by the July 3, 1947, crash of a flying saucer that had brought those alien bodies to Earth.

She took pictures of the outsides of the museums, stuffed as many pamphlets as she could into her purse, and bought several expensive books about the July 3 crash as well as the mysterious Area 51 where the government supposedly has hidden alien bodies since 1947. She knew Area 51 would fascinate her students. She smiled at the thought she had found something that would interest them.

Several hours later she had taken all the pictures she cared to, seen enough alien museums to last a lifetime, and heard enough stories about flying saucers and the existence of aliens from other planets to give her enough material to share with her students for the months to come. Her grumbling stomach told her it was time to eat. When she saw long lines at every decent restaurant in town, she decided to skip lunch, head north on US 285 till she hit I-40, and begin the long drive back to New York.

An hour north of Roswell, the rays of the afternoon sun formed a sharp contrast between the light of day and the dark of the gathering storm. Jane watched as the dark clouds steadily eclipsed the sun. When the eclipse had reached its greenish zenith, an eerie darkness descended upon the landscape. Headlights from oncoming traffic reflected off the two rubber worn tracks etched in the asphalt highway formed by countless cars that had traversed it for countless years.

Crack! The sudden sharp noise startled her. She flinched backward in the seat and let out a loud "Whoa!" She heard a second crack then a third. A fourth and a fifth raindrop exploded against the windshield.

She put the window down. She wanted to feel these raindrops. She extended her arm through the open space and flattened the palm of her left hand into the wind hoping to capture one. She didn't have long to wait. With razorblade sharpness, one struck the softness of her palm. "Ouch," she yelled as she withdrew her hand into the safety of the car and closed the window.

A chunk of ice smashed into the windshield followed by another and another. They fell so fast they fused together from the heat of the road and formed a sheet of ice covering the highway. An oncoming car skidded off the icy highway and crashed into the ditch, showering Subie with sand and gravel.

The icy pavement threw Subie into a skid. His front end rose up and shook violently. Jane heard her father's calm, reassuring voice, the voice of a much traveled New York City cabbie, telling her to take her foot off the gas, not to touch the brake, and to steer into the skid.

She did what her father told her to do. Subie slowed. His front end lowered. She could steer, but she had no idea which side of the road she was on. She put her face as close to the windshield as she could. She strained to see through the raindrops, the chunks of ice, and the blinding sea of headlights coming toward her.

A blaring horn, a sudden flash of lights on the right side, the sound of skidding tires, breaking glass, and crunching metal made her realize she was on the wrong side. A second near miss unnerved her. Her right foot shook uncontrollably. Subie jerked in rebellion when she pressed the gas pedal.

She maneuvered around cars stopped on the icy highway. All had their headlights blazing and wipers flashing back and forth, but she couldn't stop. She knew she had to keep moving. That was her father's advice: "Don't stop unless you have too."

As suddenly as the ice had appeared, it disappeared. Through the darkness, she saw an even darker swirling mass of tumbleweeds, sand, and dirt to her left. The swirling mass disappeared only to reappear a few moments later, straddling the highway directly in front of her. She slammed on the brakes. The swirling dark mass descended upon her with a roar so loud she couldn't hear her own screams. She felt Subie rock violently, heard the sounds of sand and gravel hitting him along with breaking glass. She felt the air being sucked out of her lungs. Then all was quiet.

She gasped for air. Minutes passed. She struggled to breathe, passing in and out of consciousness. Once the panic had lessened and normal breathing had returned, she peered through the cracked windshield with narrowed eyes, still gripping Subie's steering wheel with such tenacity that not even the winds of a tornado could pry it from her hands. She couldn't believe what she saw. The sun was shining and the swirling mass was disappearing into the distance.

She looked at the road ahead, a road that had disappeared under the sand, gravel, tumbleweeds, and rocks left behind by the storm. What lay before her was a road strewn with hidden obstacles. What lay behind her was ice, accidents, maybe death. After many moments of indecision, she put Subie in gear. Together they crept forward.

Subie groaned as he fought to climb the hidden rocks beneath the sand and gravel, shuddering as his undercarriage ground against the jagged, unseen obstacles. The roar of the straining engine hid the sounds of his heart being ripped apart.

Jane had no idea how far she had driven through the rock-strewn highway, but once she could see the white center line, her frayed nerves forced her to stop. She wrapped her arms around the steering wheel and collapsed into it. She was physically and emotionally drained. She desperately needed to get off the highway, but she was in middle of nowhere. She had no choice. She had to continue.

Mile after tedious mile went by with no place to stop. The sun disappeared behind dark but less threatening clouds. The temperature fell and a cold rain set in. She had worn powder blue shorts and a short sleeve white blouse since the day had started out sunny and warm. She shivered. Maybe it was the cold that made her shiver. Maybe it was fright. She couldn't be sure which. It didn't matter. She was cold and shaking.

At last she saw the sign she had been waiting for—I-40 ten miles ahead. She prayed there would be a motel. She didn't care what it looked like. She wanted to get off the highway and into a nice warm bed.

The ten miles seemed a lifetime. Night was fast approaching. Through the descending darkness, she saw bright lights ahead. Her pulse quickened. Two words in blue and red neon lights, Motel and Restaurant, stood out against the blackness of night and shimmering rain on the windshield. She saw El Satélite, words that even in her misery made her smile. It reminded her of Roswell and aliens.

She guided Subie into the motel's driveway where he coasted to a stop. She sat for a few moments, summoning up the strength to open the door. It took several tries before she managed to keep the door open long enough to swing her legs over the hump and onto the pavement. When she stood, her legs buckled. She felt the coldness of the wet pavement against her body and heard the pitter-patter of the rain as it hit the side of Subie, and that was all she remembered.

CHAPTER 2

Jane struggled to make sense of a soft knocking sound. She lay quietly, hoping whatever or whoever it was would go away. She heard the sound of a key and the soft click of an unlocking door. The bright sunlight streaming through the opening door blinded her. All she could see was a blurry figure moving toward the bed.

"Well, hello there. I see you're awake. My name is Sandi. I work here at El Satélite," she said softly as she crossed the room and stood at the foot of Jane's bed. "You gave us quite a scare last night."

"I did?" Jane mumbled.

"Yes, you did." Sandi emphasized the word *you*. "You drove in our driveway, got out of your car, and collapsed. Your car started to move backward. I was afraid it was going to roll over you. I yelled to the guys for help. Ya shudda seen 'em come a runnin'. Four of 'em. They picked you up and carried you to this room. I pulled down the covers, they put you between the sheets, and I covered you with the sheet and blanket so you'd be nice and warm and wouldn't get sick. Pepe brought in your luggage in case you needed something. The men left. I turned down the lights and left too. That's pretty much what happened except us girls, me, Rosa, and Graciela checked on you every two hours to be sure you were okay."

"I'm sorry to have caused so much trouble. I was all in but"—Jane threw back the sheet and blanket—"it's time I get up and hit the highway. I've got a long drive ahead of me."

"It wasn't any trouble. We were thankful you found us when you did. I don't think you could have driven much further, and I wouldn't advise you to hit the highway. Do you have any idea what time it is?"

"Sometime in the morning, I guess."

Sandi threw back her head and laughed. "Better try sometime in the afternoon and late afternoon at that. You've been asleep for close to a full day."

"No. I couldn't have. I just got here."

"You mean you just woke up here." Sandi's warm smile and breezy manner made Jane feel at ease. "And I imagine right about now you're plenty hungry. Am I right?"

"You must be a mind reader."

Sandi pulled her cell from a pocket, pressed a key, and said, "Graciela, please bring over the tray." She slipped the cell back into her pocket and commanded gently, "Now you slip back under those covers young lady and let us serve you late afternoon brunch in bed." Sandi's warm smile reassured Jane she wanted nothing more than to serve her brunch in bed. "Not too much, mind ya. Just a little something to give you enough strength to get dressed, walk across the parking lot to our restaurant, and eat one of our famous New Mexico steaks along with a baked potato smothered in one of Pepe's secret sauces and the best salad you've ever tasted, and for dessert pie, cake, maybe both, with a couple scoops of ice cream. Any of this sounds good to you?"

"All of it," Jane said without hesitation. "I'm gonna eat everything in sight."

"Good girl." Sandi turned at the sound of a soft knock on the open door. "Come in Graciela," she said quietly. She motioned for her to put the tray on the bed next to Jane.

"I hope you like the little things I made for you, Miss Jones."

"You know my name?"

"We all do. We were so worried about you last night that we notified our state police who notified your state police who gave us your name, address, phone number, and your parents' names, address, and phone number too. We did it as a precaution in case you needed immediate medical attention, had allergies, or drug sensitivities. I hope you don't mind. We didn't mean to pry into your personal life."

The hurt that flashed across Sandi's face assured Jane that Sandi had done what she had done out of genuine concern for her safety.

Sandi glanced at her watch. "Graciela and I must be running along. It's a little past five now—in the afternoon." Jane smiled at Sandi's joke. "Can we expect you at, say, eight o'clock for dinner?"

"Most definitely!"

"See you at eight. I'm so glad you're feeling better."

"Me too. And I'm looking forward to that steak dinner."

Sandi had no sooner closed the door than Jane attacked Graciela's creations. She had no idea what she was eating, but whatever they were, they were warm, delicious, and brought back the color to her cheeks. When she had finished, she rested, giving the food a chance to digest. Then she got up, showered, washed her hair, and made herself as presentable as she could for her eight o'clock rendezvous with a steak dinner.

Jane liked to be prompt, a trait she had inherited from her father. At eight o'clock, she opened the restaurant door and was pleased by the smells of hot bread and the sound of sizzling steaks that greeted her. "Well, come on in." She recognized Sandi's voice before she saw her. "I've been expecting you. I have a nice quiet table reserved so I can take special care of you tonight. Follow me through this tangle of tables and chairs. Ya kinda haf to know your way with the lights turned down so low." Sandi led the way to a secluded part of the restaurant. "Here we are," she said, pointing to a table set for one. "Is this all right?"

"Perfect."

"I kinda thought you might want a quieter place after all you've been through." Sandi pulled out a chair. "Please be seated," she said, sliding the chair behind Jane as she sat.

"Sandi, you don't have to go to any special trouble. You've already done so much. I appreciate your thoughtfulness more than you'll ever know."

"I'm pleased to do whatever I can to make your stay not just a pleasant one but a memorable one. I want you to relax and enjoy your dinner. I'll go get the ball ta rollin'." She turned and disappeared into the kitchen.

Now that Jane had a moment to herself, she looked at the table. The first thing she noticed was a white card with fancy gold script embossed on it. She picked it up and read By Special Invitation for Miss Jones. "Sandi, you shouldn't have," she murmured to herself.

The restaurant was nothing like she had expected. For Jane, the word restaurant meant diner with cheap Formica tabletops and butt-breaking bench seats whose springs had collapsed long ago. From the moment she had entered the dining room, she had been impressed, first by the wonderful smells and then by the ambience. She was more than surprised to see the tables were not only covered with pastel tablecloths but were decorated with delicate desert flowers in fluted vases and small lanterns that emitted a discreet amount of soft yellow light in the darkened atmosphere. She decided such fine surroundings demanded a name change. The neon sign should read Fine Dining not Restaurant.

The darkened dining room made Jane feel insecure. She never ate in expensive restaurants. She considered it a waste of money to spend so much on a single meal, but the real reason was they made her feel uncomfortable. She was a New York diner girl through and through. If she had known the word restaurant meant fine dining in New Mexico, Sandi or no Sandi, she would have stayed in her room, but here she was and here she had to stay, although every bone in her body cried out, "run, run far away as fast as you can."

The more she looked at the people in the dining room, the shabbier she felt. The men wore western hats. She had no idea how many gallons they were. All she knew was they were cowboy hats. She thought the men quite handsome in their western shirts with their ornate designs, tight fitting jeans, and pointed-toe western boots.

As for the women, they were elegant, too elegant for Jane's taste because they made her feel frumpy. Their hair perfectly styled, each one fancier than the last, their dresses, although simple in style, looked incredibly beautiful when contrasted with their flawless olive complexions, and their open shoes looked expensive with their high heels and graceful straps, but it was their makeup that made Jane feel most inferior. *These women really know how to make themselves look beautiful,* she thought to herself.

Makeup, cosmetics, whatever they were called was an area Jane had stopped investigating when she had graduated from high school. She decided they weren't for her. She thought they made her look artificial, like she was trying to be somebody she wasn't, that they made her look cheap and vulgar. Being an *unfashionista* as she proudly referred to herself, she refused to wear them, not even lipstick.

Travel can change people's opinions about many things, and as Jane sat at her table surveying the people around her, she began to rethink her position on skin color, fashion and makeup. Both the men and the women looked wonderfully healthy, so vibrant and full of life. Their gorgeous olive skin glowed in the dim light of the lanterns. She looked at the pale, lifeless white skin of her arms. For the first time in her life, she was ashamed of it, wishing it was more like the color of the people seated before her.

As for fashion, she wished she had worn a long sleeve blouse rather than the short sleeve, white one she had thrown on so she could hide her skinny arms. She was thankful the rest of her body was hidden not only by the table but by the dim light in the dining room because her knee-length, powder-blue shorts were no competition for the beautiful dresses the women wore. As for her shoes, she had bought the white tennis shoes at *Zapato Barato* (Cheap Shoe) at the mall the day before she left. They screamed cheap, but she couldn't pass up a $9.99 bargain.

Then she had a most unsettling thought, her hair—mousy brown, cut short with no particular style in mind, giving her a masculine appearance. Every day and night of her life she hadn't given her clothes or her hair a second thought but for reasons she didn't understand, tonight was different. She felt self-conscious, uncomfortable, but worst of all, inferior to the women seated in the dining room because of her blouse, her shorts, her shoes, and her hair. Sitting alone watching people eating, drinking, talking, and laughing, she concluded everything about her was wrong.

She wished Sandi would hurry and bring her dinner so she could escape this elegant world of dining and its beautiful people where she felt uncomfortable, where she knew she didn't belong. She wanted to go back to her room, get a good night's sleep, and hit the highway in the morning. As simple as it might seem, that was all she wanted. That was her life, simple and uncomplicated. That was the way she liked it, and that was the way she intended to keep it.

CHAPTER 3

"I bet you thought I'd got lost," Sandi said as she approached Jane. "That front office is somethin' else tonight. It's jumpin' like I've never seen it jump be-fore." She accented the *be* in *before* long and hard. "I brought a little libation to get you started off right. You don't have to worry. It won't make you crazy drunk. It just warms the body and stimulates the ole taste buds." She placed a small stemmed glass filled with a white liquid in front of Jane.

Jane picked up the glass and smelled the white liquid. It had a pleasing aroma. She took a small sip. It tasted light and refreshing and did what Sandi said it would do. It warmed the body. As for stimulating taste buds, they didn't need stimulation. She was hungry and ready to eat everything in sight.

Sandi returned a few minutes later. "I see you've tasted our local aperitif Cacico. It's made from the trunk of the cactus. Whataya think?"

"Delish."

"I thought you'd like it. Who da thought something so good could come from a cactus. Here's something else for you to try." Sandi placed a cup on a small plate in front of Jane. "Don't ask me about the soup. I have no idea what it is. Pepe, our chef, makes a new soup every day. I've given up trying to remember how he makes 'em. I just eat and enjoy. Bon appetit. I'll be back in a few minutes."

Jane ladled a spoonful of the soup into her mouth. It was a clear broth yet it had body and felt pleasingly warm as the liquid slipped down her throat. Sandi returned with a young man. "I thought you might like to meet the men who helped you last night."

"Yes, of course."

"This is one of them, Jimmy. He's our intern. He's nearly finished with his studies in hotel management."

"I'm pleased to meet you, Miss Jones," Jimmy said politely.

Jane looked briefly at his facial features and lowered her eyes. Years of hurt had taught her how to protect herself.

"Nice to meet you, Jimmy."

"And this is Pepe, our chef."

"How ju like sopa?" Pepe asked, more interested in the soup than anything else.

"Very much."

"*Bueno. Eez mi creación,*" he proudly proclaimed. "Ju cook, Señorita Hones?"

"Sorry, Pepe. I don't cook."

"Too bad, *mucho* too bad. Ju miss *mucho* fun. Okay. I go now. I tink your steak ready. I hope ju like. I make one way, Pepe's way. That why I no ask how ju like."

As he turned to leave, Jane said, "Thanks for my luggage."

Pepe turned and smiled. "No problema, Señorita Hones. Now to get steak."

Moments later Jane heard the sound of a steak sizzling before she saw it. A middle-aged woman placed a plate encased in a wooden frame in front of her. "Be careful. The plate is really hot," she warned.

"This is Rosa. She checked on you last night to be sure you were okay."

"Rosa. Thank you so much for watching over me."

"I'm glad it was nothing more serious than a lack of sleep. Excuse me. I've got to get back to the kitchen. Very nice to have met you, Miss Jones, now that you're awake." Sandi and Jane laughed at Rosa's joke.

"Rosa and I are going to go about our duties and let you enjoy your dinner in peace and quiet. I'll be back later to check on you."

Sandi and Rosa had no sooner turned to leave than Jane cut a small piece of the sizzling steak. From the moment she put it in her mouth, she realized she had never had a steak as good as this in her life. Sandi had lived up to her promise of a great steak, a baked potato with a delicious topping, and a most delightful salad. Each had its own distinctive taste. She had no idea why the steak, the baked potato, or the salad tasted better than any she had ever had. All she could think to do was to give praise to Pepe's way. She ate slowly, savoring each bite. She knew she would never have such a fine dinner as this for the rest of her life.

She lost track of time. It seemed only a matter of moments when she heard Sandi exclaim, "My, oh, my! You weren't kiddin'. You did eat everything in sight. Let me bring you a coffee or a tea to sip on to settle your tummy and then we'll go on to dessert from there."

"Coffee would be great."

"One coffee coming up." Sandi disappeared into the kitchen. When she reappeared she had three men with her. She set the coffee in front of Jane and said, "This is the rest of the crew that carried you to your room last night. This is Hank, our maintenance engineer. This is Diego. He's in charge of the housekeeping. And this is Aaron. He's in charge of purchasing. He bought all the things you ate tonight."

Jane looked at all three, lowered her eyes, and said, "Thank you for all you've done. My friends back in New York won't believe any of this when I tell them how wonderful you've all been."

"Our pleasure, ma'am. Those are mighty fine words of praise, and we sure appreciate 'em," Hank said looking down at Jane. "Okay, boys, I guess we'd better *vammoos* and let Miss Jones enjoy her dessert."

When Sandi returned, she brought a plate heaped with desserts. "I couldn't decide which one you'd like best, so I brought a little bit of everything."

Jane sampled the desserts, sipped her coffee from time to time, and gloried in the sweet reveries that brought to a perfect end Pepe's way. With the last bite of cheese pie and a final swallow of coffee, she noticed the dining room had emptied. *Time for me to go too*, she thought to herself, but she didn't want to leave without thanking Sandi and saying goodnight.

Moments later Sandi appeared. "I see you enjoyed our desserts." She laughed when she saw the empty plate.

"Indeed I did. They were all so good. I couldn't pick a favorite if I had to. Thank you for a wonderful dinner and for being so kind to me. I'll never forget you and the others. Now that I've got a full tummy, I think it's time for me to go back to my room and get some rest so I can be on the road bright and early in the morning."

"You can't go yet. There's one more person you've got to meet. He would never forgive me if I let you slip out now. He's the manager of El Satélite, and he's looking forward to talking to you. I've got some work to do in the office, so I can't stand guard over you. Promise you won't leave. Promise!"

Sandi's sincerity won Jane over. "Okay. I promise. I'll wait."

"He'll be along directly."

Sandi left. Jane sat in the empty dining room. She wasn't sleepy. She knew she wouldn't sleep for quite a while with such a full stomach, yet she wanted to get up and leave. She didn't want to meet any more people. She'd met enough already. She fidgeted with the napkin in her lap and waited for the manager to appear.

She heard the sound of boots clicking on the kitchen tile then muffled by the carpet in the dining room. She turned and saw a short, heavy-set man approach her. "Good evening, Miss Jones." He took off his hat and held it in his hand to show respect.

"Are you the manager?"

"Not me, no ma'am. That's one job you couldn't give me. Too many headaches. I'm the night crew foreman. Name's Wilson. Me and the boys are here to clean. Thought I'd warn ya before we got started."

"Time for me to be going." Jane stood and walked to her room.

CHAPTER 4

The phone rang. Blurry-eyed, Jane struggled to see the red numerals on the clock next to the bed. It was a little before six. She didn't remember asking for a wake-up call. Sandi's name crossed her mind. "That girl must be a mind reader," she whispered to herself. On the third ring, she picked up the receiver, held it for a moment, and hung up to prevent another mind jolting ring. She got out of bed and repacked the few things she'd taken out of her suitcase. She heard a soft knock.

"Sandi," she said to herself. She threw open the door. "San…" Instead of Sandi, she saw an unmistakable male form standing in front of the open door. "Whatchuwant?" she demanded in an abrasive Bronx accent.

"I'm Solanch Ochoa, ma'am, manager of El Satélite. Sorry to bother you so early in the morning, but I have some things I need to discuss with you."

The unexpected sight of a male so early in the morning along with the sound of a most pleasing masculine voice threw her off balance. "Not for nuttin' I won't skip without payin'. I'll pay every cent includin' last night's dinnah. Don't worry. You'll get yah money."

There was a long silence, so long that she raised her eyes so she could see the face looking down at her. She hated what happened next, but no matter how hard she might have tried to suppress it, it was going to happen. When her eyes met his face, her heart skipped a beat and without warning beat abnormally fast. The man standing in front of her was the handsomest man she had seen in her entire life. She lowered her eyes and stared at his boots glistening in the early morning sun.

"I'm sorry you feel that way, ma'am," replied the soft, deep voice, "but that isn't the reason I came so early this morning. We've got to talk."

"Yadah, yadah, yadah," she said, talking to his boots. "It's about money. It's always about the money. I told yah I'd pay what I owe so quit botherin' me." She hated every word she was saying. It was if another Jane existed inside of her. She didn't talk this way. She didn't mean the things she was saying, but years of hurt had taught her to reject men before they rejected her. Besides, he was pretty, too pretty. He needed to be hurt, to be brought back to Earth and reality, but the real reason for all her outward bravado was he intimidated her, as all men did.

She looked up to see him push the front brim of his hat a bit higher on his forehead. He moved back several paces and stepped off the curb so she could see him more easily.

"Git outta heah so I can finish packin' and load Subie. I won't skip. You got my billin' information, so why are ya harassin' me so early in the mornin'?"

"I'm, I'm sorry, ma'am. I'm sorry you feel I'm harassing you. I sincerely apologize. I'm not here about money. Please believe me when I say that." His voice and manner were so pleasing it became increasingly difficult for Jane to keep up a good mad which made her even madder because she was afraid she might succumb to his obvious charms. She was determined that wasn't going to happen. She would put him in his place and keep him there. He was never going to hurt her. Never!

"I need to talk to you. Would you meet me in the restaurant whenever you're ready? I'd like to invite you to have breakfast with me. Would you please accept my invitation?"

Jane realized she couldn't say no to his offer. She nodded her head and in so doing saw his reddish-brown lips part in a beautiful smile that revealed the straightest, whitest teeth she had ever seen. "I was hoping you'd say yes. I'll meet you in the restaurant whenever you're ready, if that's agreeable with you, ma'am."

"Yes, yes it is," she replied haughtily.

She watched every step he took as he turned and walked across the wide parking lot toward the restaurant. Each step he took was graceful with a slight rocking motion at the waist that made it appear as if he glided in mid air. His tight jeans accented his tall, lean male form to its fullest. Even the click-click of his boots on the pavement radiated authority, confidence, and sexual strength along with the hat he wore at a rakish angle. His sexuality made Jane feel frumpish, inferior. He was too good for her.

She looked for Subie so she could load up before eating breakfast. She looked up and down the parking lot. She didn't see him. A sudden thought seized her imagination.

With renewed anger, she slammed the room door shut, marched across the parking lot to the restaurant where she saw him sitting at a table. "Now I know what you're up to, you, you, *gavone* you. This place…" she shrieked, struggling for the right words. "This place is like the *Bates Motel*, only you don't murder people. You steal their cars. You're not gonna get away with it, not with me. I'm gonna report you to the police. That's exactly what I'm gonna do." She turned to leave.

He rose from his chair. "Ma'am, please. Please sit down." He motioned with his hand to a vacant chair across the table. "Let me explain. Your car was one of the things I wanted to talk to you about this morning. So if you'll kindly sit down, I'll get us some coffee, order some breakfast, and we'll talk nice and quiet. Please."

She sat at the table and watched him disappear into the kitchen. Her heart beat wildly, partly from anger, partly from fear of him, and partly about the whereabouts of her Subie.

Lost in her tangled thoughts, she stared at the kitchen door. A few minutes later, the door opened. She watched as he effortlessly carried a tray with two cups, a coffee pot, a sugar bowl, and a small glass pitcher filled with cream across the dining room and placed them on the table in front of her.

"I don't know how you like your coffee so I brought everything cream, sugar, raw sugar, brown sugar, artificial sweeteners. If you want anything else, please tell me and I'll get it for you."

"No. This'll be fine," Jane said curtly.

"May I pour?"

"I suppose so."

He picked up the pot and poured the hot coffee into two cups. "Do you take sugar?"

"Yes."

"One or two?"

"One."

He removed the lid from the sugar bowl, took a teaspoon from the table, measured out a level teaspoon of sugar and placed it in her cup. "Is that enough?"

"Yes, thank you."

"Cream?"

"No thanks."

He picked up his cup, smiled, and took a sip. She did the same, except she didn't smile.

"I hope you like it."

"Yes, it's quite good."

"Good. Now to the things I must discuss with you. I'm sorry about your car. None of us here at the motel said anything to you about it because we didn't want to upset you. The sad news is your car is totaled."

Jane gasped in disbelief. "I don't believe it. I drove it here."

"You were lucky you got this far. I called the insurance adjustor and a local mechanic while you were asleep. Both went over your car thoroughly. They agreed it isn't drivable or fixable. The frame is badly bent. We had to tow it around back and cover it with a tarp so it wouldn't become a tourist attraction. I imagine you'd like to see it."

"Yes," Jane said hesitantly, feeling as if she were going to a funeral.

When he raised the tarp and she saw Subie, tears came to her eyes. The windshield along with the other windows had numerous cracks, both headlights and taillights had been smashed, the entire car was covered with dents made by the falling ice chunks, but the worst damage was the tumbleweeds and clods of dirt sticking out of the grill that had been driven with tremendous force into the motor. He explained once he had turned the motor off, he couldn't get it started.

With tears streaming down her cheeks, she looked at him and said, "Subie died to save me." Quietly she walked back into the dining room. Breakfast had been served and was waiting on the table when they returned. They ate in silence, he not wanting to intrude into her thoughts, and she lost in them.

CHAPTER 5

Silence was the best medicine for Jane. Without it, she couldn't have swallowed a forkful of breakfast or grappled with the death of Subie whose passing she took harder than she could have imagined. Her mind replayed the sights and sounds of ominous black clouds, huge raindrops, chunks of ice, icy roads, crashing cars, and screaming wind.

She took a few sips of the strong, hot coffee. That more than anything pushed the dark thoughts of death and destruction to the back of her mind and allowed her to focus on the man seated before her. He ate with his head down. The brim of his hat covered most of his face. This gave her the breathing space she so badly needed to get her world back in order.

As she watched him eat, she realized he wasn't some god on Earth. He chewed, drank, swallowed, breathed like any other human being, a handsome human being, a male human being.

Human nature is fraught with insecurity and hypocrisy. When we humans find someone who pleases us, we look for flaws, hoping we'll find something that will bring him or her down to our level, but we don't want the flaws to be too serious because then we lose interest. So it was with Jane. She didn't mean to do it. It just happened. She noticed how he held his fork, how he cut his ham steak, how he ate his eggs, how he picked up his toast, how he picked up his coffee cup, how he handled his napkin. She could find no fault in any of these things, so she looked at the hand that held the fork looking for that one flaw that would make him human. The olive skin of his long slender fingers blended with the cuticles of his nails that ended in white, shiny, semi-long, perfectly shaped nails. His shirt was starched and perfectly pressed. He didn't smack his food, slurp his coffee, or pick his teeth.

The lack of an imperfection made her feel inferior, and yet, she was drawn to him. She couldn't help it. *How cheap I am*, she thought to herself. *One breakfast and I'm drawn to him.* It infuriated her she could be won over so easily. She considered herself a sane, practical person when it came to relationships, standoffish, not easily won. She renewed her vow, he was never, ever going to hurt her, and yet she was glad he was there.

In the past, men had analyzed and scrutinized her. They had found fault. They had rejected her. She had become defensive, developing a nasty hardness born from rejection that drove men away. She had tried this nasty, hardness tactic on the man sitting across the table, but it had failed. He hadn't run away nor had he analyzed or scrutinized her. He had allowed her to accept him on her own terms. This drew her closer to him.

When he had finished his coffee, he looked up and smiled. "How are you feeling?" His smile was warm and genuine. It was obvious he was concerned about her.

She managed a half smile and said, "So-so."

"You've had a difficult time," he said softly. "You've seen things that people who've lived a lifetime out here haven't seen. I drove down 285 to where the tornado hit. I was surprised at how much debris covered the highway. 285 is still closed. I don't know how Subie ever made it through." She smiled a full smile, pleased he used the affectionate name for her car.

"Now that we've broken bread together, may I reintroduce myself?"

"Please do."

"I'm Solanch."

"And I'm Jane."

"May I call you Jane?"

"Only if I can call you Solanch."

"Then it's a deal,"—he hesitated for a moment—"Jane."

"It's a deal,"—she hesitated as he had done—"Solanch."

"How about another cup of coffee, Jane, now that we know each other?"

"Sounds good to me, Solanch."

"I'll be right back." He picked up the half empty pot. "I'll get us a fresh one." He wasn't gone but a few moments before he returned with a fresh pot. He poured two cups, put a level teaspoon of sugar in her cup, and stirred. He banged the spoon on the rim of the cup to shake off the last drop and smiled. "Sounds like the key of C to me. What do you think?"

"I'm tone deaf. It sounds like a spoon hitting the side of a coffee cup." They laughed.

When the laughter had subsided, he looked down and fell silent. His silence didn't bother Jane. Normally silences with men would have bothered her, but with Solanch, it was different. A long silence with him didn't concern her because she knew his silence had nothing to do with her. She felt she understood him.

He played with the handle of his cup as a little boy would, a simple act that further endeared him to her. He broke the silence with, "I wish I didn't have to tell you these things, Jane, but"—he paused—"I must. I hope you understand."

Jane didn't like this new serious tone of voice. She feared it might spoil their newfound relationship.

"First I have to clear up a few things."

The old Jane took over, sensing the outside world intruding into her life. She lowered her head and focused on the clasped hands in her lap.

"When Sandi saw you collapse by Subie, it looked as if you had hit your head on the car door and the pavement. When she saw you were unconscious, she was certain you were badly hurt. She yelled for me to call 911, which I did.

"Since El Satélite is in the middle of nowhere, as you well know, there's no local EMS. All 911 calls are transferred to the state police who decide what course of action is to be taken. The police transferred my call to a doctor who asked me to keep a close check on you. He gave specific instructions that if you didn't regain consciousness within a twenty-four-hour period to notify him immediately so preparations could be made for your transfer to a hospital. He was concerned you might have suffered a concussion or perhaps internal injuries. He asked how the injury had occurred. I assumed you had been involved in a traffic accident. That seemed the most plausible explanation."

Jane breathed a sigh of relief. His soft, gentle voice had a calming effect on her. Nothing of what he had said frightened her. She looked up and saw him looking intently at her. She gave a little smile to convey she was fine with everything he had said so far.

He returned her smile with a simple parting of the lips and continued. "Yesterday afternoon, about the time you were waking up, the state police called. They said they could find no evidence of any traffic accidents on either 40, 285, or any state or county road in the area except for the fact an EF5 tornado had hit 285. They wanted to know if there was any possibility you could have been involved in that. They asked questions about the condition of your vehicle. I told them everything I knew."

Solanch stopped. He pushed his hat back a little further on his head. "Now comes the hard part, Jane. I don't know how to tell you this in any easy way except to tell you the truth. At a little past seven last night, our governor, the Governor of New Mexico, Miguel Sanchez, died along with his driver. They had been traveling south on 285 at the time of the tornado. They had reported to the state police that they were driving on icy pavement and that they saw headlights coming toward them followed by garbled transmission. The state police want to talk to you to see if you can give them any further information."

Jane's shoulders slumped.

Solanch paused a long while before he continued. "There's one other thing I must tell you. This has become a huge news story. All the TV networks have been calling here since the story broke. As of yet, they don't know your name or even that you're here. They're checking all motels for leads. One last thing and this is the most difficult of all. The state police are waiting in my office to talk to you. I had to tell them you were here. I've checked with my lawyer, Jack Burton. He's a good friend of mine. He assured me you must remember this accident was caused by an act of God. You are in no way responsible for any harm that might have come to anybody. You are not responsible." He said the last words forcefully. "Do you understand?" he said more gently.

He stood and walked around to where Jane was sitting. He touched her shoulder. "Do you understand, Jane? You are not responsible. I will be with you along with Jack who will protect your rights while the police question you. Nobody is accusing you of doing anything wrong. It was a tragic accident caused by one of the strongest tornadoes recorded in New Mexico. The state police want to get the facts straight, that's all."

His gentle voice and manner persuaded Jane there was nothing to be afraid of. She managed to stand without noticing his strong, warm hand under her arm and walked toward his office.

CHAPTER 6

The state police were nothing like Solanch said they would be. Three inspectors were brutal in their questioning once they realized it had been Jane who had caused the accident and the deaths of the governor and his driver. Jack reminded them this was an accident caused by an act of God and Jane was in no way responsible for anything that might have happened on 285 to the governor or anyone else. The police inspectors paid no heed to Jack's protestations. They questioned Jane for hours as if they were her judge, jury, and executioner.

Jane underwent a range of emotions from fear to tears to anger to resignation to tears and so on. When the questions stopped, she was as pale as a ghost and emotionally drained.

Solanch and Jack each took one of her arms and escorted her from the motel's office to the security of the empty dining room. Solanch spoke first. "You can't stay at the motel, Jane. The press will be swarming all over the place. It won't be safe. I've made arrangements for you to stay at our house. My mother will be delighted to have another female in the house since she's had to contend with my father and me for years. I promise you'll be safe there. Jimmy has put your things in the truck. With your permission, we're going to walk out the back door, get in the truck, and drive to my parents' house, but only with your permission."

"Solanch is right, Miss Jones. You must go unless you want every newsman in the country to stick a microphone in front of your face and ask lots of impertinent if not embarrassing questions."

Jane nodded her head.

Solanch turned the battered-white Toyota pickup from the narrow macadam road onto a badly rutted gravel road. He drove a few miles until he came to a tire rutted sandy road. He turned onto it and drove a few minutes until the Toyota came over a slight rise in the road. In a depression in the New Mexican desert, Jane spotted a single, desolate-looking house surrounded by sand interspersed with clumps of mesquite grass. Solanch pulled the truck up in front of the house in a cloud of dust and stopped. Once the dust had settled, Jane could see a modest, white stucco house.

The front door opened and a woman not much shorter than Jane came out. "*Bienvenida. Bienvenida,*" she said, holding out her hands to Jane. "Welcome to our home, my dear girl." She took Jane's hands in hers. "Jack Burton called, and he explained everything. *Ay, qué feo!* What a terrible day you've had. Well, it's over now. You're with friends, so come in, come in. I've made a nice lunch for us. How does a nice cup of hot coffee sound to you?"

"Heavenly," Jane answered, almost too exhausted to talk.

"I would like to give those men from the state police thunder," she said as she ushered Jane into the house, "for the way they treated you. Disgraceful! Absolutely disgraceful!" She had the same sweet voice as Solanch. "It's all over radio and TV but don't worry. They haven't reported your name. Let's hope the state police can keep a secret for a change. Ay, all this talk and I haven't introduced myself. I'm sure you've guessed by now. I'm Solanch's mother."

She held out her hands to Solanch who went over to her and kissed her on the lips. "He's such a good boy," she said smiling. Then she sighed and added, "I suppose all mothers think that about their sons." She paused for a moment to give her son a look of adoration. "Now for that cup of coffee. Follow me into the kitchen. The coffee's hot and ready to be poured. Solanch, would you please pour?"

The cups had been laid on the table. As Solanch poured, his mother said, "I must warn you. You'll have to get used to my Spanglish as I call it. I forget sometimes and use a Spanish word or phrase here or there."

Solanch gave her a son look that said she hadn't spoken the entire truth. "You see the look my son gives me now. He knows my English is hopeless when I'm sad. Everything flies out the window. I can't remember my English. Only Spanish comes to mind, but when I'm happy or angry, the happy part is often, the angry part is never, I think, *mi inglés es perfecto.*"

"Ahem." Solanch faked a cough.

"All right. Not so *perfecto* just pretty-well good." She looked adoringly at her son and then at Jane. "I don't understand why it is this way, but that's the way it is with me. I hope you don't mind."

"Of course not," Jane said. "I understand."

"See, she understands." Mamita looked knowingly at her son. "Papito is like me. His English is very good when he's in business. But at home with me, he speaks a little English mixed with a little Spanish but Solanch," she said proudly, "is *mucho* better than both of us. Papito and I like to say he's *puro gringo.* He never gets confused. The only time he speaks Spanish is with Papito and me, with a few of his friends, or with business associates. Anyway, he calls me Mamita, which means 'little momma' in Spanish. It's a term of endearment, one I hope you'll use too."

Jane paused for a few moments and said, "I, I don't think I can. I don't know you well enough. Please, I would feel more comfortable if I called you Mrs., Mrs...."

"Solanch. You haven't told her your last name?" She wagged her finger lovingly in Solanch's direction. "Shame on you. It's Ochoa," she said turning to Jane. "So you can call me Mrs. Ochoa, Señora Ochoa, or Mamita."

"It's just that I'll feel more comfortable calling you Mrs. Ochoa."

"If we're going to be formal then I'd better call you Miss Jones. Solanch has poured the coffee, Miss Jones, so let's all sit down, have a few sips, and then I'll put some food on this table."

"Please, Mrs. Ochoa. Call me Jane. Miss Jones makes me feel so uncomfortable and so, so…"

"Old?" Mrs. Ochoa finished the sentence for her. "And how do you think Mrs. Ochoa makes me feel?"

"It's just that…"

"I understand Jane, and I will call you Jane. You're in a strange house with people you hardly know in the middle of nowhere. I don't blame you for wondering what in the world is going on here. Let me put your mind to rest. We are friendly and peaceful. We don't argue. We don't fight. We don't lie to each other. We have no secrets. That way none of us do or say anything we'll be ashamed of later. We enjoy each other as much as we can from one day to the next, but enough talk. Let's eat."

"Good idea, Mamita," Solanch said as his mother began taking dishes out of the refrigerator and oven. "And don't talk Jane to death either. Let her eat in peace and quiet. She likes it that way."

"Whatever you say, *mi querido*, which means"—she turned to Jane—"my most loved one or something like that in English. No matter what it means exactly, it has special meaning to me," Mrs. Ochoa said confidentially to Jane.

Solanch's demand was met. The three sat at the table eating and not saying a word yet enjoying each other's company. It wasn't what was said. It was what was felt.

When they had finished eating, Mamita said to Solanch, "Would you show Jane her room? I'm sure she'd like to rest."

Jane looked at her wearily. "I would." She had no sooner entered the room, kicked off her shoes, and collapsed on the bed then she was asleep before Solanch could close the door.

When Jane awoke in the dim light of dusk, she smelled unfamiliar but delicious smells. She realized Mrs. Ochoa had been busy in the kitchen while she had been sleeping. She got up and went to the door where she found her suitcases waiting outside in the hallway. She took them into the room, took out a brush, quickly brushed her hair into some semblance of order, and headed toward the living room where she was certain someone would be. She wasn't wrong only it wasn't Mrs. Ochoa or Solanch who greeted her but a tall, lean man with snow-white hair.

He stood with his hand extended. "*Buenas noches, Señorita* Jane. I hope you don't mind if I call you Jane."

"Not at all, Mr. Ochoa?" Jane asked hesitantly.

"Well, yes and no. I mean everyone in this house calls me Papito. *Espero*, I mean, I hope you will too." Before Jane could protest, he put up his hand and said, "I know. I know. Mamita told me you insist on calling her Mrs. Ochoa but with me, I hope things will be different. *Por favor*, please call me Papito." He had a wonderful glint in his eyes that made Jane want to go over and give him a big hug, but she suppressed her feelings. She didn't feel comfortable hugging a man she had just met nor did she want him to think she was cheap and vulgar with such a display of affection.

"I couldn't, Mr. Ochoa. I hope you don't mind."

"Yes, I mind, but I want you to feel comfortable." He looked like a motel manager's father should look and sound, plainly dressed and soft-spoken.

"And of course you'll call me Solanch."

She turned to see Solanch enter the living room. He held out his hand to her. She took it, noting how big and soft it was, not the hand of a cowboy flashed through her mind.

The next hour was spent with the four of them talking about a variety of breezy topics that gave them great enjoyment and made them laugh while they sipped the most delicious margaritas Jane had ever tasted. She complimented Solanch on his bartending skills.

After a second round of margaritas, they ate Mamita's excellent dinner at the kitchen table, for the little house had no dining room. Then they adjourned to the living room where they sipped brandy. Well past midnight, Mamita said, "Papito, it's time we sleep," to which he agreed. They both stood. Mrs. Ochoa reached out her hand to Jane and said, "This has been the nicest evening we've had in a long time, Jane. In fact, I can't remember any night quite like it. I think you missed your calling. You should have been a comedienne. Your stories about your students are priceless."

"She's right, Jane. You are one funny lady," Papito agreed. "But the one story you told not only was humorous but very moving, the one about the Hispanic boy who stood on his desk, lit a match, and with outstretched arm, said, 'Look Miss Jones, I am the Statue of Liberty.' I won't forget that story as long as I live, and I'm going to tell it often with your permission."

"Permission granted," Jane readily replied.

"I like this story because it shows how much a boy, a Hispanic boy, loves this country. We don't have enough of these types of stories to convey the love we Hispanics have for this magnificent country called the US of A."

"*Tienes razón, Papito.* You are so right," Mamita agreed, "And you are so funny, Jane."

"I'm afraid it was the margaritas talking, not me," Jane demurred.

"Whatever it was, it was fun. I haven't laughed this much in years. *Hasta mañana,* Jane. Until the morning, when we get to eat again," Mamita teased. She and Papito said good night. Hand in hand, they disappeared into the back of the house.

Jane turned to Solanch and said, "And it's time for me to get some sleep too. Seems as if that's all I've been doing the last few days is sleeping, getting up, eating, and sleeping some more."

"Don't go just yet. Please sit with me for a few more minutes." Solanch motioned to a chair opposite the sofa behind him. "I have news for you, and I'm afraid not such good news."

Jane sat in the chair, he on the sofa. "No one knows you're here, not even the state police, although I'm certain they've figured that out by now, but who knows." He shrugged his shoulders and smiled. "I talked to the chief of police this afternoon. He asked me if I knew where you were. I told him I did, but I would turn you over to him only with a court order."

Solanch could see panic return to Jane's eyes. "I know all this makes you sound as if you're some kind of a criminal. You are not. Jack has worked on this, and he assures me no judge in New Mexico will grant the chief such an order. However, he has taken the preventive step of invoking a restraining order that denies you the right to leave the state until he is satisfied this was an accident and nothing more. For political reasons, he's prolonging the investigation so he looks as if he's doing something about the governor's death."

Solanch stood and walked around the sofa that served as a divider between the living room and kitchen. He leaned over the sofa, clasped his hands, and said, "For now, you must obey his order. You'll stay with us for as long as you want, and yes, Jane, for free. I promise we won't charge a cent." He smiled his beautiful smile. "Just like we won't charge for the room at the motel, not for last night's dinner, not for today's lunch, or tonight's dinner, or for any other meals you will eat in this house. Everything's free. We're glad you're here with us." The smile that accompanied those words was as genuine as the one he had smiled at breakfast.

He had done so much for her in such a short period of time. She felt comfortable with him, as if she had known him for years.

CHAPTER 7

With the bad news dispensed, Solanch asked Jane if she would like a cup of coffee. "Strangely enough, that sounds good," she replied. A few minutes later, he placed a coffee with one sugar on the table next to her chair and put his cup on the table in front of the sofa. He sat on the sofa, reached for his cup, took a sip, and said, "Not bad, even if I made it myself."

"Excellent in my book."

"I hope this will keep you awake after the margaritas and brandy because I'm in the mood to talk, and I don't want you to get sleepy. I'm going to be selfish and talk your ear off. I hope you're in a talkative mood."

"My favorite sport."

"Good." He smiled, and asked, "Would you mind if I do one more thing?"

"What's that?

"Take off my boots. They're killing me."

Jane had just taken a sip of her coffee. It was all she could do to swallow it as she fought back a laugh. "It's your house. Be comfortable."

"Thanks." As he took each boot off, he uttered a sigh. "That feels so good," he muttered, as he wiggled his toes. "I love to wear boots but after so many hours, they can become a bit much."

"You don't have to tell me about shoes killing your feet. I have a whole closet-full that do the same thing."

He wrinkled his brow. "I hope my feet don't smell. Tell me if they do, and I'll put my boots back on. Boots can make your feet smell, you know," he admitted sheepishly, like a little boy revealing a top secret.

Jane smiled a smile of contentment. There they were. Two imperfections. Boots hurt his feet, and his feet smelled. He was human after all.

Solanch was true to his word about talking her ear off. He talked about New Mexico and its problems, then about problems the West faced. Jane talked about New York and its problems and problems the East faced. From there they moved onto problems the United States faced, then the world, with economics, politics, and religion being the focus of their discussion. They didn't agree on every topic but that only made their discussion livelier. Even in disagreement, they respected each other's point of view complimenting the other for a well-made point.

As the hours flew by, and the cups of coffee mounted, their respect for each other grew exponentially. Finally Jane asked, "How do you know so much about so many different things?"

"I was about to ask you the same?"

"I try to stay informed. I read newspapers, magazines, watch informative TV shows, the news, and listen to what people are saying. That's about it. What about you?"

"Same here."

"Have you ever gone to college?"

"Yes. What about you?"

"I went to a state school," she said lowering her eyes. "It was all my parents could afford. What about you? Where'd you go to college?"

He paused for a moment and said quietly, "Hayverd and from there to The London School of Business."

Her eyes widened. "Wow!" was all she could say, keeping her eyes lowered. She was silent.

"Jane, it doesn't matter where one gets an education. It's what one does with it after they've gotten it. Look at the Hayverd graduates who run our state and federal governments. Look at the messes they've created. The chaos they've caused. These are high-priced educations gone to waste."

Jane threw her head back and laughed. "You've just made another very good point."

"Ah-ha. See? East does meet West. Don't let names of prestigious universities impress you. Believe me, they graduate loads of nincompoops, nincompoops who think they're smarter than everyone else and try to run everybody's lives with their nincompoopish ideas."

"*Touché*," Jane replied. "Down with the nincompoops, and up with the common man and his common sense."

As night faded into daylight, they saw each other in a new light. The late night hours with its intense intellectual stimulation had been an electrifying experience for both, one that neither had ever encountered and one that neither would ever forget. Without realizing it, they had, during those few hours of discussion, become one in a mental marriage, a bond not so easily broken.

CHAPTER 8

The next day, Jane took notice of her new surroundings and the people in them. The floors of the little house had no carpets, not even a throw rug, just tile, far different from her carpeted New York studio apartment. The kitchen had most of the modern conveniences with a washer and dryer in a small room off the kitchen but conspicuously missing was a dishwasher. It was a clean, functional house with three small bedrooms and a single bath. The furnishings were modest but comfortable, about what Jane would expect for the family of a motel manager, although she wondered why anyone would waste such an excellent education to be a motel manager in such a remote place. She was curious but knew better than to pry into other people's business, especially the business of someone who had been kind to her. She remembered her father's advice, "Some questions are best left unasked."

Jane liked Mrs. Ochoa. She admired her vivaciousness, her unpretentious attitude, a woman who accepted herself for what she was, and a woman who accepted Jane for what she was, no questions asked. It pleased her that Mrs. Ochoa allowed the gray to replace a good part of her natural black hair and wore it in a simple Native American style with a single braid down her back. None of her facial features by themselves were outstandingly beautiful yet each blended with the others to give her that rare feminine quality of muted, distinguished beauty that was as much an expression of her inward beauty as her outward attractiveness.

Mrs. Ochoa's figure resembled that of a woman Jane's age more than a woman with gray hair. She had a robust look about her that exuded health and happiness accentuated by her flawless olive skin that had a tinge of red behind it that made it glow in any light. She was an inch shorter than Jane and a foot shorter than Solanch, about five feet three, but it was Mrs. Ochoa's outgoing personality that made her the likeable woman she was. It certainly wasn't her dresses because they were loose fitting of nondescript style and unflattering washed-out pinks and yellows over which she wore a faded-blue, half-apron tied around her waist.

When Mrs. Ochoa found out Jane didn't know the first thing about cooking, she insisted on sharing a few of her basic recipes that Jane mastered in a single try. In return for the cooking lessons, Jane insisted she help with the housework whether it was washing dishes or mopping the tile floors. None of it seemed like work as they talked and laughed. Mrs. Ochoa thought to herself, if she had been able to have another child, she would have wanted a little girl just like Jane. She wouldn't have changed a thing.

Each day at five o'clock Mr. Ochoa arrived home. He dressed about the same each day. He wore jeans, a different western shirt, and cowboy boots that made him almost, but not quite as tall as Solanch. Jane couldn't be sure if it was a difference in height or if the heels on Solanch's boots were a bit higher, but it made no difference. Both were tall and lean. Jane could tell where Solanch got his chiseled good looks because he and his father looked much alike. It pleased her to see them together because she knew how Solanch would look in thirty years with snow-white hair, lean body, and a still handsome face, but a time she knew she would be long forgotten by him and his parents.

She enjoyed the hour she and Mr. Ochoa spent together talking about a variety of subjects. She was surprised how much he knew about various topics, and he was surprised to find out how much she knew about business.

One afternoon during one of their business conversations, Jane forgot her father's advice and asked, "May I ask if you're in business since you seem to know so much about it?"

"Of course, Jane. Perfectly natural question. I own a couple of motels between here and Albuquerque and since they're so far apart, I asked Solanch if he would run El Satélite." He put his open hand to the side of his mouth and whispered in a confidential tone, "I'm testing him to see if he knows what he's doing."

"I see," Jane whispered back. She knew she shouldn't inquire any further, but curiosity got the best of her. "And how is he doing?"

"Adequately, Jane. Adequately." But she could see the proud glint in his eyes that revealed more than words could that he was more than pleased with the way his son was running his business.

At six each afternoon, Solanch returned for the cocktail hour that prompted Mrs. Ochoa to exclaim, "I don't know what's gotten into these two men to keep such regular hours. Papito is never home before seven and Solanch, heaven only knows when he's going to blow in, so I know it's not me that's got these men home at regular hours. It must be you, Jane."

"Or the margaritas," Jane quipped to which they all laughed.

Dinner was served *tiempo latino* as Mrs. Ochoa liked to call it which was any time after nine. They enjoyed a leisurely meal at the kitchen table after which they adjourned to the living room until twelve o'clock sharp when Mrs. Ochoa would say, "Papito, bedtime for us." He would agree, and they would excuse themselves, leaving the room with his arm around her waist and her head resting against his arm.

The time after twelve became a special time for Jane and Solanch. They sat for hours drinking coffee and talking, talking, talking about everything they could think of. It was as if they couldn't pick each other's brains fast enough. It was only after sheer exhaustion had consumed them both that they confessed to each other they were talking nonsense and it was time to call it a night. Reluctantly, they retired, despising the fact that sleep was interfering with sharing their ideas, discussing their ambitions, their inner thoughts, their anxieties, and their fears.

On the sixth day Jane had been in the Ochoa's house, Solanch arrived home with his father at five. Neither looked happy. Jane and Mrs. Ochoa saw it immediately. Jane's heart sank at the thought some judge had issued a warrant for her arrest and she was headed for jail. *What would her parents think? What would her sister on Long Island think? What would the teachers at school think? I'm ruined* were the thoughts that raced through her brain.

She went into the living room and slumped into a chair. Solanch followed and said, "I have good news for you, Jane."

Jane wrapped in her thoughts of ruination heard nothing of what he said. "The chief of police has rescinded your restraining order which means you are free to leave New Mexico whenever you wish." He looked at Jane to see how she responded to the news. Much to his surprise, she looked straight ahead and said nothing. "And there's one other piece of good news for you as well. Whether someone at the state police made a mistake or it's the chief's way of apologizing, your name has been released to the press but your first name is spelled J-A-Y-N-E and your last name is James, not Jones. I promise you no one will ever trace you to this unfortunate accident, and before I forget, when you return to New York, a new Subie, exactly like the one you had, will be waiting for you." He hoped this last bit of news would cheer her up, but she sat motionless.

Solanch looked at his mother. Mamita tried to smile, but Solanch could see her heart wasn't in it. She crossed the room to where Jane was sitting and put her hand on Jane's shoulder. "It's good news for you, Jane. It means you can leave us as soon"—her voice trailed off—"as you want."

CHAPTER 9

Late the next afternoon, Jane was in her New York apartment. True to Solanch's word, there was a message on her answering machine from the dealership where she had bought Subie. They had a replacement ready for her. The next morning she was pleased to look out her third story window and see Subie 2 parked in front of the apartment building.

Solanch called to find out if the car had arrived. She assured him she and Subie 2 were fine. They talked but the conversation was more strained than if she had been sitting in her favorite chair and he on the sofa. After a few minutes of strained conversation, Jane thanked him and asked him to convey her many thanks to his parents for the umpteenth time. She felt she had fulfilled her obligation to them with one exception. She intended to send them a thank you note as well as the motel staff for all they had done.

Now that she was back in New York and in her own surroundings, her old feelings of inferiority and insecurity returned along with her innate-New York-suspicious attitude not to trust anyone, especially those who had been kindest to her, an attitude that demanded answers as to why the Ochoas had been kind to her, and what had been in it for them? She had liked them well enough while she had been with them, but why should they like her, Jane Jones, a nobody? What was done was done, finished, forever. She had to look forward and forward meant getting ready for the opening of school. She had much to do to get her classroom ready for the first day of school.

Several nights later Solanch called. She had to admit she liked hearing his voice, but her strong sense of suspicion about his motives weakened the bond between them. She was determined he would never hurt her emotionally. She decided it was better to talk to him as little as possible. He tried to talk about various topics, but she was curt with her answers and said good-bye after several agonizing minutes of forced conversation.

A few nights later, he called to thank her on behalf of his parents and everyone at the motel for the beautiful thank you notes they had received. He told her everyone was pleased to hear from her and was looking forward to her next trip west. Jane smiled, pleased everyone remembered her, but when she hung up, she had no intention of going west, ever.

School started and with it came mountains of work. It was all Jane could do to stay awake in the never-ending after school meetings, face the long drive home, stick something in the microwave for dinner, prepare lessons for the next day, fill out daily reports for the principal, and fall into bed in a state of mental and physical exhaustion so she could face another day of the same. A week after school started, she had gone to bed early and had just gotten to sleep when the phone rang. She picked up.

"Jane? Hello? Are you there?"

She recognized the voice. "Yes, I'm here. I'm in bed and really tired."

"Sorry I bothered you. I'll try another time."

"Whatevah," she said coldly.

At least once and sometimes twice a week, he called at six in the evening New Mexico time so it would be eight in New York.

He didn't want to repeat his mistake of bothering her after she had gone to bed. He struggled to have conversations with her, but she ended them, telling him she had things to do. He respected her wishes and ended his conversations as gracefully as he could.

Jane couldn't understand why he kept calling. It was obvious they didn't have anything to say to each other. Everything had been said. Hearing his voice reminded her of painful events best forgotten and a life far more complicated than she wanted or could handle. She had her old New York life back, simple and uncomplicated, and she intended to keep it that way.

Nevertheless, she needed to rationalize her nasty behavior and suspicious attitude for her own peace of mind. These rationalizations came in the form of magazine and newspaper articles she read while waiting in line at the supermarket, the first of which contained a magazine cover story about clubs men formed to see how many women they could have sex with. The man who had the highest provable number won the jackpot worth thousands of dollars. She knew she was the perfect target for this handsome motel Romeo who considered her nothing more than a sex object. She wasn't some object he could take whenever he felt like it. She was a person with feelings, with integrity. He was never going to have the chance to hurt her high moral ideals. If winning the prize money depended on him having sex with her, then he might as well count himself a loser. He wasn't going to get away with that kind of stuff, not with her.

An article in the *Daily News* about a different type of sex club where men bet on how many women they could get to commit suicide if they pretended to love them heightened her suspicions. *The scoundrel,* Jane thought to herself. *If he thinks for one New York minute I'm committin' suicide so he can win some bet, he's got another think comin'.* These two thoughts, sex and suicide, reinforced her growing hatred of him.

The phone rang. She jumped to attention. She let it ring several times before she picked up. "Jane? Is that you?" It was him, with that sickening sweet voice of his. Without hesitation, she pressed the block button.

Chapter 10

Jane had no idea if Solanch called after she had blocked his calls. She didn't care whether he did or didn't. She wanted no part of him. She never wanted to see him or hear his voice. She decided she would never, ever utter his name. If she had to talk about him, she would use nameless pronouns like he, him, or his. She had her life to protect, and she was going to protect it no matter what she had to do.

Her life consisted of going to her parents' house in the Bronx for Sunday dinner, occasionally visiting her sister on Long Island, and sometimes going out to lunch and dinner with other teachers at school, but the most important aspect of her life were her students who needed her. That was her life, simple and uncomplicated, and it suited her just fine.

It was an unusually warm night for mid March. Jane had her windows open enjoying the fresh night air, wishing the weather would stay this way until next winter, but she knew as did all New Yorkers that a warm night like this was one of a kind not likely to be repeated any time soon. She was watching an old movie on TV when the phone rang. She picked up.

"Jane?" It was a thin, fragile voice almost impossible to understand.

"Yes, this is Jane."

"Mamita."

"Who?"

"This, Mamita."

"I'm sorry. I don't know anybody by that name."

"Me!" the voice shrieked. "Señora,"—the voice paused—
"Mrs. Ochoa." The voice sounded so strange and strained Jane
couldn't focus on what was being said.

"Mrs. Ochoa?" Jane was stunned. Why would Mrs. Ochoa
want to talk to her? She didn't want to talk to her or any Ochoa.
She wanted to hang up but the voice sounded so weak and fearful
she didn't have the heart.

"It Solanch, Jane. He, he broke."

So that's their game, Jane thought to herself. *They're nothing but
a bunch of con artists trying to steal my money.* She promised herself
Mrs. Ochoa and the rest of the Ochoa gang wasn't going to get a
single cent out of her.

"I sorry, Jane. I so upset. *Mi inglés* no good."

Jane hardened to Mrs. Ochoa's strained voice. She marveled
at how good she was in trying to con her out of money. She
decided not to hang up so she could report her and the rest of the
Ochoa gang to the police.

"Not broke. Broken, broken."

"What?" Jane yelled, annoyed by English that didn't make
any sense to her.

"Seek. Solanch seek." Mrs. Ochoa stopped to catch her
breath, then added, "I tink maybe dying. I, I…" She struggled to
say more, but uncontrollable sobs cut off her voice.

"No," was all Jane could think to say. She couldn't decide if
this was some sort of trick or on the up and up.

It took considerable time for Mrs. Ochoa to regain her
composure and continue. "Many week back, Solanch, he come
home from work, early, tree in da afternoon. I in kitchen. He walk
by me. He no say hello, he no kiss, he walk by like I no exist and
go to room." She stopped to compose herself.

"Maybe one hour go by. I hear him crying. I know he crying loud. If I hear him in kitchen and he in bedroom, then he crying loud. He never cry. Not since he little boy."

Mrs. Ochoa paused. Jane waited for her to continue. "I go back to him. He lying in bed, crying in pillow. I worry. I… I no like see him like this. He tell me between cries, 'I tried, Mamita. I tried. I failed. I failed.' I no idea what he talk about. I taught maybe bad ting at El Satélite happen. I call Papito. He come home fast. We call doctor who not know what *problema* but give him *medicina* make him sleep only it no work. Solanch only cry more. We call best doctors. All say same. What they call it, Papito?"

"Nervous breakdown, Mamita."

"Is that you, Mr. Ochoa?" Jane asked, disbelieving her own ears. This wasn't the Mr. Ochoa voice she had heard when she had stayed at the little house. That voice had been soft, humble. This new voice commanded attention.

"Yes, Jane. This is Mr. Ochoa. We're on a three-way conference call. I hope you don't mind."

"I thought I was talking to Mrs. Ochoa." Jane's suspicious nature was aroused.

"She made me promise to let her talk first, woman to woman. Mamita and I hate to involve you in our family problems, Jane, but you are our last hope. Solanch has given up." Mr. Ochoa's voice cracked with emotion. "He doesn't want to live." The sound of his voice frightened Jane.

"But why? Why would he want to do such a thing?" she asked unable to comprehend any motive that might make him do such a drastic thing.

"Please, Jane. Please. Please come," Mrs. Ochoa pleaded. "I beg you on my son's life. Please come."

Jane could hear Mrs. Ochoa's sobs. She felt helpless. "I don't see what I can do? If the doctors…"

"Please! Jane! Come! Solanch needs you. Papito and I needs you. What more I say you promise you come. *Estoy loca! Completamente loca!*" Jane could hear sobs catching in her throat.

"Mamita said she is out of her mind with fear. I'm close to it myself only I can't let myself go. There's too much at stake."

"But I can't just pick up and come. I've got a job, students who need me, responsibilities."

"All those things have been taken care of. Dr. Carlson has given you an unlimited leave of absence. I have provided your substitute, Mrs. Zeigler, who is quite capable. She will take over your classes until your return."

"But," Jane protested.

"Our time is limited," Mr. Ochoa continued. "I have much to explain to you. Things are not as you supposed them to be. Go to your window and look at the parking lot."

Jane did as he asked.

"Do you see the black car?"

"The limo?"

"Yes, the limo. Just a moment." She could hear his muffled voice talking to someone.

"Do you see a man getting out of the car?" The car door opened. "That's Steve. He's going to wave." She could hear his muffled voice. Moments later Steve waved.

"There's no time for you to pack, so I'm going to put Miss Zocalo on. She will ask you some questions about size and color so the appropriate clothing will be available when we land."

Miss Zocalo was efficient. She asked Jane five questions and was finished.

"By the way, Jane, be sure to close your windows before you leave the apartment."

"How do you know my windows are open?"

Mr. Ochoa laughed. "Don't worry, Jane. No spies. Steve told me." Then he became serious. "Please go down to the car. I know this all sounds strange to you, but you must trust me. Our family needs your help more than you know. Steve will drive you to Butler Aviation next to La Guardia. I'm on the company plane. We'll take off as soon as you get here."

CHAPTER 11

Steve drove Jane to the waiting Learjet. The moment she was seated on the plane, a young woman in a long, colorful dress that was a swirl of reds, yellows, and oranges blended together in a most pleasing, tropical manner greeted her. "Good evening, Miss Jones. Please allow me to help you." With the click of the seatbelt, the plane's engines revved. The plane rolled to take-off. Within minutes it was airborne.

Jane's attention had been focused on the take-off. She hadn't had time to think about Mr. Ochoa. She looked about the small cabin. She didn't see him. She looked for the young woman. She didn't see her either. Panic seized her. She closed her eyes and screamed.

"Are you ill, Miss Jones?"

When Jane opened her eyes and saw Miss Zocalo standing beside her, she stopped screaming. She saw a worried Mr. Ochoa looking over Miss Zocalo's shoulder. "My deepest apologies, Jane," he said. "I should have known better. It's that I love flying so much I assume everybody does."

Mr. Ochoa said something to Miss Zocalo who turned and left. He sat in the seat opposite Jane and deftly lowered a side table. "I've asked Miss Zocalo to mix you a margarita. Sorry I can't join you, but I'm officially on duty since I'm the pilot of record," he said smiling, but the smile disappeared when he saw a sudden look of fear cross Jane's eyes. "Don't worry. The best pilot we have is at the controls. He was kind enough to allow me to be the lead pilot so I can get in my flying hours to satisfy the FAA. I hope my take-off wasn't the reason that upset you. It was rather steep, but it's because of the noise abatement regulations. Ah, here's your margarita. Taste it and see if it's as good as Solanch makes."

Jane took a sip and nodded her approval.

Miss Zocalo smiled and said, "Thank you, Miss Jones. It's high praise when I can compete with Mr. Ochoa's bartending skills. May I bring you a blanket?"

"Yes, please!" Jane replied. She had left her overheated apartment wearing nothing more than a pair of shorts and a light sweater.

Miss Zocalo brought the blanket, wrapped it around Jane, and disappeared to the rear of the plane.

For the first time, Jane had the opportunity to get a good look at Mr. Ochoa, a much different Mr. Ochoa from the one she had seen at the little house. His snow-white hair that had been tousled by the desert wind was perfectly combed. His expensive gray suit, shirt, and tie were coordinated to bring out the whiteness of his hair and the magical glint in his eyes.

"I know this is quite a shock to you limousines, private jets."

"To say the least," Jane muttered between sips of margarita.

"Mamita and I like the simple life. I know none of this looks simple." He gestured at the interior of the plane. "But it's as simple as I can make it and still do business around the world. I'm sure you've never heard of us, Ochoa Industries. The name doesn't appear anywhere except on the New York Stock Exchange, but we're a company that has holdings in every country in the world. Ochoa Industries is the name behind the name. Ever hear of Zapato Barato?"

"Yes," Jane said sheepishly, embarrassed she shopped at such a cheap store.

"Don't be embarrassed. I see you're wearing one of our most popular products, the TSW999, a low-cost shoe with high value. You've chosen well, Jane."

Jane smiled, pleased with her shopping skills.

"So much for business." Mr. Ochoa motioned to the back of the plane. "I don't know about you, Jane, but I'm hungry. How about you?"

"Me too."

Miss Zocalo placed their dinners on the table. Jane couldn't believe how good everything tasted at forty thousand feet.

Three hours later the plane landed. Mr. Ochoa and Jane boarded the waiting helicopter for the short flight to The Big House as Mr. Ochoa called it. As the helicopter settled onto the landing pad, Jane was shocked to find it wasn't a house but a massive hotel. Security guards rushed her off the helicopter. Huge glass doors swung open as she entered the building. More security guards rushed her down a hallway to a waiting elevator where she was whisked to the top floor. When she stepped out of the elevator, more security guards greeted her and asked her to follow them through a large room that was elegantly decorated and into another hallway where she saw Mrs. Ochoa talking with two men outside a double oak door.

"Jane," Mrs. Ochoa said quietly when she saw her approaching. Mrs. Ochoa extended her hands. They felt cold and trembled in Jane's hands. "*Gracias por venir.* Thank you for coming." Mrs. Ochoa's eyes filled with tears. "He so bad, Jane. I'm not sure how long he live like this. You our last hope. Oh, *excúsame.* I forget to introduce Dr. Spinoza and Dr. Silverstein." Both doctors shook Jane's hand showing her great respect. They looked at her not as someone who would interfere with their medical decisions but as a healer, the one person who might save a patient they couldn't.

Dr. Silverstein spoke, "We're hoping you can get him to eat, Miss Jones. We forced fed him for a week. Now we're feeding him intravenously. That's the only reason he's still alive. We can keep his body alive but not his mind. Without the will to live, intravenous feeding is only a means to an end, the end meaning his complete recovery or..." his voice trailed away in despair.

Jane could hear Mrs. Ochoa's choked sobs. Whether she'd heard Dr. Silverstein's words or not was of no consequence. She knew her son was dying on the other side of the closed double oak doors.

"So that's the situation, Miss Jones. Do what you can to get him to eat on his own. Just do the best you can," he added as words of encouragement.

Instead of his words giving Jane hope, they frightened her. What could she do the doctors hadn't already done? She had no idea how she could help let alone cure the dying person on the other side of the doors. Dr. Spinoza swung the doors open. Jane stood motionless as if rooted to the floor. Her legs shook so badly she wasn't certain she could walk. How long she stood transfixed she had no idea, but somehow she managed to take the few steps into the room because she heard the soft click of doors closing behind her.

CHAPTER 12

Jane stood many minutes getting used to the grandiose if not grotesque scene that lay before her, a scene that looked more like a movie set than someone's bedroom. The room was immense, more than twice the size of her New York studio apartment, but what caught her attention was the huge chandelier that hung from the ceiling in the center of the room. Its brightness seemed out of place when contrasted with the life and death struggle that was being waged under its intense white brilliance.

Once her eyes had become used to the intense brightness, she looked across the room to its far side, a side hidden by tall white medical screens that shielded whoever was behind them from the intense light. The sight of the screens renewed her fears. She knew who was on the other side of those screens. Someone she never wanted to see in the best of times let alone the worst. Slowly she made her way across the room. Each shaky step she took felt as if she were walking on eggshells, her feet sinking into the deep white-piled carpet, each step guided by soft beeping sounds that came from behind the white screens.

As she rounded the screens, the beeping machines that had guided her steps came into view. She stared at them, not understanding what the flashing green numerals meant. It was a long while before she could bring herself to look at the bed where he lay somewhere in the dark shadows.

Her eyes started at the foot of the bed. She saw a slight rise in the sheet that outlined his feet pointing outward. The rest of his body seemed to disappear beneath the whiteness, a whiteness that looked more like a death shroud than a sheet. It wasn't until her eyes came upon the upper body did she see a slight rise in the sheet. She became aware of a new sound not made by machines but by him, the unmistaken sound of labored breathing.

When she looked at his face, she gasped in shock for her gaze had fallen on the part of the face she would never have dared look at in any man—his eyes. These were the eyes of a dying man. Even with the lids closed, she could see they had receded into their sockets with heavy dark circles beneath them. She stared. She couldn't help herself. If it hadn't been for the labored sound of his breathing, she would have been certain the eyes had been closed by death and not sleep.

How long she stared at those eyes she had no idea until she became aware of his long black hair with its once sexy curled ends. Now it looked lifeless and brittle. She lowered her gaze to the facial features that had made him handsome but handsome no more. The skin had shrunk and was nothing more than a thin, leathery covering for the bones that lay beneath. The lips were no longer reddish-brown but an ashy-bluish gray. They had lost their fullness and were pulled back so as to give him a ghoulish smile, revealing his white teeth contrasted by purplish gums that had an unhealthy look as death worked to snuff out the last vestiges of life within him.

Mrs. Ochoa hadn't exaggerated. He appeared to be preparing for the last breath of life and to pass into the unknown. Jane couldn't believe the once handsome face now resembled a death mask rather than that of a living being and how the once strong body had shriveled to nothing more than skin and bone. She knew it was an unworthy thought, but it was one that in the briefest of moments crossed her mind, that even the handsomest look ghastly before death, for he no longer looked like a vibrant young man, only the black hair belied his true age.

She put her hand over her mouth to stifle the sob she felt welling up inside her throat as she studied the broken body before her, but it was no use as one strangled sob followed another making it nearly impossible for her to breathe. Tears flowed down her cheeks. She collapsed into a red leather chair by the bed. It took many minutes for the tears to stop flowing and her breathing to return to normal. She was thankful he had been asleep and hadn't heard her sobs.

Minutes passed into hours. She put her head against the back of the chair. She couldn't be certain if she nodded off or not for reality had become intertwined with surrealistic dreams, and in the mental state she was in, she couldn't distinguish between the two.

CHAPTER 13

A scream made Jane bolt upright in the chair. She looked over at the bed. He was sitting, screaming as loud as his tortured lungs would allow.

She jumped to her feet. Without a thought, she said in the same voice she used to reprimand her students, "Stop the screaming! Right now!" To her surprise, the screams stopped.

"Now lie back," she commanded. When he didn't obey, she said in a louder voice, "Lie back, this instant! And no more screaming! Do you understand?" She put her hand on his shoulder and placed several pillows behind him lowering his body against them. She heard what she thought was a chuckle, but she couldn't be certain if it was that or air escaping from his lungs.

"What's the idea of you scaring the wits out of your mother?" She paused while she straightened out the sheet. "And your father too," she added, placing another pillow behind his back to support his semi upright position. "They're out of their minds with grief. They're...they're..." she struggled to remember the Spanish word, "they're *loca*, yes, *loca*." She emphasized the last "*loca*". "Everyone at the motel is *loca*. Are you satisfied you've managed to make *loca* everybody who knows you, making me come all the way out here to see you like this? Well, buster, I think you've overplayed this scene, and I for one am pretty well tired of it." She put her hands on her hips to accentuate her no-nonsense attitude. "Now, I'm going to order a little something for you to eat, and you're going to eat it, like a big boy. Do you understand? Blink once if you understand." He didn't blink.

"Now listen, Mister! Make up your mind! Blink once if you want to eat like a gentleman, or else I'm going to pry open your mouth and pour it down your gullet. Your choice!" The long awaited blink appeared along with a sound Jane knew was a chuckle. "I'm going to step out of the room. I won't be gone long."

She walked around the screen. She jumped in fright at the sight of two security guards seated in red leather chairs on the other side of the screen not far from his bed. She blushed, ashamed of the things she had just said, but shame vanished when suspicious thoughts flooded her brain. *They don't trust me. They've sent guards to spy on me. Do they think I'm going to kill him?* Jane realized that was exactly what they thought. *So that's why they dragged me out here. They expect me to kill him so they don't have to do it themselves. They don't want his death on their hands, so they're framing me,* Jane's suspicious mind concluded.

She decided he wasn't going to die, not to save him, but to save herself. The battle lines had been drawn. He was going to live no matter what she had to do, and once she had accomplished that feat, she was going to get out of this gilded house of horrors with its spying security guards. "I suppose you heard what I said," she said to the guards.

"Yes, ma'am," they said in hushed unison.

In a voice more severe than necessary, "Would one of you go get a cup of chicken broth and a small glass of orange juice?"

One of the men got up and headed for the door while the other pulled a cell out of his pocket, pushed a button, and whispered something unintelligible into it. She had no sooner sat down in the chair next to the bed than the guard who had left the room appeared carrying a small tray with what she had ordered.

Without a word to the guard, she took the tray out of his hands and put it on the table. She picked up the tepid bowl of broth, sat on the edge of the bed, and placed the broth filled spoon in his partially parted lips. He swallowed as much as he could with considerable difficulty.

"You're so dried out, you can't swallow," Jane said unsympathetically, wiping his chin with a white linen napkin.

She reached for a glass of water on the table and lifted his head high enough to pour a bit of the liquid down his throat. She alternated with a teaspoon of broth followed by a sip of water until all the broth had been eaten. "Now drink this orange juice," she coldly commanded. He drank it willingly.

She wiped his mouth with the linen napkin. "I'm going to do this every two hours until you're strong enough to feed yourself. Then I'll order one of those famous New Mexico steaks Pepe's way with baked potato smothered in one of his secret sauces and a delicious, nutritious salad. You'll need something green by then. Once you've eaten, it's back to New York for me. Do you understand?"

She saw him blink. Now that he had eaten, she could rest. She set her cell for two hours, leaned back in the chair, and fell into a sound sleep.

CHAPTER 14

When the cell sounded two hours later, Jane jumped to attention. He was awake. The look in his sunken eyes told her he was pleased she was there, but his look meant nothing. She didn't want his appreciation. She wanted nothing from him. She had a job to do, to get him well, nothing else. She knew she had to escape his charm, his wealth, and his sickness as soon as possible. He meant nothing to her, nothing.

Under Jane's watchful eye, he made tremendous progress. Within a week, he was sitting up and feeding himself liquids with some soft food mixed in. If she hadn't seen it with her own eyes, she wouldn't have believed it, but as the first week passed, his eyes and cheeks became less sunken. His lips regained some of their color and fullness. She could see an improvement in his overall skin color, a bit of the redness shown through, and the skin didn't look as leathery as it had a week earlier. She was fascinated to watch Mother Nature at work as she sought to repair the damage death had tried to inflict.

As his strength returned, so did the strength of the Ochoas who came to see their son every day. Sometimes Mamita and Papito came together. Sometimes they came separately. When they came together, they talked about the weather, friends, and a little bit about New Mexico politics. When Mrs. Ochoa came by herself, she fussed over him, holding his hand, and wanting to know how he felt while praising Jane for saving her son. When Mr. Ochoa came, he too praised Jane for her good work, but he focused more on business.

Jane asked to be excused from these family conversations, but the Ochoas insisted she stay. They trusted her. She had saved their son. Besides, she made them and their son laugh.

By the end of the second week, he looked almost like his old self. His good looks, the beauty in his eyes as well as his sweet voice had returned. Jane knew it was time. She had the stewards prepare a table fit for a proper executive luncheon in the bedroom and ordered steak Pepe's way. Solanch relished every bite of his steak luncheon. She relished it too. She knew this was the last one she would have.

When they had finished, they talked for a few minutes. Jane excused herself from the table, telling him she had something important to do. He stood when she stood and remained standing long after she had left the room.

She asked one of the security guards seated outside the oak doors if she could make an appointment to see Mr. Ochoa as soon as possible. The young guard looked surprised. "Miss Jones. You never have to make an appointment. You are always most welcome in Mr. Ochoa's office. Let me call ahead and let his secretary know you're on your way." He pressed a button on his cell, said a few words, then looked at Jane, and said, "Please follow me."

He led her to a waiting elevator that whisked them many floors downward. When the doors opened, she was surprised to see hundreds of people milling about talking. "This is the conference hall, Miss Jones. Executives from the various companies Mr. Ochoa owns meet here to discuss economic trends and how they relate to the world economy and their own particular companies."

"So many people," Jane muttered in awe.

"Oh, this is nothing. You should see this place when it really gets busy. We've had more than a thousand people in this room. You should hear the noise level with so many different languages being spoken. It's like the UN. But all that changes when Mr. Ochoa appears. Then there's total silence. Everyone thinks very highly of Mr. Ochoa," he said reverently. "It's their way of showing respect for a man who started with nothing and built up his companies to be the largest, most influential in the world. They trust him with everything they have. When he speaks, they listen."

Jane wished the security guard hadn't told her this about Mr. Ochoa because it was going to make it all the more difficult to do what she knew she had to do.

"Would you believe, this *big house* as Mr. and Mrs. Ochoa call it, has four hundred bedrooms, five hundred bathrooms, four ballrooms, the conference hall you just saw, five different dining rooms, an Olympic size swimming pool, a gym with all the latest equipment plus an indoor running track, a bowling alley with fifty lanes, a billiard room, a library better than most big city libraries, and a kitchen that can feed over two thousand people five meals a day. This isn't a house. It's a hotel, easy to get lost in if you don't know your way around. I've gotten lost a couple of times."

All Jane could do was shake her head in awe, intimidated by the hugeness of the place the Ochoas called home.

While Jane and the security guard had been talking, they had crossed the conference hall, gone down a corridor, and entered a large office filled with men and women working intently. At the rear of the room was a large oak door with a gold plaque on it that read Personal Secretary of Mr. Solanch Ochoa and underneath that, Mrs. Gabriella del Rio.

Jane felt more intimidated and inferior with each oak door she passed through, but she knew she had to do what she had to do and she was going to do it no matter what.

"Miss Jones, if I may address you in that way." An attractive middle-aged woman with graying hair stood in front of her desk, smiling, with her hand extended as Jane walked across the room to take her hand.

"I'd prefer you call me Jane."

"Then Jane it is," Mrs. del Rio replied in a most pleasing voice. "Mr. Ochoa is waiting for you. Please allow me to escort you to his office."

Mrs. del Rio opened the large oak door at the rear of her office and led Jane down a carpeted corridor where another set of huge oak doors loomed at the far end. In front of the doors sat four security guards with rifles lying across their laps. "Security, Jane. It's everywhere. We can't be too careful these days, especially since terrorists have vowed to attack every corporate headquarters they can, but don't worry. None of the guards will shoot you," she paused for effect and then added, "as long as I'm with you."

"Oh," Jane said, so intimidated she didn't know how to respond properly.

As Jane and Mrs. del Rio approached the massive oak doors, they opened. "I'll see you on the way out, Jane. Until then, good afternoon." She turned and left Jane to enter Mr. Ochoa's office alone.

"Jane, I'm so glad to see you. You honor my office," Mr. Ochoa said, standing just inside the opened doors. "Please take a chair so we can both relax and talk more informally." He motioned to two chairs opposite each other separated by a highly polished small table. "Big desks are much too formal to have a friendly conversation over." He smiled a mischievous smile. His eyes glinted as he added, "And a smaller table makes it easier for us to have something nice to drink. I know you've just finished having luncheon with Solanch, so I'm going to take the liberty to offer you an after lunch drink, if that's all right with you."

"Yes," she muttered softly.

As if by magic a female attendant appeared. Mr. Ochoa ordered two of something Jane couldn't understand.

When the attendant left, Mr. Ochoa continued. "First of all, Jane, Mrs. Ochoa and I will never be able to find the words to express our gratitude for all you've done. You not only saved my son's life but Ochoa Industries as well because Solanch will take over all this when I retire." He motioned with his hand around the huge, exquisitely decorated office.

"Mr. Ochoa," Jane said as matter-of-factly as she could. "I came here to do a job, nothing more and nothing less. I'm pleased I was able to help."

"Good, our drinks have arrived. I hope you like it," Mr. Ochoa said cheerfully, brushing aside what Jane had said and the way she had said it.

Jane took a sip of the drink she had been offered. She had never tasted anything like it before.

"What do you think?" Mr. Ochoa asked, sitting on the edge of his chair.

"Hmmm. Very good," Jane said in a more pleasant voice.

"I was hoping you would say that."

"What's it called? I'd buy a bottle right away."

"Doesn't have a name yet. Experimental. One of our companies in India has been working on it since the beginning of the year. I'll tell them they have one customer who's willing to buy their product." Mr. Ochoa laughed. Jane managed a forced smile.

"As I was saying, Jane, Mrs. Ochoa and I are most appreciative of all you've done. Words can't even begin to express how we feel about what you've done and how we feel about you."

"That's very kind. Please thank Mrs. Ochoa when you see her."

"I had hoped you would tell her yourself, over dinner, tonight."

"My purpose for being here no longer exists. I need to leave as soon as possible on a regular airline in coach class and not on some private jet. You've spent enough money on me already."

Mr. Ochoa sat back in his chair, dumbfounded. "But, Jane, can't you stay a few days longer? Everything is settled at your school. You can stay here or at the little house for as long as you like."

"Please, Mr. Ochoa. I want to leave as soon as possible."

Mr. Ochoa stood and went to his desk. She could hear him talking softly, to whom she couldn't be certain, but she imagined it was Mrs. del Rio. She could distinguish only a few words like *reservation*, *New York*, *as soon as possible* and not much more.

When Mr. Ochoa had finished talking on the phone, he sat down in the chair opposite Jane and said, "Mrs. del Rio is checking to see which airline leaves the earliest." Jane could see he was upset.

After what seemed an eternity of silence, he spoke. "Under the circumstances, you have made what I have to say next very difficult. I don't want you to get the wrong impression about what I'm going to say, but I made a solemn promise to Mamita, Solanch, and myself that I would." He could see Jane wince in her chair.

"You have done a great service, Jane, more than you realize. On behalf of Mamita, Solanch, and me, as an expression of our gratitude and our respect for you, we have opened a bank account in your name for five million dollars, tax-free I might add. We hope this token of our appreciation will enrich your life in many ways, and," he stressed the word *and*, "we hope you will come visit us often and stay as long as you wish," he added with a smile.

Now it was Jane's turn to be stunned but only for a few moments. She feared if she waited too long she would give an answer she would regret. "Mr. Ochoa." She paused, weighing her words carefully, looking into her lap. "It's a very generous offer. One I'm certain I should take. But I'm not going to. You and your family were very kind to me when I needed help. I have simply repaid my debt. Consider our accounts balanced and equal, nothing more, nothing less."

"Jane, the money is a token of our gratitude. This is our way of saying thank you. Please accept our gift. No strings attached." The look in his eyes conveyed the hurt his gift wasn't going to be accepted.

"I know this sounds crazy, and most people would say I'm crazy for not accepting it, but I'm old-fashioned. I'm not interested in money, at least not large amounts of it. For me to enjoy money, I must work for it. I must save for something I want, like my car, Subie. That way and only that way can I appreciate the things I've bought and the things I have. Five million dollars wouldn't do me much good except make me fat, lazy, and arrogant. Three things I don't intend to become. I like who I am, and I don't want money to change me."

Mr. Ochoa went to his desk and picked up an envelope. He returned to where Jane was seated. "At least you can accept this envelope that contains all the information you will need to access the account."

"Thank you but no thank you. I don't want the envelope. That would be a temptation I would have to fight every day of my life."

A long silence followed before Mr. Ochoa spoke. "I can understand your feelings, Jane. Just remember. The money will always be there in your name if you ever need it." He smiled the best he could.

The phone on Mr. Ochoa's desk rang. He answered, listened for a few moments, and said quietly, "Yes, yes, I'll tell her. Thank you, Gabriella." He turned to Jane. "A car is waiting to take you to the airport. Your plane takes off in little over an hour. We'll send your clothes to you."

"Please don't bother. They don't belong to me. They belong to you." Jane stood. "Once again, thank you for your kindness, generosity, and hospitality. They won't be forgotten." Jane knew her last words were a lie because she intended to forget the Ochoas as soon as she could. They weren't going to hurt her or run her life. Not for five, ten, twenty, or even a hundred million dollars. Jane Jones was Jane Jones and she was going to stay that way the rest of her life.

A week later Solanch called. Jane knew he would, and she was prepared to do what she had to do. She was polite. She answered all his questions but asked none so the conversation remained one-sided. She had to admit his voice was charming, but she reminded herself of his good looks, looks that were too good for her, his wealth, wealth that threatened to destroy her individuality, and his mental instability, instability that had nearly killed him and might do the same to her. She considered his mental weakness his rightful curse for being so good-looking, so charming, and so rich. He called once a week for the next several weeks, then once every other week, once a month, and then not at all. When the calls stopped, a sense of relief swept over her. Now she could be herself.

CHAPTER 15

Fate has its way with us humans. Just when we think we are in control of our destinies, events occur that destroy even the most carefully planned lives, and so it was with Jane. As the years passed, her well-ordered life fell apart bit by bit. It began with her father. It was as if some unseen force inside his head had flicked a switch. One day he was his fun-loving, gentle self. The next he was an unrecognizable man who flew into rages over the most trivial of things. Sunday dinners for Jane became hours spent in fear and despair. If she or her mother forgot to put the salt shaker on the table, he flew into a rage. If his coffee wasn't hot enough, he called Jane and her mother vulgar names, names he had never uttered to either of them in his life.

Jane feared Alzheimer's. When she suggested he see a doctor, he flew into such a rage she and her mother cringed in fear. It wasn't until a neighbor overheard his yelling and threatened to call the police that he settled down.

Jane could see the terrible toll her father's rages were having on her mother. Each Sunday she visited she couldn't help but notice how increasingly withdrawn her mother had become. She realized she was now the mother and her mother the daughter, a daughter who needed care, a daughter who sought refuge in remembering past events, whether it was her daddy kissing her when he got home from work, the day of her wedding, or the birth of Jean,

Jane's older sister by three years. Her mother's fondest memories were reserved for Jean. She talked endlessly about Jean and all the cute and funny things she had done. She wished Jane would marry someone as important as Jean had and have lots of babies so she would be a grandmother many times over, ignoring the fact it was Jane, not Jean, who was there when she needed help.

This was a bitter pill for Jane to swallow. For the first time in her life, she realized it was Jean her mother loved. Her mother had used her to get the things she needed like a half gallon of milk here and a few pounds of steak there, things Jane paid for because her mother had no money of her own, but the bitterest part of the pill was Jean could have cared less about her mother. Her interests focused on herself, herself, herself, and then her children, in that order. She cared little for her husband, Terrence, whom she regarded as nothing more than someone to provide the luxuries she demanded. Jane realized her sister would be no help in the crises their parents faced in the months ahead.

Crises have a way of striking when we least expect them even when they're expected, and sometimes it isn't the crisis we expected. Jane knew her father was slipping away day by day, and there was nothing she could do to stop it. He had been diagnosed with inoperable cancerous brain tumors that as they grew in size pressed against those parts of the brain that had made her father the strong, intelligent man who had shaped her life in so many ways. She knew his days were few. She was determined to be the best daughter an ailing father could possibly want. When the phone rang at three in the morning, she thought his end had come. She had prepared for this moment the best she could, but her heart beat wildly as she picked up the phone.

"Jane?"

"Yes," Jane answered hesitantly.

"Come! Quick!"

In the background, she could hear a low-pitched, menacing male voice shouting, "Shut up! Shut up!" while the voice on the phone sounded fearful and breathless.

"What?" Jane asked, trying desperately to wake up and understand what she was being told.

"It's your father! He's got a knife! He's trying to kill me!" her mother shrieked. Jane heard sounds of furniture being overturned and breaking glass, screams followed by muffled sounds followed by more screams. "Get away from me!" her mother snarled in a voice Jane had never heard her use.

Jane sat upright in bed. "Mother!" she screamed. She could hear her mother pleading, "Don't hurt me. Please don't hurt me, Harold," followed by several loud blood curdling screams followed by several quieter screams.

"Shut up!" a male voice shouted.

The phone went dead. Jane sat on the edge of the bed stunned. When she regained her senses, she pushed her parents' number. No one answered. She hung up and called the New York City Police Department who informed her that a neighbor had reported loud noises coming from the apartment in question and a police unit was entering the building. The dispatcher asked her to hold so he could give her accurate information. When he returned, his voice was grim. He asked several questions to confirm Jane's identity and reported a female had been killed at the address Jane had inquired about.

When Jane turned the corner onto the street where her parents lived, the street was a mass of flashing red, white, and blue lights. Her worst fears were realized when she entered the apartment building. A policewoman informed her that a male had killed his wife. The man's name was Harold Jones, the woman's name, Elizabeth Jones.

Jane didn't know how to feel. The man she had adored, who had taught her about morality, patriotism, and the ways of the world, had murdered his wife, her mother, a woman who cared little for her. She leaned against the wall trying to understand what had happened when she heard footsteps in the stairway along with the jangling of keys and the squeaking of leather. She saw her father being lead out of the building in handcuffs by two burly policemen. As he passed her in the hallway, his glassy eyes revealed the inner soul, the light of her life, had been extinguished. He passed in silence. Neither had anything to say to the other. All the years they had spent together laughing, loving, and surprising each other would become distant, blurry memories, but this one moment would forever be seared in her brain.

When Jane informed Jean of their mother's death and asked for help in making the funeral arrangements, Jean told her she couldn't possibly fit a funeral into her busy schedule because she had filed for divorce from her no-good, rat of a husband. Jane wasn't surprised her sister refused to help. She had known she would have to make the funeral arrangements for her mother without Jean's help, but for her own conscience, she wanted to give Jean one last chance to redeem herself, a chance Jean cast aside without a moment's hesitation.

CHAPTER 16

Murder doesn't make a comfortable companion with death. People focus not on the death but the murder, especially one as grisly as Jane's mother's murder had been. Some people thought she had been the cause of her own murder. If she had acted differently, she never would have been murdered. Others didn't want to be associated with anything as sordid as murder and did everything in their power to disassociate themselves from it. Only Jane, the funeral home staff, and a priest were present to bury her mother.

The night after the funeral, Jean called to apologize for her lack of attendance and to convey her condolences, not like a daughter who had lost her mother but as a distant friend who thought it her duty to call. Jean's call had nothing to do with grief but everything to do with Jean. She ranted how she was going to make her high-flying husband pay big bucks for all the awful things he had to done to her. She talked of all the sacrifices she had made, how she had taken care of the children while he had been off gallivanting around New York with every cheap floozy he could get his hands on. She had had enough staying at home, playing the devoted housewife role while that cheap, no-good husband of hers was... Jean continued on until Jane had heard enough.

"Thank you for calling, Jean. I know mother would have appreciated it if you could have attended her funeral, but under the circumstances, I know she would have understood your personal matters would naturally come first." Jane's voice dripped with sarcasm, a sarcasm she couldn't restrain.

"Well, yes, I mean, I just thought…" Jean sputtered for words.

"With that thought in mind, good night," Jane replied and folded her cell shut. She knew the relationship with her sister she had once treasured would be strained if nonexistent in the future.

Several weeks later Jane's father passed away. From the moment the hospital informed her of his passing, she felt a deep emptiness. She had lost the anchor of her life. She was alone. Her tears weren't just for her mother, or her father, but for herself. Both funerals had been sad, desolate affairs, especially difficult for Jane. No acquaintances, friends, or family members came, visual proof she was alone in the world. She realized there was no one, not a single person on the face of the Earth who loved her. That thought frightened her more than she cared to admit. Her life seemed purposeless. She had no place to go, no one to visit. She tried to take comfort her students needed her, but that wasn't enough, not nearly enough. That was a professional relationship, not a personal one. She had no hope for a personal relationship.

It is said that bad news comes in threes. That may well be true, but in Jane's case it came in fours. The death of her mother, the death of her father, and the living death of her sister—these three riders of the apocalypse had struck and struck fast removing all the joy and happiness from the life Jane had known. The last remaining joy was her students, but as events unfolded, the fourth rider of the apocalypse rose up to destroy this one last refuge of happiness.

The world was changing and none for the better. So it was with teaching. Jane's new principal, Dr. Sidney Carter, insisted new methods of instruction be employed, and any teacher who did not comply with his directives was subject to disciplinary action if not dismissal. It wasn't that Jane resisted change, but she resisted change that lowered academic standards, weakened teacher authority, and created chaos in the classroom.

She fought as hard as she could against Dr. Carter's directives. One afternoon she received a note from the superintendent who wanted to see her in her office at the close of school. During the meeting, the superintendent made it clear to Jane if she did not cooperate with Dr. Carter's directives, she would initiate disciplinary actions against her. She stressed the word *actions* because Jane was in violation of more than one of Dr. Carter's directives.

Leaving the superintendent's office, Jane was furious and afraid, furious that incompetence had taken control of a profession she loved and afraid, not just for her teaching career but for her life. She felt the will to live ebbing from her body, mind, and soul. Her last refuge for happiness was being taken away by bureaucratic, senseless madness. She felt more alone and empty than she ever had. Suicide never seemed a more welcome friend. No longer did she think about it. She thought how to do it.

CHAPTER 17

Meaningless days passed, one by one in slow succession. Jane got up in the morning, drove to school, taught her classes, drove home, stuck something in the microwave for dinner, did her schoolwork, went to bed, and did the same day after day after day. On the weekends, she got up, cleaned her studio apartment, did the laundry, watched TV, and went to bed. She left the apartment to go to the supermarket, the dry cleaners, the gas station, and occasionally the car wash. These repetitious days became repetitious months that became repetitious years. Years and years passed in this meaningless manner.

The thoughts of suicide had faded long ago to be replaced by an uncaring awareness of life and the people around her. She had no personal relationships, not even her sister, whom she hadn't spoken to since her mother's death. The only people she could count as friends were several teachers who invited her to their homes for a holiday here and there, but they were busy with their families. They had scant time for Jane who trudged through life waiting for it to end in its own good time.

Jane knew she shouldn't complain. She had an uncomplicated life. She had her freedom. She could be who she was, Jane Jones. Her deepest wish had been granted, only it was a wish that brought her no happiness.

Winter was the most depressing time of year for Jane. Its dark days and even darker nights dragged on endlessly. One such night she had settled into an old TV rerun of *Sex in the City* when the phone rang.

"Yes," she screamed into the phone, hoping the person on the other end would hang up.

"Jane? Jane Jones? Is that you?" It was a calm, male voice.

"Yes," she said not as angrily as before.

"I don't know if you remember me or not, Jane. It's Solanch Ochoa calling."

The sound of his name, the sound of his sweet voice was like a punch in the stomach, rendering her speechless.

"Jane? Are you there?"

"Yes," she managed to utter.

"I know my call is unexpected. I hope I'm not disturbing you in any way."

"No. Not at all."

"I'll get to the reason why I called. I was wondering if you would have dinner with me Wednesday night about seven, if the time works for you."

"Dinner? Seven? Let me think." She paused a long time before she had the courage to say, "Yes, I can make it."

"I'll send a car to pick you up at six thirty, if that's convenient for you."

"Yes," she said, feeling more like a woman than she had in years.

Even in the cold, dark depths of winter, the sun shone brightly on Jane. Her life had meaning. She had something to look forward to. She felt giddy, like a schoolgirl. She had to admit his voice had sounded wonderful even though he had only said a few words. Her body tingled at the thought of seeing him. She had missed him more than she had allowed herself to believe. Her loins longed for him. *Maybe after Wednesday I won't be a virgin.* She giggled in ecstasy at the thought.

On Wednesday morning, she did something she had never done in her teaching career. She took a day off to go shopping. Her first stop was the most expensive dress shop in town. She felt uncomfortable when she entered the shop, but an attentive older woman greeted her warmly. She offered Jane a cup of coffee and then showed her a variety of dresses she thought Jane might like. Jane was enchanted. It was as if she had entered a world of make-believe. An hour later, she and the woman decided a low cut, knee-length, black dress along with a pair of open shoes with black straps and stiletto heels that came from the shop next door would be appropriate for the dinner engagement. Jane explained she would wear her mother's pearl earrings and necklace as accents. The woman agreed they would be proper accoutrements. Jane left the shop feeling young and carefree.

Her next stop was the beauty parlor where she had the least amount of hope. She joked to herself that *maybe somebody in this place can work miracles with scraggily, mousy-brown hair.* The hair stylist greeted her as warmly as the woman in the dress shop had. After looking at Jane's hair for several minutes, she smiled and said, "We have lots of options."

"We do?" Jane squeaked, surprised that anything could be done with her *unruly mop* as she called it.

"We do," the hairstylist reconfirmed.

The stylist described various styles along with coloring options. Jane showed her the dress she had bought. The stylist complimented her on her good taste and said, "That narrows it to two choices." She combed Jane's hair into both styles so she would have some idea of what each would look like. After considerable discussion, she and the stylist made a decision. Jane snuggled back in the chair, closed her eyes as the stylist went about the task of transforming her *unruly mop* into a modern hairstyle. The warmth of the stylist's soft touch, something no one had done since she had been a little girl, relaxed her into a state of blissful oblivion.

"Tah, dah!" were the next words Jane heard. When she opened her eyes, the stylist had turned the chair so she could see herself in the mirror.

Jane gasped when she saw the reflection and shrieked, "That's me?"

"That's you," the stylist assured her.

"I don't believe it. Are you sure you didn't paste someone else's picture on the mirror?"

"No ma'am. That's one hundred percent you."

"You really are a miracle worker. I love the strawberry blond coloring, and you even managed to hide my broad-English forehead. I don't believe it."

After the beauty parlor, Jane decided to splurge and have an expensive lunch. It was just a little after one. She wasn't going to have dinner until sometime after seven, maybe later if she had her way. Her heart jumped at the thought. She settled on a nice bistro and was pleased how cordially the waitress greeted her and ushered her to a table. During the course of lunch, she was delighted that several female patrons noticed her hairstyle and smiled their approval. Jane didn't feel lonely as she relished each sip of wine and each bite of food placed before her.

It was well past two thirty when she left the restaurant. She made her way to the most expensive department store in town for its special makeup makeover. The cosmetologist couldn't have been friendlier, praising both her and the hairstylist for their selection of color and style which, as she explained, would determine the shades and tones of cosmetics she would recommend.

Jane's interest in cosmetics waned as a tummy full of wine and good food soothed her into a wonderful hypnotic world of half awake and half asleep. How much time she spent in this blissful state she had no idea. She would have remained there for hours if it hadn't been for the cosmetologist who said in a pleasant voice, "There now. I think we've finished. Let's let you have a look."

The cosmetologist turned the chair so Jane could see herself in the mirror. Jane couldn't believe her eyes. She stared in disbelief for some moments before she spoke. "My lips, my pale, thin lips look so much fuller, and my eyes, I never knew I had such pretty eyes."

"I'm so glad you're pleased. The moment I saw you, I knew I wanted to concentrate on your emerald eyes to accentuate their fiery greenness."

Jane turned to the cosmetologist. "You have performed a miracle. I don't know how you did it, but you did. I never dreamed I could ever, ever look like this." For the first time in her life, Jane felt pretty, and what a wonderful, glorious feeling it was for her. This was her moment, and she savored every second of it.

CHAPTER 18

When Jane returned home, she rested for an hour in preparation for her next task, learning to walk in stiletto heels, a feat she had never tried. She surprised herself. She walked better in them than she had expected. After a few turns in the apartment, she took off the shoes, showered, spritzed herself with the high priced perfume she had purchased from the cosmetologist, shimmied into the black dress, slipped on the stilettos, attached the pearl earrings to her ears, and secured the pearl necklace around her neck.

She stood in front of the mirror for a last minute inventory. She decided to be as critical as she was sure he was going to be. She checked her hair, perfect. She checked her makeup, perfect. She checked her dress, perfect. She checked her figure. Much to her delight the dress accented all the right curves of her trim, petite figure even more than it had at the store. Her figure was perfect. The shoes were perfect. She had to admit the extra three inches in height added to her well-proportioned figure. Everything was perfect. "Well,"—she breathed in heavily—"this is as good as it gets." She glanced at the clock. Two minutes before six thirty. She looked out the window. The limo was waiting in the parking lot. "It's show time," she whispered nervously to herself.

As Jane approached the waiting limo, the driver had the rear door open. "Good evening, Miss Jones. I'm sure you don't remember, but I drove you to Butler Aviation many years ago. My name is Steve."

"Good evening, Steve," she replied good-naturedly. "Where are we headed tonight?"

"Trump-Tower-Twelve-on-the-Hudson, ma'am."

"Ex-pen-see-ive." She accented each syllable.

Steve laughed. "You can say that again. I can't afford the electric bill in that place let alone the rent."

"You and me both." They laughed.

She snuggled back in the seat while Steve talked about a snowstorm that was expected to hit the city in an hour or two. "Doesn't seem like it could snow tonight," she heard him say. "It's too warm for snow, but that's what the guys at The Weather Channel are predicting."

She didn't hear much of what Steve said because she was lost in her own thoughts about what she was going to say to him, things he was going to say to her, romantic glasses of wine, maybe a little something to eat, she would sit on the sofa, he would sit next to her, he would compliment her on her perfume, her hair, her dress, her breasts. She felt warmth shoot through her body as she imagined his warm breath against her cheek, him kissing her lips with those full, reddish-brown lips of his. She could feel his soft, warm hands on her breasts.

"They say it's going to snow a foot or more tonight and maybe another foot tomorrow." Steve looked in the rear view mirror so he could see her better. "Man, oh, man. That's really going to foul up traffic. Rainstorms and snowstorms along with heavy traffic make a chauffeur's life a living nightmare."

They drove for many more minutes in silence until Steve said, "Here we are, Miss Jones, Trump-Tower-Twelve-on-the-Hudson." He turned the limo into the circular driveway. As soon as the car had stopped, he got out, walked around the front of the car, and opened the rear door for her. He took her hand to help her out of the car, and said cheerfully, "Have a great evening, Miss Jones. I'll be waiting for you whenever you're ready to leave."

From the moment Jane stepped out of the car and was escorted by the uniformed doorman through the huge glass doors of Trump-Tower-Twelve, she was surrounded by opulence rivaled only by the Ochoa's *big house* in New Mexico. The doorman clicked a button on his cell. The elevator doors opened. He said quietly, "Mr. Ochoa is expecting you, Miss Jones." The doorman pushed another button. The elevator doors closed. When the doors reopened, there he was.

"Good evening," he said flatly, gesturing for her to enter the apartment.

"Good evening," she answered in a coquettish manner, accepting his gesture to enter.

As he led her across the large room to the sofa, he inquired, "I trust you had a satisfactory ride."

"Most satisfactory," Jane replied playfully.

"I'm not surprised. Steve's one of our best men."

He motioned for her to sit on the sofa while he took a nearby chair. A distinguished white-haired man approached. "I thought we should have a change of drinks since we're in New York so I've asked Rogers to make us each a Manhattan. I hope that's satisfactory."

"How appropriate. A Manhattan in Manhattan," Jane said breezily.

Rogers retreated for a few moments and returned with a small tray containing two stemmed glasses filled with an amber liquid. He placed the drinks on the coffee table in front of each of them.

"Have you had a Manhattan before?"

"No, can't say that I have." Jane took a sip and nodded her approval. Rogers smiled that his drink had been accepted. When he had gone, she leaned as close to him as possible and whispered in a soft, sexy voice, "It's very good, but I like your margaritas much, much better." She crossed her legs, displaying as much thigh as her close fitting dress would allow. She took another sip of her drink never taking her eyes off him, her fiery green eyes conveying a sexual yearning that needed to be satisfied.

"I see. I should thank you then," he said politely, avoiding eye contact. He raised his glass and said, "Thank you."

"You're very welcome." She laughed and held up her glass in his direction. He didn't move to clink his glass with hers. He took a small sip and set his glass on the table. Disappointed, she did likewise.

He inquired into her health and hoped all was going well with her. She was careful not to mention anything sad like the deaths of her parents or the estrangement from her sister. She steered the conversation away from any topic that might bring him or her embarrassment.

She had taken a few sips of her drink when Rogers reappeared. "Dinner is served, Sir."

"Thank you, Rogers." He motioned for her to follow him to the dining room where he pulled a chair out and seated her properly. Rogers brought their partially finished drinks to the large glass dining room table.

Conversation was limited as Rogers brought this and took away that, but his intermittent appearances didn't inhibit Jane altogether. Whenever he was out of the room, she made little jokes and laughed more than she should have.

Halfway through dinner, Solanch's cell chimed. "Excuse me," he said rising from the table. He left the dining room for a few minutes. When he returned, Jane could see he was concerned.

"That was Walt McKinney. He's my personal pilot. He's onboard waiting for my arrival. He says the weather is deteriorating rapidly with heavy rain and falling temperatures, but he's most concerned about the wind. I hate to be rude, Jane, but I'm going to have to leave in a few minutes. I've asked Rogers to clear the table and serve dessert." He looked at her, his handsome face contorted in an expression of worry and profound sadness.

Rogers was prompt. He cleared the table so quickly, Jane didn't have a chance to respond to what Solanch had said. She sat transfixed, watching Rogers go about the job of resetting the table.

Dessert was a hurried affair. After a few bites of whatever and a sip of coffee, he asked her to join him in the living room. He motioned for her to sit on the sofa while he seated himself on a nearby chair.

He sat for a few moments trying to remember the words he had so carefully planned to say, words that would make it easier for them both but with the constraints of time, he forgot every single one of them. He leaned forward, folded his hands in front of him, and stared at the coffee table. "I invited you here tonight." He stopped. "I thought…well…I hoped…I need…I see that…" At a loss for the right words, he blurted, "Tonight I'm flying to an island we own in the Bahamas. The truth is I'm going to be married on Saturday, there, on the island. It'll be televised on *The Rich Get Richer* if you care to watch. We've invited several thousand of our nearest, dearest friends," he added sarcastically.

He stood up. "Sorry," he cried out in pain. "I shouldn't have subjected you to this. I've made a terrible mistake. I'm sorry, sorry for doing this to you. This has been a rotten joke I've played on you just like this loveless wedding has been a rotten joke played on me. It's made me crazy. I apologize to you."

He paced in front of the sofa, running his fingers through his hair. He turned and faced Jane. "Do you know who I'm marrying?"

Jane moved her head. Whether it was a yes or a no, she had no idea, because her brain had shattered into a million pieces.

"Juanita Sanchez. You've never heard of her, I'm sure." A harsher, grimmer sound replaced his usual sweet voice. "But you've heard of her uncle, Miguel Sanchez, the Governor of New Mexico." He stopped to let the irony sink in. Her startled, fearful expression told him she remembered Miguel Sanchez.

"The Sanchezes are all alike, they're corrupt. Juanita is a true Sanchez, pampered and imperious. She cares for no one but herself. She's as corrupt as her uncle in her own way. This marriage won't be based on the love of body and soul as it should be but on the love of money. My family is the fourteenth richest family in the world. Hers is the twenty-second. When we marry and combine the two fortunes, the Sanchez-Ochoa Familia," he said *Familia* with disgust as if he were describing a mafia family, "will be the fourth richest family in the world. Only two Chinese families and one Indian family will have more money than we. For us Ochoas, this marriage is a hostile takeover. For the Sanchezes, it's just another acquisition," he said with bitterness and sarcasm.

He sat in a chair. "I don't expect you to feel sorry for this poor little rich boy. Rich boys never get sympathy, just scorn, because everyone knows if you're rich you have everything. Well, I don't have everything." He stood and cried out, "I won't have a wife I care about. I won't have a family. I won't have anyone to come home to. I won't have a son to carry on the family name. I won't have anyone to call me *papi*. I won't have anyone to take over Ochoa Industries when I'm gone. No one! This'll be a lifeless, childless marriage.

A silence came over him broken only by Rogers who reminded him that he should be leaving. "Thank you, Rogers," he said so softly Jane barely heard him. He sat down. "When you were staying at the little house, I felt needed. I know that must sound strange to you, but it's true. No one in my life besides my parents ever depended on me as much as you did, and I liked it very much. I'm used to people needing me on a professional level. That's one thing, but I've never had anyone needing me on an unconditional, personal level as you did, and that was something altogether different. It felt wonderful. An experience I shall never forget and one I fear I may never experience again.

He paused a long while before he continued. "I have never forgotten our late night discussions. I've used many of the things you taught me in those few nights in my speeches. People all over the world have been exposed to the wit and wisdom of Jane Jones."

Jane was in such a state of shock she couldn't react to the compliment.

"Now comes the most difficult part of what I have to say to you. You see, Jane, in those few short nights, I thought I had found someone with whom I could share my thoughts, my fears, my hopes, my dreams, my everything, but I was wrong." He stopped, his voice choked with emotion. "You are not the woman I thought you were."

Jane sat on the sofa frozen in time and space, her emotions numbed by the strange sound of his voice, his facial expressions of hurt and betrayal, and his stinging words. "I never ran away from you, Jane, never, but you deserted me, not once, but four times. The first time was when you ran away from my parents and me as soon as the chief of police lifted your restraining order. We understood why you left, but you'll never know how much we missed you.

"The second time was when you refused to talk to me when I called. All I wanted was to hear your voice, continue our talks, and learn from you. I had several business problems I wanted to discuss with you to get your point of view. You see, Jane. I valued your thoughts and insights.

"You deserted me a third time when you blocked my calls. That's when I realized you never wanted to talk to me again, that our time together was finished. I can't tell you how saddened I was by that single thought, a thought that nearly cost me my life.

"The fourth time, well, what can I say? I was so happy you came to take care of me when I had my nervous breakdown. I thought you had come back to me, but you left me standing in my bedroom without so much as a good-bye."

"It really is time to leave, Sir."

"Yes, I know. I'll be along in a moment," he said impatiently. He waited until Rogers had departed and added, "You built the walls too high, Jane. I can't get over them, around them, under them, and most certainly not through them. I tried. I tried, but I failed." His voice trailed off, "Failed." He put his head in his hands for a few moments, then looked up and said, "You have judged me, Jane. You have judged harshly. Perhaps I deserve such judgment.

CHAPTER 19

When the elevator doors opened, Jane ran past the surprised doorman and across the large atrium as fast as her tight fitting dress and three inch stiletto heels would allow. She pulled open one of the huge glass doors. She raced past Steve with the waiting limo and out into the cold rain where she slipped and fell head long onto the sidewalk badly skinning both knees. She tried to stand, but the stilettos slipped out from beneath her on the rain-slicked sidewalk. She kicked them off and ran in stocking feet. She ran blindly, guided only by instincts that told her to *run as fast as you can. Run until you can't run any more.*

She crossed the main street and ran up a steep hill on a joining side street. The rain smeared her makeup, destroyed her new hairstyle making her look like the distraught woman she was, and soaked her once stylish black dress that clung to her like a second skin becoming tighter and tighter as the delicate fabric rebelled against the brute force of the storm. Her breathing became increasingly labored. His words, "You're not the woman I thought you were," drove her to run as hard and fast as she could. Halfway up the hill, her stamina failed. She could run no more. She stood motionless, dazed, as the huge flakes of snow surrounded her.

A car stopped on the deserted street in front of her. She heard a voice. She saw a figure approach her. She shivered uncontrollably.

She felt something warm around her shoulders along with a hand that guided her toward the waiting car. She felt herself being lowered onto the seat where she lay soaked, cold to the bone. The warm car moved down the steep hill and turned a few corners. Jane heard the familiar soft hum of tires on highway. Between the warmth of the car and the blanket that had been put over her, the shivering subsided. She was too emotionally spent to fear for her safety. She drifted in and out of consciousness.

The car seemed like a magic carpet for in a blur of time, it stopped. The rear door opened. "You're home, Miss Jones." She recognized Steve's voice and felt his warm hands pull her out of the car and carry her into the apartment building, up the stairs, and to her apartment. She mumbled that he should knock on the neighbor's door for the key to her apartment. She assured him she would be all right standing in front of the door while he went for the key.

Steve did as he was told. As if in a distant dream, she heard him knock on the neighbor's door and heard her ask in a shaky voice, "Who is it?"

"It's Steve, ma'am. I'm Miss Jones' chauffeur. She asked me to get the key from you."

"Oh, okay. Okay. I'm coming. Wait just one moment."

"Yes, ma'am," Steve replied.

"Wait just a minute. I'm coming. I'm coming. I'll be there. Just wait a moment more."

Jane felt lightheaded and slumped against the apartment door. She heard footsteps fast approaching and felt Steve's strong, warm hands lean her securely against the closed door.

"I'll be all right," she muttered as she heard her neighbor in a distant haze say, "Just a minute. I'm coming. I'm coming." Jane heard a loud click that echoed down the hall. The neighbor's door opened a few inches, restrained by a thick security chain.

An elderly woman with a cane in her right hand squinted through the narrow opening. "Oh, it's you," she said. "Are you Steve?"

"Yes, ma'am."

"I thought so. Jane told me your name a long, long time ago when you drove her. She said you were an excellent driver. She said she felt very safe with you. I don't doubt it. A good lookin' fella like you. I saw you out in the parking lot tonight. I thought to myself, *now there's a right smart lookin' young fella.* Yes, I did."

"Thank you, ma'am. May I have Miss Jones' key?"

"Oh, oh yes, of course. I keep it right here in the ashtray. My husband used to smoke, you know. That's why I have ashtrays. I never did, smoke. I knew they weren't good for you, the cigarettes. When he died eleven years ago, I kept the ashtrays as a remembrance so I…"

"I'm afraid Miss Jones doesn't feel well, that's why I'm here and not Miss Jones herself," Steve interrupted.

"Oh, what a shame. She looked so pretty when she went out tonight. I haven't seen her look so nice."

"Yes, ma'am. May I have the key, ma'am?"

"Oh, the key. Of course, that's what you came for, not conversation with an old lady. These old arthritic fingers of mine can't get the key out of the ashtray. Would you mind doing it for me?"

Steve reached through the narrow opening and retrieved it from the shaking ashtray. "Have you got it?"

"Yes, ma'am."

"Good."

"Thank you for your help, ma'am," Steve said politely as he held the key in his right hand.

"No trouble at all, young man. No trouble at all."

Jane heard Steve's approaching footsteps and felt him hold her steady as he inserted the key into the lock. She felt him lift her semiconscious body in his arms and carry her into the apartment. She motioned to the neatly made twin bed in a corner of the room. He laid her on it, covered her with the blanket he had given her, placed the key on the kitchen countertop along with her shoes, locked the door from the inside, and left the apartment as soon as he could, not wanting the slightest hint of any improprieties.

He returned to the elderly neighbor's door and knocked.

"Just a minute. I'm coming. Just a minute," came the voice from the other side of the door.

"Can you hear me?" Steve said in a loud voice.

"Yes, yes, I can hear you. No need to shout."

"I'm leaving now. If you look out your window, I'll wave to you from the parking lot."

"Oh, that would be nice," she answered in a coquettish voice, for looking at Steve even from a distance brought joy to her heart.

CHAPTER 20

The buzzer sounded at six a.m. With great effort, Jane forced herself out of bed. She felt feverish. Her head ached. Her knees hurt. Her legs felt like stilts. She silenced the buzzer. She tugged and pulled, but the wet dress had molded itself to her body. In desperation, she grabbed a pair of scissors and cut it off.

She felt better after she had showered except for the terrible taste in her mouth. She ate her usual breakfast of an egg and a piece of toast with butter and strawberry preserves that she washed down with a cup of instant coffee. She brushed her teeth and swished with mouthwash, but she couldn't rid herself of the terrible taste in her mouth. She dressed, got in the car, and drove to work. The bright morning sun aggravated her headache.

As she pulled into the school parking lot, she sneezed several times. *Oh great! I'm catching cold.* She didn't feel like teaching but since she was there, she figured she might as well finish the day, promising herself if she didn't feel better she'd take a sick day, something she rarely did.

When she entered the building, the first words she heard were, "It's not fair. They said it would snow two feet and it barely covered the ground."

"Who are they?" another student asked.

"My mother let me stay up past midnight," another added.

Students in the hallway complained bitterly they deserved to have a day off even if it hadn't snowed.

"Good morning," the school secretary greeted her as she entered the main office to check her mailbox. "Looks like you believed the weatherman too and stayed up past your bedtime." She laughed. "I think we all did. Have a good day."

"Thanks," Jane rasped in reply.

She sneezed as she entered her classroom. The shrill noise of students arguing made her head hurt. Like a voice from another world, she heard someone say, "Gesundheit."

"Thanks," she said automatically amongst the chaos of students complaining about having to come to school. The bell rang for class to begin, but no one paid attention.

"Everyone sit down and please be quiet," Jane said in the loudest voice she could, followed by a coughing spasm. When it had passed, she said, "Take out your math workbooks everyone." No one did as she asked. She raised her voice again to ask them to sit down and be quiet, but every time she spoke, she coughed violently. "Turn to page forty-seven. Is everyone on page forty-seven? Ashley? Are you on page forty-seven?"

Ashley nodded her head although her workbook was closed.

"Ash…" Jane stopped in mid name to cough. "Lamont. Are you on page forty-seven?"

"I don't wanna do math. I wanna play video games." Lamont pounded on his desk in rhythm with, "I wanna play video games. I wanna play video games."

Alex picked up the chant, "I wanna play video games." The two boys pounded their desks, flashing menacing stares at the other seven students in the room.

Without warning, Lamont stopped pounding his desk, picked up his pencil, and threw it as hard as he could in Jane's direction, missing her head by a fraction of an inch, and crashing into the smart board behind her.

"Miss J! Miss J! Lamont just threw his pencil at you," exclaimed Josh.

"Lamont! Alex! Be quiet!" Jane demanded, but coughing silenced her voice so she was unable to respond to Josh's warning and discipline Lamont for his pencil throwing. Realizing he had done a bad thing, Lamont resumed pounding his desk and chanting, hoping to escape punishment. The other students joined in the chant, "I wanna play video games."

Jane's head throbbed. She felt hot and weak. She swallowed several times and yelled as loud as she could, "Lamont! Alex! Everyone! Be quiet! Settle down before I call the principal." The class quieted. "Turn to page forty-seven," Jane said forcefully, but her small show of force caused her to cough uncontrollably.

"You don't look so good Miss J. You all right?" Chris asked.

"Yes, Chris. Just a little cough, that's all," Jane assured him, but she felt weak. Her legs felt as if they might buckle under her weight at any moment.

She remained seated, something Donna noticed. When Alex yelled at Chris to shut up, Donna looked at Alex and said, "Don't you see Miss J don't feel good?" whereupon Alex told her to shut up too.

"Ouch!" Wanda screamed in pain.

"What's the matter, Wanda?" Jane wheezed.

"Lamont stuck me with his pen."

"I did not."

"Yes you did."

"You're such a retard, Wanda. You know you are."

"Lamont," Jane coughed out more than said. After a few moments of coughing, she said, "You know better than to call anyone that word. That's a word we never use, never, ever."

"I do," Lamont proudly proclaimed.

"No you don't. Now apologize to Wanda."

Lamont sat unrepentant. "You apologize to her right now or I'm going to report this to Dr. Carter." Lamont didn't say a word. Jane picked up the classroom phone. "Dr. Carter, please."

"I'm sorry, Wanda. I'm sorry. Please don't tell Dr. Carter what I said, Miss J. Please don't."

Jane hung up the phone. Alex got out of his seat to sharpen his pencil, one of his favorite activities because he liked the whirring sound of the electric motor.

"Who can," she paused to cough several times," write an example of…"

"*Ew,*" she heard the class exclaim in unison.

"Look at Alex, Miss J," Wanda exclaimed pointing at Alex.

Jane turned and saw Alex had removed the tray from under the pencil sharpener, run his hands through the lead filled shavings, and put his lead stained hands on his white shirt. "Alex, stop that right," she coughed violently, "now." She asked him to sit down and keep his hands in the air, dirty hands that he waved at everybody near him, pretending he was going to smear them with his lead stained hands.

"Page forty-seven everyone. Ramón, are you on page forty-seven?"

"Jes, I eez."

Jane smiled.

Ramón was one student she could count on to be on the right page at the right time. His English was limited as were his abilities, but his bright smile and sweet disposition made it impossible not to like him. "Good, Ramón."

"Ewwww," the class cried in unison looking at Alex.

Jane turned in Alex's direction. He had put his lead laden hands in his mouth and run his fingers down his face.

"Look, Miss J. I'm an Indian." He got up out of his seat and began running around the room screaming war hoops. Lamont joined him, jumping on desks and kicking anybody who might be in his way.

"Quiet, both of you." Jane tried to sound as forceful as she could. She coughed for a few moments before she continued. "Alex, Lamont. Sit down!"

Chris, with a worried expression on his face, asked, "Why is there a whistling noise when you breathe, Miss J?"

Jane ignored the question and asked one of her own. "Who thinks he or she can go to the board and give an example of the commutative property?"

None of the students spoke so Jane wrote one plus two equals two plus one.

"That's so easy," Lamont said. Jane asked him to go to the board and write his example. He wrote one plus nine equals eight plus two.

"That isn't the correct answer, Lamont."

"They both equal ten and that's all that matters," he retorted.

"But it's not the commutative property," Jane corrected him.

As the morning progressed, Jane coughed harder and longer. She removed her sweater. She wore just a short sleeve white blouse and a light pair of slacks. Having no success with the commutative property or page forty-seven in the workbook, she moved onto spelling which turned out as badly as the math lesson had.

During the social studies lesson, while students colored in a map of the South American countries and labeled their capital cities, Jane helped individual students at their desks, an activity that required her to bend down. Student voices became distorted. The room spun. She lost her sense of balance and collapsed to the floor.

Lamont was the first to see her fall. He ran to her side and asked gently, "Miss J? You okay?"

"I theenk she no good," said Ramón bending over Jane's body.

"Miss J? Miss J?" asked an uncomprehending Ashley.

"I'm gonna get help!" Lamont yelled.

"Yes! Go! Run!" Chris screamed. Fear spread to the other students. They didn't understand why Jane had fallen and not gotten up.

Lamont ran from the room. Moments later he returned with the school nurse and Dr. Carter, who asked the students to step outside the room. While the nurse made Jane as comfortable as she could, he called 911.

When the EMS crew removed an unconscious Jane from the classroom, students gathered in the hallway. They expressed their affection and fears.

"We love you, Miss J."

"Get well fast."

"I hope you don't die."

As the gurney carrying Jane disappeared around the corner, a tearful Lamont said quietly, "I'm sorry I was bad today, Miss J."

Jane was rushed to the intensive care unit of the hospital. Doctors pumped her full of antibiotics, but her condition worsened with each passing hour. On a sun-drenched island in the Bahamas, Juanita and Solanch exchanged their marriage vows. As the last note of the wedding ceremony passed into nothingness, so did Jane, for she breathed no more.

CHAPTER 21

Doctors pronounced Jane dead and left. Fifteen minutes later, a male nurse, disconnecting tubes that connected her to machines heard what he thought was breathing. He leaned over. He felt a soft, warm puff of air on his cheek. He summoned doctors who ordered the machines reattached, and so Jane, who had nearly met her maker, lived, but her retreat from the grave was slow. She remained in intensive care for ten days. The first week was the most critical. Her unstable condition showed a little improvement one day followed by serious setbacks the next, but as the second week progressed, her condition improved.

After a three-week stay in the hospital, doctors permitted her to return home, provided she didn't go back to work for at least two weeks. She followed the doctors' advice. Once the two weeks had passed, she returned to work and life, the same life she had had before her illness, a life without friends, without love, and without hope. As the years passed, she wished the pneumonia had taken her so she wouldn't have to face the many years of emptiness, alone.

CHAPTER 22

Jane weighed the pluses and minuses of her life. The pluses outweighed the minuses but just barely. She had her health. Once she had recuperated from pneumonia, she had an occasional cold from time to time but nothing more serious than that. Secondly, she was grateful to those who had protected her identity after the accident in New Mexico. No one had connected her to the death of the governor after all these years, and thirdly was the five million dollars waiting for her in some bank somewhere. She knew she would never use it, but the thought was reassuring. She was grateful money wasn't a problem. Her teaching salary plus the small inheritance from her parents was enough for her to live a comfortable life, for Jane, unlike her sister, had no desire for an extravagant lifestyle.

Those were the pluses, but, as with all things positive, they are forgotten. We humans focus on the minuses of life. So it was with Jane. One plus that had become a minus was her teaching career, a career she had depended on to fill the void in her loveless life. She was to be denied this last refuge of happiness.

As the years passed, she became increasingly disenchanted with meddling politicians who catered to the never satisfied, ever changing whims of educational experts, psychiatrists, interest groups, and angry parents. These meddlers made Jane's daily teaching assignments a nightmare instead of the joyous activities they should have been. She railed against meaningless instructional activities and found it increasingly difficult to maintain the type of discipline necessary for serious study, but most of all she hated what these meddlers had done to her students. Too many of them had become unruly, uncaring, and worst of all intellectually uncurious.

Jane did her best to comply with the maze of ever-changing rules and regulations, but her best was never good enough. Parents, unable to cope with their out- of-control children, looked to Jane and her colleagues to provide a magic bullet to cure their children's problems. They expected her and the other teachers to do what they and a multitude of doctors and psychiatrists had been unable to accomplish. This placed Jane and her colleagues in a mission impossible position and the perfect scapegoat for a failed educational system as well as failed parenting.

As big as this minus was, two bigger minuses dominated Jane's life. Although she no longer admitted it, she wanted a husband and children. She knew her biological clock was winding down. If she didn't have children soon, she would be too old to have them. This single thought saddened her.

Jane's summer vacation had begun. As she had done in years past, she planned to avoid places where young couples would be walking hand in hand hopelessly in love. The sight of others embraced in love had become a sight too painful for her to bear. She would spend another dreary vacation in her small apartment catching up on her rest, reading a few books, watching TV, and cleaning. She had decided long ago she had no other choice than to isolate herself from others and life itself.

Whenever the phone rang, its ringing stirred no anticipation or excitement within her. She had become a walking, talking zombie, retreating into a numbed existence. One evening at eight thirty, the phone rang. Tired of hearing its persistent ring, she picked up and heard a voice that sounded familiar.

"Jane? Jane Jones?" she heard a no-nonsense, feminine voice say before she had a chance to say, "Hello". "It's Mrs. Ochoa calling."

"Mrs. Ochoa?"

"Yes. I'm no beat the bush, Jane. I'll come to point. I have a serious problem, with Little Solanch. I need your advice and your help. I want you come here for summer vacations. Yes, I know you just started your vacations. I know I ask a lot of you, but I need you come. You no need be afraid. No mens will be here. Papito will be in Asia for summer and Solanch will be in Europe and Russia. It will be just we two womens, here, in the little house, with Little Solanch.

"I've booked you on Continental flight 759 leaving La Guardia at ten tomorrow morning. A car will pick you up at eight. Nothing fancy, Jane. No private jets. I bought you a coach ticket. I know you want it that way. I expect you here in time for an early lunch. We eat and then get to work. We don't have a moment to lose. I explain everything when you get here. I know you have to make the suitcase. Don't' worry if you forget something. We have stores here too." She laughed. "You will come, yes?"

Jane weighed her options. Her summer vacation plans were dull to say the least. She liked Mrs. Ochoa well enough. The idea the two of them would be together to solve some problem appealed to her not to mention she was curious what kind of problem could exist with this Little Solanch person, someone she had never heard of.

"Yes," she heard herself saying. "I'll be ready at eight."

As soon as Jane hung up, life had meaning. She was needed. What a wonderful feeling it was to be needed.

CHAPTER 23

The dusty, black Lincoln Town car stopped in front of the white stucco house. The dust settled. Mrs. Ochoa stood in the doorway. She waved for Jane to come into the house. Jane did as she was directed. The chauffeur brought in the luggage while Mrs. Ochoa motioned for Jane to follow her to the kitchen.

"First a cup of coffee to get rid of the dust," Mrs. Ochoa said formally. "Sit at the table while I prepare lunch." Jane sat while Mrs. Ochoa went about the business of pouring coffee and putting the finishing touches to lunch. When lunch lay upon the table, Mrs. Ochoa said a brief prayer, crossed herself, and ate quietly, remembering Solanch's advice years ago when the three of them had had their first lunch, to allow Jane to eat in peace, advice more suitable to Solanch than Jane.

When they had finished, Mrs. Ochoa sighed and said, "Now we can talk." She folded her hands in her lap, looked at Jane, and began. "The reason why I ask you to come Jane is that Little Solanch, my son's son, is ill, seriously ill. Doctors think it autism. I don't. I won't go into my suspicions at this moment. I just want to think about the child. That's why I call you. You're a specialist. You know about these things. I need you to help find a way to cure this child. I know it can be done. The doctors want to give him high-powered drugs. I said no." Her voice became animated. "This child no need drugs! That much I know! Don't ask how I know! I just know!"

"What's the matter with the child?"

"His poor little body is hard, tense, like board. It no move. When he in my arms, he feel like bundle of sticks, not soft like child. Sometimes his eyes is closed, but most of time they open, but no blink much. He never talk, no mama, no papa, no nothing. He used to scream, but no *más*." Mrs. Ochoa stopped and looked pleadingly into Jane's eyes as only a woman can when a child's life is at stake. "I thought together we might save him."

Jane looked at Mrs. Ochoa's face. The once vibrant, reddish-brown skin looked ashen, dark circles under the eyes, and the eyes themselves looked weary as if they had the weight of the world bearing down upon them. "Does he eat?"

"No *mucho*. His face all shrunken. He so skeeny for having more than two years. I no like him like this. I wish he were fat, happy baby, like baby should be." She put a hand on Jane's arm. "*Por favor, por favor, ayúdame.* Please save my grandson! For me!" She grasped Jane's hands.

Mrs. Ochoa's plea moved Jane. Tears welled up in her eyes while her mind formed a course of action.

"When can I see him?"

"He at big house. He be here in one hour."

"Mrs. Ochoa, I have no idea if what I'm going to suggest…"

"You have plan? Ideas?" Mrs. Ochoa's eyes lit up with this glimmer of hope.

"I don't want to get your hopes up. I have no idea if what I'm going to suggest is going to help in the slightest."

"Jane. I try whatever you say. I trust you. That's why I call you. Whatever you say, Jane. Whatever you say."

"I'm a little hesitant to say…"

"No, don't be. Say it. Say it now. I want know."

"We need a rocking chair, one that creaks."

"Yes. We do."

"Turn off the air conditioner so we sweat. Just let the fans run. Bring in extra fans. We'll need them."

"I turn off now." Mrs. Ochoa jumped up and turned off the air conditioning, allowing the fans to run.

"Ask them to bring the child to us now."

"Okey dokey, as we Americans say," the playfulness returning to Mrs. Ochoa's voice. She flipped open her cell, pushed a key, and said, "Please bring Little Solanch. And bring a rocking chair too. Make sure it creaks." She paused a moment and said, "Yes, I said creaks. Make sure chair creaks, and if it doesn't, then do something to make it creaks, and bring fans too. Lots of them." She flipped shut the cell and smiled. "I don't know what you plan, Jane, but I feel better already. At least we have plan. We're doing something."

An hour later a Suburban pulled up in front of the house. Mrs. Ochoa ran to it and carried Little Solanch into the house. A man followed carrying a rocking chair. Mrs. Ochoa turned to him and said, "Does chair creaks?"

"Yes, ma'am," the man answered. "I tested it myself."

"Good," Mrs. Ochoa replied. The man returned to the Suburban, brought in the fans, and then left, glad to leave the hot house and escape to the coolness of the Suburban.

"You sit in the chair, Mrs. Ochoa. Hold him with his ear next to your heart. The house must be kept quiet. We'll speak in whispers and walk in our bare feet."

"*Sí*," Mrs. Ochoa whispered.

"He needs everything to stay the same as much as possible, to hear our heartbeat, feel our warmth next to him, smell our bodies, and hear the gentle creaking of the chair and the whir of the fans along with the rush of air over his body. We'll feed him in the chair. We'll change him on the floor. Those tiles might feel good after being next to two sweaty women like us." They both smiled. "He must be in our arms twenty-four hours a day. In a few days, we'll hum and talk to him. I promise you nothing, Mrs. Ochoa. I have no idea if any of this will work. Only time will tell."

The two women took turns holding Little Solanch next to their sweating bodies. They rocked, they hummed, they whispered, but the child showed no sign of improvement. Days became one week, two weeks, a month, and then seven weeks. The desert heat, the physical exhaustion of constant rocking, the frequent whispering and humming, the lack of rest, and the lack of appetite took their toll on the two of them as late August rolled around. They both agreed they had done their best. If he didn't show improvement soon, they would allow the doctors to inject him with high-powered drugs.

As the end time drew near, Mrs. Ochoa in the wee hours of an exceptionally hot night raised her head to the sky as she had done on many a night. Her unshakeable faith in Him and His healing powers had given her the strength to do all she had done thus far. She closed her eyes. She knew she didn't have to utter a sound for He was with her as He always was. This she believed. This she knew. As she rocked back and forth with the child in her arms, she felt something different this particular night, something she had never experienced before. She felt her spirit merge with His, that He and she were one.

She felt a powerful strength within her, a strength that knew no earthly bounds, a strength that had its own curative powers far more powerful than rocking, humming, or words could ever have. It lasted only a few seconds and was gone.

With the last bit of energy her mind and body could summon up, she whispered with tears streaming down her cheeks, "*Tu abuelita te ama tanto, mi querido. Por favor, mi querido, mi nieto*, my dearly beloved grandson, please, please get well. Your grandmother loves you so very, very much." She laid her head on the back of the chair. Exhaustion overcame her. The rocking stopped.

CHAPTER 24

Jane awoke as the first glimmer of light streaked across the cloudless desert sky. Wearily she crossed the room to the bathroom where she washed her face not in cool water as she would have liked but in sun-heated water. Without the air conditioner, the sun had its way with the water temperature, but even hot water felt refreshing against her face, washing away the sweat of the night.

She made her way to the kitchen. She glanced at Mrs. Ochoa in the chair with Little Solanch in her arms. She smiled when she didn't hear the creaking of the chair. *Good. She needs her rest,* she thought. She went into the kitchen, flicked on the coffee maker, and sat at the kitchen table mesmerized by the sound of falling water through coffee grounds as the black liquid filled the glass carafe.

Exhausted, she struggled to her feet as the last drops of black liquid fell into the carafe, poured a cup, and took several sips. She decided to check on Mrs. Ochoa and the baby. As she approached the two of them, she noticed something different. What that different was, she couldn't say, but something about the child was different. When she got closer, she realized his breathing sounded normal, not in little gasps as before but normal as any baby would. She looked more closely. Her eyes opened wide. She couldn't be certain. She stared in disbelief. Could it be? She reached out and felt his left leg. It felt like the soft leg of a normal baby. Relaxed.

Not stiff. She looked at his toes. She couldn't restrain herself. She had to touch them, to see if they were soft and relaxed. They were.

Jane slumped to the floor and sobbed. Her muffled sobs were enough to awaken Mrs. Ochoa. "Mamita, mira," Jane blurted, pointing to the baby.

Through sleep-filled eyes, Mamita felt more than saw a difference in the child. Her eyes widened. "Jane!" she exclaimed. "Can it be? Can it be?"

Jane sobbed, "Yes, Mamita. I think it is. I think it is."

Little Solanch let out a huge sigh and blew a spit bubble. Mamita and Jane looked at each other in amazement. Mamita stood up. She felt his arms and legs. "Jane!" she exclaimed excitedly. "He's let go. He's let go. He's relaxed. No more stiff like board." The two women looked at each other with tear filled eyes. They hugged the sleeping baby. They hugged each other. Then they both melted into uncontrollable sobs of exhaustion and exhilaration.

CHAPTER 25

Exhilaration won out over exhaustion. Jane and Mamita were too excited to think about anything except the rebirth, as Mamita called it, of Little Solanch. Jane covered the kitchen tiles with a blanket and laid him on it so he could have freedom of movement.

"Can we turn the air conditioner on?" Mamita asked.

"I thought you'd never ask."

"I'm tired of this straggly, dripping hair I've had for weeks. It'll feel good to have it clean and dry."

The welcome sounds of the air conditioning and the first puffs of cool air cheered them both.

"I smell hot coffee. A cup would taste good."

Jane poured. "Mamita, may I make a suggestion?"

Mamita smiled and touched Jane's arm. "That's the second time you've called me Mamita. Please, always call me Mamita."

Jane's brain reeled at the thought of calling Mrs. Ochoa mamita. Her New York formality placed barriers on such affectionate names. She had never called anyone such a name except her father whom she had called daddy, but that had been years ago when she was a little girl. "I wasn't thinking. It just popped out."

"That's because it was natural. Please, Jane. No more Mrs. Ochoa. Just Mamita. Please."

Jane looked at her in a standoffish manner, but Mamita's pleading voice, the affectionate look in her eyes, and her warm, gentle touch on Jane's arm broke the barrier between them. "You win. Mamita it is."

"Good," Mamita said with such joy in her voice that made Jane smile and laugh at the same time. They joined hands in friendship. "Now," Mamita broke the silence, "you said something about suggestion."

"The baby can't stay on the floor like that forever. He needs a bed."

"You're right. I'll call Pedro and see what he can do." Mamita reached into an apron pocket and pulled out her cell. She pushed a button and said, "*Hola*, Pedro." The rest Jane couldn't understand as Mamita spoke Spanish.

When she had finished, she turned to Jane. "Pedro says when Little Solanch was born they made a crib and several beds that would be age appropriate. He'll be here in an hour with a bed he and Alejandro made for a two-year-old. I'm excited to see what they came up with."

True to Pedro's word, an hour later the Suburban rolled up outside. Two men carried a small bed into the house. Both Mamita and Jane were pleased when they saw it. They laughed and clasped their hands together in joy at the beautifully handcrafted bed. They realized Pedro and Alejandro had worked to create not just a bed but a work of art. The sideboards illustrated popular children's stories. Pedro demonstrated how the bed could either rock or remain stationary and how the wheels could be locked or unlocked so the bed could be wheeled from one room to another. It was made and ready to be used.

Mamita picked up Little Solanch and placed him in it. He did two things no one had ever seen him do. He smiled and laughed.

"I think he likes his new bed," Pedro said and smiled. He put his arm on Alejandro's shoulder.

"I think you're right," Alejandro replied, thrilled the baby appreciated his hard work and creativity. He had been the artist who had decorated the sideboards.

After Pedro and Alejandro left, Mamita and Jane returned to the kitchen table to finish their coffee. As they looked at the bed and the child in it, they talked about the bed, about the thoughtful men who had made it, and about Little Solanch. Mamita made it a point to call him Little Solanch, not the child, my grandson, or the baby. His name was Solanch, and she intended to say it whenever necessary even if the name Solanch made Jane uncomfortable. Mamita knew it did. She saw Jane wince whenever she said it, but she also knew that Jane had to get used to hearing it.

"Look, Mamita!" Jane exclaimed. "The baby's stretching. He's working the kinks out of his muscles."

They marveled as Little Solanch moved his arms and legs. Mamita put her hand on Jane's arm as she watched in awe a child come to life before her eyes. With tears in her eyes, she quietly uttered, "You've done it, Jane. You've brought my Little Solanch back to me."

"I don't know, Mamita. Maybe it was something we did. Maybe it was some unseen force, maybe both, and maybe none of them. We'll never know. It'll forever be one of those unanswered mysteries of life."

Little Solanch yawned, smiled a baby's smile of love, closed his eyes, and entered into blissful sleep.

"It takes my breath away to watch him," Mamita whispered. For many minutes, both women sat speechless in awe of the life taking shape before their eyes.

"We'll keep Little Solanch here," Mamita said. "He'll feel more comfortable than he would at The Big House with all those people and security guards. Better he stay here, in the little house. He'll be the third Solanch to stay in this house."

Mamita poured herself another cup of coffee and continued talking. "This little house is very important to Papito and me. He built it for us many years ago. It wasn't nearly so big then, just one room. This small section of the kitchen and that small section of the living room was the entire house.

"We didn't care. We were happy. Of the two of us, I think I was the happiest. I never dreamed I would marry such a handsome, successful man as Papito. My father was Mexican. I almost never saw him. My mother was Navajo. She and I lived on the Navajo Reservation. We lived in a small, adobe hut with only a small fireplace for cooking and heating, no running water, and no indoor plumbing. It was a hard life for us." She took a few sips of coffee and pushed the cup and saucer aside.

"So you see why I thought I'd never meet, let alone marry a man like Papito. As for Papito, he was born and raised in a little village in Mexico. His parents had come from Spain to Mexico to make their fortune, but Mexico being Mexico ruined their plans. He and his family lived like my mother and me, in poverty. When he was seventeen, he decided to come to the United States to seek his fortune. Not so many Mexicans did that back then, so the gringos didn't care if there was one more Mexican or not. They needed cheap labor. His first job was unloading pipe from trucks in the Texas oil fields. They paid him next to nothing. That's how he got started in the oil business.

"A few months after he had worked in Texas, the company moved him to New Mexico. They thought they might find oil here too. They didn't, but Papito and I found each other, by accident. It scares me to this day to think I could have missed meeting him."

She picked at some breadcrumbs on the tablecloth. "I worked a few days a week in a tiny store in El Morro. Another girl worked more days than me. She said she was tired of working and wanted a day off. She asked me if I would fill in for her. I needed the extra money, so I told her I would. It was early afternoon. I hadn't had a customer all day. Finally someone came in, a tall, lean, young figure. It was a man. When he saw me, he took his hat off. He had long, black, curly hair. My heart skipped a few beats at the sight of those curls, his handsome face, and that long, lean body of his. When he spoke, his voice was like an angel." She giggled a school-girl giggle and added, "I thought he was very sexy." She giggled again. "I still do."

Mamita played with the handle of her cup as she relived past events before she continued. "I guess he thought I was Mexican because he spoke Spanish to me, and when I answered him in Spanish, I think that's what got him interested in me. He was still just a boy and homesick. Someone who could speak Spanish was a comfort to him.

"We talked quite a while. Not a single customer entered the store so we were alone. After much time had passed, he said he was hungry and asked me if I was. Believe me, Jane, I didn't play hard to get. I told him I was hungry. He asked me to have something to eat with him. I accepted. Then I had a terrible thought. I couldn't leave the store. He asked how much money I made in a day. I told him four dollars. He pulled a twenty out of his pocket.

"In those days, we never saw a twenty-dollar bill so to me this was a fortune, the whole world. He leaned over the counter, put it in the till of the cash register, and said, 'Close the store,' which is what I did. I couldn't get over the fact that he would spend twenty dollars on me. It sent shivers up and down my spine even in the heat. I was afraid to question my good luck for fear I would put a bad spell on myself. I hoped he liked me as much as I liked him. To be honest, I didn't like him. I loved him. For me, it was love at first sight. He said it was for him too.

"We went to the cantina, the only place in El Morro that served food. Since the cantina didn't have many customers, the only thing to eat was rice and beans, but it made no difference to

THE IRONIES OF LIFE

us. He told me how lonely he was, how he wanted to settle down, how he wanted a family. We talked the rest of the afternoon until nearly sunset. I had to be back on the reservation before sunset. He asked if he could see me again the next day. Of course I said yes.

"As we left the cantina, he took my hand in his. My heart pounded in my chest. I was afraid I might have a heart attack. He drove me home, promising he would see me in the evening of the next day. After he had left, I thought I had lived a wonderful dream. I could hear his angelic voice, feel his soft, warm touch, and remember the earnest yet affectionate looks of a beautiful young man spilling his heart out to me, to me, Nascha. That's my Navajo name. It means owl. Nobody except Papito uses it now, but it's my official name. Nascha Ochoa.

Mamita stopped. "Maybe I talk too much about past. I don't want to bore you with such stories. Maybe they are no interest to you."

"Of course I'm interested, Mamita. You're answering some of the questions I had about you and Mr. Ochoa." Mamita frowned. "I mean, Papito."

"That's mucho better," Mamita smiled.

"Go on, please," Jane pleaded.

Mamita needed little encouragement to continue her story. "When I got home, I told my mother I had met a man and he was going to call for me the next day. My mother was a stern, serious woman. She seldom talked, seldom smiled, and stayed in the hut almost never leaving it. At the time, I had no idea she was ill. She hid it from me, but when she heard I had met a man, she rallied her strength. I'm sure she wanted to see me married and happy before she passed on."

Mamita sat quietly for many moments thinking of her mother before she continued her story. "She said she would do my hair. The next morning bright and early we spent washing, cutting, and styling my hair not in an Indian fashion but a modern Mexican style she had seen in a magazine. I couldn't imagine my mother looking at a magazine let alone remember a hairstyle, but you wouldn't believe what a beautiful job she did. She put her heart and soul into that hairstyle. When she had finished and I saw myself in the mirror, I couldn't believe what I saw. I looked so nice and I felt so pretty. Those few hours were the happiest my mother and I ever spent together. I loved her as I had never loved her before. She passed away a few weeks later, but she left me with an everlasting memory.

"The next afternoon my angel arrived when he said he would. There wasn't anything to do except walk and talk which is what we did until it was time for me to return to the reservation. We did this for six wonderful nights. On the sixth night, he told me he had to go away. He didn't know when he would return. He promised he would, but I didn't believe him. I was certain I would never see him again.

"Many weeks passed. They were not happy weeks for me. I was alone. No friends, little money. I felt abandoned as if nobody in the world cared about me. Months passed. No word from him. I gave up all hope."

She paused to reflect on those awful times before she continued. "Then one morning he came into the store. Without a word, he pulled a twenty-dollar bill out of his pocket and put it in the cash register. I stared at him in disbelief. 'Time is short,' he said in Spanish. I had no idea what he was talking about. My mind was going in all directions. Before I knew it, he had taken off his hat. His long beautiful curls fell about his face. He got down on one bended knee in the middle of that store and asked me to marry him. I hesitated. It wasn't that I didn't want to marry him. I couldn't believe he wanted to marry me. He waited patiently for me to say something. Slowly he repeated the words, 'Will you marry me?' Finally I came to my senses and said yes.

He got up off his knee and asked, 'May I kiss you?' I nodded my head yes. When his soft, warm lips joined with mine, I thought for sure I was going to faint. I think we both did because we lost our balance and fell to the floor. He laughed and so did I. He said it was safer for us to kiss on the floor so we wouldn't fall. He was right."

Mamita leaned back in her chair and smiled as she recalled those first flavorful kisses between them. "Then he told me he didn't have a ring and would I mind waiting to get one. What did I care about a ring? It was the man I wanted. He said I had to go away with him. I explained there were a few things I wanted to take with me and told him about my mother's passing. I could see sadness come over his handsome face as I told him. I could see what kind of a man he was even though he was just seventeen. I knew he was someone I would be proud to call my husband, bear his many children, and grow old together."

Mamita shook her head in disbelief and mumbled, "So many years ago." She looked at Jane and continued. "After I had collected my few belongings from the hut, we got in his old, battered truck and drove from one side of the state to the other. I had no idea where we were going. I just knew I was happy as we drove through the night, me sitting next to him with his arm wrapped around me tight. When the road was straight and no cars coming, we treated ourselves to a few kisses. That was the most wonderful drive of my life. Papito said it was the same for him. We had what we wanted. Each other.

"It was a little after dawn when we drove down this little dirt path." Mamita motioned to the path outside the house. "In the early morning light, I saw a little house. I looked at him. "It's our new home," Papito said in English. 'It's all ours. It has fresh running water and indoor plumbing. I built it for us.' His voice choked with emotion as he spoke the words *for us*." She paused as she reflected on the meanings of the words *for us*.

"I started to get out of the truck. He put his arm around me and said, 'There's something else I want to show you.' I couldn't imagine what it could be. We drove out into the desert. The sun had risen and its blinding light made it difficult to see very far ahead. The truck stopped. He pointed off in the distance. I couldn't be sure what I was looking at. It was kinda high, made of wood. 'What is it?' I asked.

"'It's an oil well,' he told me. He said when he was drilling for water he had hit a pocket of oil. Then he added with that sweet smile of his that it was just a small one, but he assured me it'd be enough so we wouldn't starve.

"He told me from the moment he had left how he had worked night and day, alone in the heat of the day and the cold of the night. Every second, all he could think of was me and how worried he was I would go away or find another man. He said those two thoughts made him work harder and faster than he ever imagined he could. Then he said something I will never forget until my dying day. He said he couldn't face life without his Mamita beside him for always. We fell asleep in each other's arms in the front seat of that old truck."

CHAPTER 26

Darkness fell over the desert. Jane could see Mamita was exhausted. Since she was a light sleeper, she suggested Little Solanch sleep in her room. Both knew he wouldn't sleep through the night. Mamita agreed. A few minutes into darkness, the house was quiet.

Sometime after midnight, Little Solanch awakened Jane. She heard him talking to himself. She slipped out of her bed and looked down into his. He was sitting in the middle of it playing with his toes, talking and laughing to himself. When he saw her, he held out his arms and yelled, "*Mama.*"

Jane couldn't believe her ears. "You little scoot," she whispered. "You've been listening and learning all this time, haven't you."

Little Solanch laughed and waved his arms up and down when he heard her speak. "*Mama,*" he repeated, holding up his arms so she would pick him up. She knew it was useless to try to get him to go back to sleep since that was all he had done for a full day.

"Someone must be hungry." She smacked her lips imitating the sounds of eating. He understood. He smiled and stood holding onto the sideboard. He held out his arms to her and stomped his feet up and down. "Yes, someone is hungry." He threw back his head and laughed.

She picked him up and went into the kitchen. She held him close as she prepared hot cereal. He sighed, a deep baby sigh, put his arms around her neck, laid his head on her shoulder, and patiently waited as she went about the cereal preparations. When it was ready, she sat him on her lap and fed the lukewarm cereal spoonful by spoonful to a willing body that enjoyed every mouthful that was offered him. When he had finished, she made preparations to burp him even though he was no longer a small baby. Because of the condition he had been in for such a long period of time, she and Mamita considered it the prudent thing to do. She put a towel over her shoulder and gently patted his back. After a few pats, his response wasn't what she expected. She heard loud gurgling coming from his body. Then she smelled it. As unpleasant as baby smells can be, this one pleased her. She knew his body was returning to normal since he hadn't gone for many days.

She took off the soiled diaper, cleaned his bottom, patted it dry, and put on a clean diaper. He yawned and clenched his fists glad to be clean and dry. She laid him in his bed. Within moments he was asleep and so was she.

"*Mama! Mama!*" Jane jumped out of bed not fully awake. Daylight filled the room. Little Solanch was standing in his bed with arms outstretched. "*Mama!*" She looked up to see Mamita come running into the room tying her bathrobe.

"*Díos mío, está hablando*," she exclaimed. "He's talking."

Mamita reached down to pick him up. He screamed, "*Mama!*" holding out his arms to Jane.

"He wants you, Jane."

"I can't hold him all the time," Jane said coldly. "Besides, I'm not his mother."

"Jane, is it so terrible a small child loves you? I can see he wants to be with you. I'm not hurt. At this moment, you're the most important person in his life. It's perfectly natural. I know he'll come to love me as he loves you. I can wait. I'm thankful what you've done."

"*Mama!*" he hollered, demanding Jane pick him up.

"Pick him up, Jane. He's an Ochoa all right. He knows what he wants when he sees it."

Jane reached down and put her arms around his little body. "*Mama, Mama,*" he muttered quietly and laid his head against her shoulder in contentment.

As Mamita made the morning coffee and Jane prepared hot cereal for Little Solanch, Mamita said, "There's something I've got to tell you about Ochoa men, Jane, and you might as well know it now." She reached into the cupboard, took down two cups and saucers, and placed them on the table. "Once they've made up their minds, they don't change and that includes women.

"To look at them, the handsome devils they are, you would think all they thought about day and night was sex, but that's not my Solanches. The fact is they're one-woman men. Most men want the prettiest, sexiest woman in the world. I think they call them trophy wives these days. Not my Solanches. I know what you're thinking. I'll get to Juanita Sanchez some other time."

Mamita poured the coffee. She and Jane sat down. "There is a plain, hard fact you and I already know. We're plain women. We think because so many women are prettier than us, we have nothing to offer handsome, intelligent, successful men like my Solanches, but we have so much more to offer than outer beauty. Outer beauty fades with time, inner beauty, ah, that grows with time if properly nourished. I know all this sounds ridiculous, that you don't believe a word I'm saying. Most people focus only on the outer shell, a shell that none of us can control. We are born, live, and die the way God made us, handsome, plain, or ugly, and there's not a whole lot we can do about it. But inner beauty, now that's something we can develop by listening to the hopes and fears of others, by being a friend when others need help, by not being judgmental when others confide in us, by never betraying someone's confidence, by learning from our experiences, by not being selfish thinking the world exists just for us and our pleasures, and by not expecting the world to bow before us because we're pretty or handsome for a few short years. What kind of ridiculous rubbish is that? The outside changes every few years and not for the better. I can tell you that from experience. The inside changes too, and if we do the things I just said, the changes can be for the better. Let Little Solanch call you mama, Jane. After all, you're the only mama he's ever had."

CHAPTER 27

In the weeks Jane had spent with Mamita and Little Solanch, a strong bond of friendship and love had developed between them, but even the strongest of bonds are sometimes tested. Jane thought long and hard about what Mamita had said about Little Solanch calling her mama, but in her heart of hearts, she knew it was wrong. She wasn't his biological mother. She decided he must call her Aunt Jane and the sooner the better so when he called out to her "*Mama! Mama!*" she told him to call her Aunt Jane.

When Mamita heard this, she lashed out with unexpected fury. "I thought you were going to let him call you mama!" The sudden harshness of Mamita's voice shocked Jane.

"I'm a teacher." Jane spoke even more harshly. "I teach facts not fiction. I am not his mother and that my dear Mrs. Ochoa is a fact." Both their breasts heaved in the sudden heat of anger. A long silence followed, each finding some meaningless task to keep them busy while both felt the hurt that had been inflicted upon them and the hurt they had inflicted upon the other. Both regretted the words they had spoken in anger and yet there they were. They couldn't be taken back. They had to be dealt with.

"I see we're back to Mrs. Ochoa."

"I'm sorry, Mamita. I misspoke, but I will not permit that child to call me mama when it's a blatant lie. It's not fair to the child to be taught such a lie, and I won't be a part of it."

Tension filled the air as each went about her meaningless task. Mamita motioned to a chair at the kitchen table and said, "Jane, please, sit down." Seated at the table, Mamita looked into Jane's eyes and said, "The only claim Juanita Sanchez has on motherhood for Little Solanch is that she donated a few of her precious eggs. That's it!" The blank look on Jane's face told Mamita that Jane hadn't fully understood what she had said.

"That Sanchez woman and my son never had sex. She wanted no part of him. On their wedding night, she locked him out of the bedroom, a bedroom that was theirs to share. What woman in her right mind, on her wedding night, won't let her husband be in the same room with her! She's crazy that one is.

"The day after the wedding she flew from the island in the Bahamas to The Big House. She demanded the penthouse bedroom. She demanded it be redecorated in pink. That once beautiful room looks like the room of a prostitute. She demanded Solanch never set foot in her room, ever. The nerve of that woman! Living in his house all these years and demanding the man she married stay out of her bedroom and away from her!

"Solanch didn't fight her. He never raised his voice. He respected her wishes. He asked just one thing. He wanted a child. Since natural sex was out of the question, she said she would give him one but only on her terms. She would donate the necessary eggs if she could select the surrogate mother who would carry the child to term. Solanch hated the thought of what he would have to do to supply the necessary sperm, but he had no choice. He had to go through with it if he was to have a child."

Mamita stared at the white tablecloth, hoping she had made the point clear that her son was an honorable, unfulfilled man. She had told Jane the part that hurt her the most. She dreaded the next part she might have to tell, the part that would hurt Jane. Her heart sank when Jane asked, "Why did he marry her?" That was the question Mamita dreaded.

Mamita kept her eyes on the tablecloth. "Solanch didn't want to marry that woman. He didn't want anything to do with her. Papito didn't want the marriage, and you can guess how I felt about it."

Mamita's breathing became labored as the anger welled up in her. "God forgive me, but I have hated that woman more than anyone I have ever met in my entire life. She's brought anger and misery to this family since we got mixed up with her and her spiteful family. I once told you we don't argue or fight in this house. That was true until Juanita Sanchez was forced on Solanch. Even though she has never set foot in this house, she has trespassed on our happiness and caused us to do all the things we vowed we would never do. Look! She's got us yelling at each other." Mamita lowered her voice. "Please, Jane, no matter what we say to each other, I want us to be friends, always. Promise me that much." Jane nodded her head.

Mamita sighed in relief. A renewed anger made her say, "From the first moment I laid eyes on that Juanita Sanchez I knew she was no good. To me she was the devil, the worst kind of devil because she cared about herself, her fine figure, and money, money, money, and more money but not at all about my Solanch."

Mamita stood, went to the counter behind her, and poured herself a cup of coffee talking all the while. "Lawyers arranged the marriage. This was just another business deal for the Sanchezes. They could have cared less if anybody loved anybody or not.

"Those Sanchezes. Everything they do is for money. They hired lots of lawyers. The best money can buy. Those shysters did their job. They are the ones who did the Sanchez's dirty work for them."

Mamita put the coffee carafe back in its holder and sat down. She looked into Jane's eyes so there would be no miscommunication between them. "Those shysters sifted through all the documents pertaining to the death of Governor Miguel

Sanchez. They discovered that a Jayne James from New York had been responsible for the accident. They checked out every Jayne James in New York and found none of them had been in New Mexico the day the tornado struck. That didn't stop them, not those kinds of lawyers. It inspired them to dig deeper."

Mamita could see Jane's eyes widen in horror as she realized what Mamita was telling her. "Those lawyers found an old log book in the New York City Police Department that recorded a request from the New Mexico state police for the address of a Jane Jones on the date of the tornado. That was all they needed. They checked you out as well as every other Jane Jones in New York to be certain they had the right Jane Jones. Once they were certain it was you they were seeking, they reported what they had discovered to the man who had hired them, Hugo Sanchez, Juanita's father.

"The lawyers dug deeper and discovered you had stayed in this house for six days. When Hugo heard this, he knew he had us right where he wanted us. He knew he could ruin Solanch and Ochoa Industries with a barrage of trumped up charges based on the ridiculous notion that Solanch had committed a criminal act by hiding a hit and run driver from the law. Hugo didn't care if the charges were true or not. Truth didn't matter. Public perception was what mattered, and he knew the public would believe anything he and his lawyers told them to believe. The Sanchezes blackmailed Solanch into marrying their spiteful daughter."

CHAPTER 28

Mamita got up from the table to check on Little Solanch. Jane sat still, stunned by what Mamita had told her. The thought that someone somewhere knew her identity unhinged her. The little house became too small. The kitchen closed in, suffocating her. She wanted to get up and run, run as far away from the Ochoas and this little house in the middle of nowhere as fast as she could. Life had turned ugly and become complicated.

Mamita brought Little Solanch into the living room so he could crawl on the floor. Within moments he crawled past the sofa and into the kitchen. "*Mama.*"

Mamita laughed. "You can't hide from him, Jane. He's going to find you wherever you are." Jane didn't hear a word of what Mamita had said.

Little Solanch climbed the leg of the chair and stood. He laughed and stomped his feet up and down pleased he was standing. Then he did something that stunned Mamita but was lost on Jane whose mind was locked in its own fear-filled world. He took a few steps away from the chair before he collapsed in a heap on the kitchen floor. He looked at Jane and laughed. He struggled to his feet and took the few steps back to the chair. "See?" he asked in a high-pitched voice.

Jane stared at the kitchen wall. "Did you see that, Jane? He took his first steps." Mamita clapped her hands in joy, jerking Jane back to reality.

She forced a smile and tried her best to sound cheerful. "Yes, Aunt Jane sees." Little Solanch laughed the gleeful laugh of a child who's proud of what it's done. He turned and walked a few more steps away from Jane until he collapsed on the floor.

Mamita watched him run his hands over the floor tiles making happy gibberish sounds. She smiled at the thought he was having quite a conversation with himself and thrilled the happy babblings of a small child filled her home. She had missed these babblings more than she had ever imagined. She sat in silence, listening, enthralled. She loved this child with all her heart. No matter what might happen in the future, she would be grateful to Jane for saving her son and now her grandson.

"It's been less than a week since his illness and he's already talking and walking. I can't believe it. I wouldn't have believed it if I hadn't seen it with my own eyes, and what a sweet child he is. I can't believe how happy he is. His happiness brings me such joy. I hope you feel the joy too."

Jane nodded her head, but she felt no joy. Her mind focused on just one thing. Unknown individuals knew her true identity, where she lived, where she worked. They knew all about her. Her head went in circles. She felt unstable, unable to concentrate on anything but these cold, hard facts.

"Little Solanch has waited until he's with you to take his first steps. He wanted to show off just for you, Jane. You should be honored."

She stopped, lost in thought.

"Anyway," Mamita said, coming back to reality, "I'm going to teach Little Solanch to say Mamita today. That's close to Mama. He should be able to say my name." She heaved a sigh of contentment. "Having a baby in the house does me such good."

Then she said as much to herself as Jane, "I wish I could have had more babies. Poor Papito. The accident." Tears came to her eyes. "We couldn't have any more. That's why I'm so thankful for Solanch. At least Papito will have him to take over Ochoa Industries when he retires, which isn't that far away. That's why I'm so thankful for Little Solanch, who will take over the business when Solanch retires, many more years from now."

Mamita paused a moment to collect her thoughts. "It scares me to think we almost let doctors give this sweet child high-powered drugs for a condition that didn't exist. I don't even want to think what damage those drugs could have done. I told you, Jane, I never thought he had autism. Never!"

She lowered her voice to a whisper. "I've never told my suspicions to anyone. Not even Papito or Solanch. I can't prove a thing. That's why I never mentioned it to either of them, but as far as I'm concerned Juanita Sanchez is a criminal. Yes, a criminal. She terrorized Little Solanch."

Jane forced back to reality by the word *terrorized*, exclaimed, "No!" in disbelief.

"I'm certain of it," Mamita said forcefully. "One afternoon I needed to talk to her. Her security man at the door let me in unannounced. I guess I wasn't on the forbidden to enter list. I didn't see her in the bedroom. I noticed the bathroom door was open. I looked inside. I saw her giving Little Solanch a bath. She was holding his head under the water."

"No!"

"When I ran to save him, she raised his head above water and said she was washing his hair. She's a cold-blooded liar that one is. Little Solanch didn't scream. He stared at me, wide-eyed. He no blink. She screamed at me to get out of the bathroom and called security. I had no choice. I had to leave but at least that woman knew I knew what she was up to. She was terrorizing my grandson. She wanted to either drive him insane or kill him,

CHAPTER 29

Jane's world spun out of control. She heard a car outside the kitchen door. She ran out of the kitchen into the living room and sat on the sofa. She heard Papito's voice. She blocked it out. She needed to get a grip on herself. Papito stood in front of her, his arms outstretched so he could hug her. She didn't move.

Through the mental haze, she heard Solanch's voice talking to his son. She panicked. She jumped to her feet, pushed past Papito, and started for the front door. Mamita ran past her and threw herself against the closed door. The fierceness in her face stopped Jane in her tracks.

"Sit!" Mamita commanded, her breathing heavy from anger. Papito retreated to the kitchen table along with Solanch.

Jane felt trapped. She couldn't think. "Sit down! Right now!" Mamita demanded. Jane stood still. Mamita moved toward her. The fierceness in her eyes frightened Jane. She took a step backwards. As Mamita came closer, Jane took several steps backward until she fell onto the sofa.

Little Solanch sitting on the kitchen tiles screamed, "No! No want!" He wiggled free from his father's loving hands.

"I knew you would run from men and love. Yes, from men and love. You've done that all your life. You can run. This isn't a prison. The Suburban is waiting to take you to the airport, but before you leave, I have a few things I intend to say to you and you're going to listen. Which do you want? Scotch or whisky." Jane looked at her blankly.

"Papito, get a whisky to clear her head. She can't think straight. Anyone can see that from the look in her eyes. When she's finished her drink, she and I will have a little talk."

Papito poured Jane a small whisky and handed it to her. Jane's hands shook. "Drink it! Every drop!" Mamita commanded. Jane hated the smell let alone the taste of straight whisky, but she did as Mamita commanded. As the amber liquid flooded her taste buds, she grimaced and shivered.

"*Mama! Mama!*" Little Solanch screamed. His shrill screams filled every corner of the house. Papito reached down to try to comfort him. "No!" he screamed. "No want!" He screamed the screams of a child who knew bad things were happening and hoped if he screamed loud enough, the bad things would go away. "*Mama! Mama!*" Papito's shushes made him scream louder. He held out his hands to Jane sitting on the sofa. "*Mama! Mama!*" he screamed in a hysterical frenzy, fearing he was losing the one thing in life he loved most, and he was going to fight with every ounce of strength his body possessed. "*Mama! Mama!*"

"Mamita, do you want me to take him to the bedroom?" Papito asked. Mamita nodded her head. Papito reached down to take hold of the screaming child. Little Solanch screamed and kicked with such ferocity that Papito couldn't pick him up. Solanch rushed to his father's side, holding Little Solanch's legs so he couldn't kick Papito, while Papito restrained the wildly flailing arms. It took all of Papito's and Solanch's strength to take the screaming child into their arms and carry him to the bedroom. Little Solanch's heartbreaking screams could be heard retreating into the distance then muffled by the closed bedroom door. A few moments later, Papito returned, shaken by Little Solanch's ferocity and sat at the kitchen table while Solanch remained with his son.

Mamita waited for the whisky to take full effect on Jane. She scrutinized her eyes. When the wildness had faded, she knew Jane's mind had sufficiently cleared for her to begin.

"People think because we're rich, we've lost our fear of God, lost our humanity, that all we think about is how to make more and more money, that we don't care how we get it, that we cheat everyone to get it, and ruin anyone who dares get in our way. Look around you. Look! Does this look like the house of a rich family? Does it?" Mamita's voice rose in anger.

"We live in this little house because it contains the history of our lives, all three of us. This was Papito's and my first and only home, not a house but a home, a home filled with love and memories. It represents our humble beginnings, beginnings we never want to forget. I choose to wash my own dishes, mop the floors, wash and iron the clothes of those I love, and cook the meals that nurture us. By doing these things, I reaffirm my love for them and renew my understanding for those who don't have all that I have."

"This house is full of memories, good memories. Solanch was born on a rickety old bed where you're sitting. That's why the sofa is where it is. It celebrates the birth of my only child. The edge of this coffee table,"—Mamita paused and pointed to the table in front of the sofa—"was the outer wall of the house that Papito built with his own two hands."

"Whatever we have as a family, we have earned as a family. No one ever gave us anything we didn't earn, and we wouldn't want it any other way. Yes, we have money. Most people would call us filthy rich with the accent on filthy because they believe everyone who has money is indecent and corrupt, but for us, money doesn't even enter the top ten reasons that drive us to make money. Our first goal is to serve God. Our second is to honor and obey his son Jesus Christ. Our third is to serve our Holy Mother Mary. Our fourth is to honor God's representative on Earth, the Pope, and to support his benevolent causes. Our fifth is to honor the Ochoa family name, that our actions never dishonor our proud heritage in business or social relationships. Our sixth is to honor and love each other, to tell the truth, and to admit our mistakes. Our seventh is to honor the United States of America, a country that has given us the opportunity for the pursuit of happiness and the freedom to express our personal thoughts. Our eighth is to honor capitalism, the economic system that enables us not only to provide for ourselves but to employ thousands of people in countries all over the world. Our ninth is to honor our social responsibility to our fellow human beings who can't help themselves. We help millions of people every year by donating millions of dollars to build schools, and hospitals, and to provide life saving medicines for those who can't afford them. Our tenth goal is to help those charities that do research for diseases that are now incurable. To them we donate millions of dollars. So you see, Jane, money for the sake of having money never enters our minds. It's what we can do with the money that's most important to us. That's who we are and that's what we stand for."

"There are two things I have left to say to you. The five million dollars is yours whether you stay or walk out that door." She pointed in the direction of the front door. "But if you walk out that door, I promise you, you will never hear from any of us ever again, no matter what might happen." Mamita fell silent. The silence in the living room quieted Little Solanch. He lay in his bed exhausted from his outburst. Solanch tiptoed out of the bedroom, returned to the living room, and kissed his mother. She hugged him as only a mother can hug a son. Neither said a word. They didn't need to.

Papito crossed the room and kissed Mamita on the lips. She slipped her hand into his and put her head on his arm as the two of them walked slowly toward the bedroom.

CHAPTER 30

Solanch sat next to Jane on the sofa. Her mind was in such a state of confusion she couldn't remember her own name let alone have a conversation. He too was at a loss for words. Both sat lost in their different worlds. He reached over and put his hand on her arm. Jane leaned forward and buried her head in her hands. A violent sob convulsed her body. She looked up at him and said, "I'm not good enough for you. I'm not good enough for any of you." She sunk her head back into her hands and sobbed.

Through the tears, she heard him softly say, "That's not so, Jane. That's just not so." He put his arm around her shoulders and listened as she cried herself to sleep.

When she awoke, she had a splitting headache thanks to the single shot of whisky and rivers of tears. She felt something pressing against her left arm and shoulder. When she opened her eyes, she saw him asleep, his head resting on her shoulder. She wanted to jump up and run for the door. Instinctively she moved. He awoke, smiled, and said quietly, "Night, Jane." He got up and went to his room.

The smell of coffee woke her, the same smell that greeted her every morning but a welcome smell nevertheless. She looked at the clock on the table next to her bed. Ten twenty-one. She had

had a full night's sleep but her head still hurt. She could hear the sounds of Little Solanch playing. She smiled at the thought of Mamita making coffee and teaching Little Solanch to say her name, Mamita. Jane knew it was time to get up and help with the morning chores. She hoped that would show Mamita, despite all she had said the night before, that they were still friends. She threw back the covers, got up, and looked in the mirror. She looked worse than usual, which was a polite way of saying haggard. She combed her hair, dressed in shorts and a blouse, and opened the door to her room.

"*Mama, Mama*," Little Solanch cried out the moment he saw her. He held up his arms so she would pick him up. She started toward him when she heard the rattle of newspaper. She stopped. Solanch was sitting at the kitchen table, dressed in a blue, terrycloth bathrobe. She averted her eyes, picked up Little Solanch, and sat down at the table across from him.

"Good morning," he said cheerfully peering around the side of the paper. "Let me get you some coffee." He put the newspaper down and went to the counter. With his back to her, he poured the coffee. She stole a look at him. The bathrobe came down to his knees. She could see the reddish-brown color of his legs covered by dark hair. "One sugar and no cream. See, I remember."

She looked at him more closely. The legs although thin looked muscular. She allowed herself to look higher. Her heart took a leap as she looked at his small, firm buttocks, well defined by the bathrobe. She couldn't help but think this was the male form at its finest. She marveled at his male beauty. *Much too good for me,* she thought as she put Little Solanch back on the floor to play with his blocks.

He banged the spoon on the side of the cup. "You're tone deaf so I won't make my usual joke about the key of C." He smiled and put the cup on the table in front of her. Because the robe was open at the top and he wasn't wearing an undershirt, she caught a glimpse of his chest. The skin had a healthy reddish-brown glow, smooth, hairless.

He is so beautiful. She couldn't help but think such thoughts, thoughts she had buried years ago and had hoped they would stay buried forever, but they hadn't. As he sat down, she got up and started to prepare hot cereal for Little Solanch.

"Oh, he ate a while ago. I prepared it myself. Listen to this." He held out his arms to Little Solanch who said, "Papi."

"He knows me. I didn't think he would," he said pleased with his son. He reached down, picked him up, and kissed him on the cheek.

"Papi, Papi," Little Solanch happily repeated.

"He's only seen me a few times in his life, yet this morning when he got up, he called me 'Papi'. I couldn't believe it. I still can't." His face beamed with happiness, because now he was a father, a real father. He kissed Little Solanch several times, told him how much he loved him, and put him back on the floor.

"Sit down and let me prepare breakfast for you. Anything your heart desires as long as it's ham and eggs and hot buttered toast. I'm afraid that's all Mamita left us to eat this morning."

"I'm not hungry."

"Two aspirin, ham and eggs, and hot buttered toast will make the headache go away." He got up, went to the cupboard, took down a bottle of aspirin, and shook out two tablets on the white tablecloth. He poured her a glass of cold water from the refrigerator, and said, "Doctor Ochoa says to take two of these in the morning after a shot of whisky the night before. Sit down, take the aspirin, let me get some breakfast in you, and I guarantee you'll feel much, much better."

Jane sat at the table, took a long sip of water, and swallowed the aspirin. She picked up Little Solanch even though he hadn't asked to be picked up and put him on her lap. She felt safer with him close to her so she could hide behind him.

"I'm hungry too. I hope you don't mind if I eat with you."

His words reminded her of Mamita's story when she was in the store and Papito had asked her to eat with him. Her words, 'believe me, Jane, I didn't play hard to get,' came to mind.

"Yes, of course," she heard herself saying. She pretended to be more interested in Little Solanch, who was being a perfect gentleman, quiet, and well-behaved, as if he hoped something good would come from this breakfast, but even the best behaved children can do the unexpected. He suddenly threw his arms in the air with his fingers extended. One of his fingers went up Jane's nose. "Little Solanch! No fingers up nose!" Jane cried out. Little Solanch laughed.

"He did the same thing to me a while ago. I'm afraid he's learned a new trick." Solanch turned back to the skillet and cracked two eggs together releasing their contents into the hot skillet. Then he cracked two more eggs, carefully arranging them in the skillet around the sizzling slabs of ham. Jane held Little Solanch's arm so he couldn't launch another surprise nose attack.

"How do you like your eggs?"

"Whatevah."

"I like mine sunny-side up with the yolk medium. Is that okay with you?"

"I guess so." She was in a state of confusion seeing him in the kitchen instead of Mamita.

She studied his male form even more. The back of his head caught her attention. The pretty curls she admired were twisted into a matted mess. He had gotten out of bed and not bothered to untangle them. She lowered her gaze not feeling it was right to look at him in his present unkempt condition.

"Voilà." He placed a plate with two eggs, several slices of ham along with two slices of buttered toast in front of her and then served himself. He sat down, said a short prayer, crossed himself, smiled at Jane and said, "Let's eat." Without another word, he cut a slice of ham and started eating with gusto. Jane sat, not eating. She couldn't take her eyes off him. He hadn't shaved. His beard intrigued her. It didn't grow in clumps but formed a covering over his face that looked like a medium grade of sandpaper, forming a perfect line on his cheekbone between dark beard and reddish-brown skin. He looked up and shook his fork at her. "Eat, before it gets cold!" Jane did as she was told.

CHAPTER 31

Breakfast eaten, Solanch washed the dishes and cleaned the kitchen while Jane took care of Little Solanch's needs. When she had finished, she sat at one end of the sofa. A few minutes later, Solanch joined her, sitting at the opposite end. He put his bare feet up on the coffee table and stretched out to relax.

Jane was anything but relaxed. Breakfast had been a tense, wordless affair. She was glad when it had ended. She stared at the front door.

"Do you know what day this is?"

"Tuesday, maybe Wednesday." She hated the tone of her voice.

"I didn't mean the day, but its significance."

"I haven't the slightest."

"It isn't to the exact day. In fact its twelve days too late, but it's close enough to celebrate. It was ten years ago you drove into El Satélite. Ten years ago you drove into my life."

"I want to forget all that."

"Jane, look at me, please."

With arms folded across her chest, she turned and gave him a look filled with senseless hostility.

"I once told you, you built the walls too high. I'm trying to tear them down, but I need your help. I can't do it alone."

"Maybe some walls shouldn't be torn down," she answered nastily, sounding more like a snotty brat than a mature woman.

She hated what she was saying. She hated the way she was acting, but she was into the scene. She couldn't turn back. She had to play it out, yet the smell of his unwashed body aroused her more than she cared to admit.

"I'm sorry, Jane. I don't agree with you. You seem to think that walls make good neighbors, but walls separate people from each other. When people live behind walls, they grow apart, they stop understanding each other, they stop liking each other, in time, they despise each other, and finally they become enemies. Friendship and love disappear, forever. No Jane, walls do not make a good neighbor.

"When we met ten years ago at the motel, you built your first wall, but it wasn't so high I couldn't get over it. I thought the wall had been smashed for good after we talked for six of the most memorable nights of my life. Then you left, went back to New York where you built new walls, higher than the old one. You talked to me less and less until you refused my phone calls altogether. In time, you grew to despise me. That's when you built your walls so high I could no longer climb over them. That's when our friendship and love ceased to exist. That's what walls do. They divide and destroy. That's what they've done to us. Please, Jane. Tear down your walls, for both our sakes. Haven't we hurt each other enough?"

"What do you care? You don't even know me."

He paused to reflect and said, "You're half right, but this much I do know. I know you took excellent care of me when I had my nervous breakdown. Without you, I would have died. You saved my life. You also saved the life of my son, something I will be grateful for the rest of my life. I know my son loves you like a mother. I know that Mamita and Papito love you like a daughter. I know I have strong feelings for you as well. I also know you're an intelligent woman."

"You know no such thing." She stole a look at his long, muscular body draped from the sofa to the coffee table. Even in anger, her heart skipped several beats as she surveyed his perfectly formed body from his head to his long, slender toes.

"Yes I do," he fired back. "Mamita, Papito, and I, we all three agree on this point. You're a shrewd woman with a good sense for business."

"I'm a teacher, not a businesswoman."

"True, but that's of your own choosing. We have been impressed by your knowledge about a vast array of business subjects, but here's what none of us can understand. I once told you, you weren't the woman I thought you were. What I meant was, why do you shut out the people who love you?"

He ran his fingers through his unkempt hair. "I've talked about your high walls, but I have one of my own that must be torn down and destroyed forever if you and I are to come to any kind of understanding, my so-called marriage to Juanita. You already know about our sexless marriage and Little Solanch. What you don't know is that she has filed for divorce, claiming there's a lack of communication between us, that I lack a commitment to the marriage, that there are serious sexual problems between us, and that she has failed expectations of me. If these charges weren't so serious, they would be funny, considering she locked me out of my own bedroom, refused to let me see my own son, and I've only seen her a few times in all the years we've been married even though she's lived in my house. Unfortunately, I can't tell you the divorce is final. It isn't, so technically we're still married, but in name only."

"Papi? Papi?"

"My son wants me." He smiled. "That's the only decent thing Juanita has done in all this mess. She's given me custody of my son for which I'm grateful." He got up and went into the bedroom.

Jane heard Little Solanch's soft voice. "I love Papi. I love Papi."

"Papi loves you too. Do you want to get up?"

"No."

"Okay, my sweet son. Papi loves you very much."

Jane could see he was going to be a loving father and the relationship between father and son would be a strong, enduring one.

He came back into the living room and sat at the far end of the sofa. He should have looked happy after having had a loving moment with his son, but he looked troubled. He sat quietly for a long time. When he spoke, he spoke slowly, unsure of how to say what he knew he had to say. "There's one other subject we must discuss if we're to find happiness. It's a subject I fear. I fear it because it might split us further apart rather than bring us closer together, but it's something that makes you feel insecure. I don't ever want you to feel insecure because of me. At the moment, I have a beautiful wife, a beautiful wife on the outside but one who is rotten to the core on the inside. Her beauty has brought me no happiness, only misery."

"I have known you for many years, and in those years, I have traveled the world. I have met hundreds if not thousands of women, many extraordinarily beautiful women of every nationality, and yet they have been of no interest to me. There's only been you. No other woman has ever made me as happy as you have. That's why this wall of insecurity is driving me crazy. It makes me unhappy because I know if it would go away, you and I would be very happy together."

His cell chimed. He spoke in Spanish. Jane could only understand one word, Suburban. "That was Mamita reminding me of the dinner at The Big House tonight. The Suburban will pick us up in a couple of hours. Time is short for us, Jane. I realize school starts in a few days. You have a day, maybe two at the most to decide if you're going to stay or leave. The decision is yours."

CHAPTER 32

Jane shouldn't have been surprised at Solanch's transformation in a few hours from an unkempt male to a distinguished businessman, but she was. He appeared elegant in his tuxedo with his freshly shaven face and perfectly groomed hair. She detected, however, an unexplained sadness, an ingrained grimness about him she couldn't explain. Her excitement about the dinner party caused her to cast aside all concerns and focus on the party, for this would be a night to remember.

Solanch escorted her into the conference hall and to a table in front of the speaker's dais. Once seated, he introduced her to CEO's of several companies and their wives. Jane couldn't help but notice an unexplained tension amongst those seated around the table.

The dinner was far superior to the diners and TV dinners she had become accustomed to in New York and the plain meals she and Mamita had shared during the recent weeks, yet those seated around the table picked at the food on their plates. Dinner conversation was strained and even that was precious little. Jane paid little attention because nothing was going to spoil this magical evening.

When the last plate had been removed, Mr. Ochoa stood behind his chair on the dais. An immediate hush came over the room. He walked slowly to the lectern. Jane saw sadness in him she had never seen before. He didn't stand his usual straight self. He looked pale, old. Her immediate fear was he had taken ill.

Mr. Ochoa stared at the people in front of him for what seemed to be an interminable amount of time. No one seated at the tables said a word. "As you know," his voice thin and strained as he began, "my son Solanch and I have just returned from an extended overseas trip that lasted over two months. Solanch went to Russia and the eastern European countries Poland, Romania, Bulgaria, Serbia, and Hungary. I went to Japan, China, Thailand, and Indonesia. Our purpose was to secure new contracts. I must report to you neither he nor I was successful in our efforts.

"Prior to this dinner, Solanch and I met with our Board of Directors, our lawyers, and our accountants who informed us that all existing governmental contracts have been canceled. Let me assure you we are doing everything legally possible to save as many of our companies not affected by government contracts from hostile takeovers by Sanchez Securities. These unexpected events have put Ochoa Industries in a serious financial situation. To underscore the seriousness of our financial position, we may, and I emphasize the word may, have to close The Big House at least temporarily if not permanently. I hope I don't sound too maudlin by saying this may be our last supper at The Big House.

"No matter what happens in the future, I want to thank all of you for your loyal service to Ochoa Industries. I wish you all success. Thank you for coming. I only wish it could have been under happier circumstances. Good night and God bless each and every one of you."

The people at the tables stood and in unison said, "God bless you, Mr. Ochoa." Quietly they filed out of the room. None of them knew what lay ahead for their companies or their own financial futures.

Alejandro drove Jane and Solanch to the little house. When they arrived, they found Little Solanch asleep. "Thank you for watching him, Miss Clark," Solanch said to the babysitter.

"No trouble at all, Mr. Ochoa. He played with his blocks most of the evening. I put him to bed a little while ago. He's such a happy little boy. Night Mr. Ochoa. Night Miss Jones."

As the sound of the Suburban's tires on gravel disappeared into the night, Solanch threw his tux coat on the sofa, loosened his tie, unbuttoned his top shirt button, and slumped into a chair. Jane sat on the sofa across from him.

"I don't understand. What's happened?"

"It's Juanita and her father. They're trying to bankrupt us, and at the moment, they're doing a very good job of it," he said in a tired, weak voice, rubbing his forehead with both hands. His eyes were glassy, sunken.

Jane felt anger surge through her veins directed at Juanita and her corrupt family. "How are the Sanchezes able to do this? Don't you have a pre-nuptial agreement?"

"Yes. We had," he corrected himself, "have one."

"She's entitled to a good chunk of your wealth, but how is it she and her family are getting so many of your companies?"

He was silent for a long while. The weight of his failing, financial world pressed heavily on his shoulders. "I've agreed to many things."

"What kinds of things?"

"I would do it again."

"Do what?" Jane asked impatiently, the anger rising within her.

"Jane, forget it. What's done is done," he said in a depressed, exhausted voice.

"No!" she said sharply. "It is not done. I want to know why you've done things that have bankrupted Ochoa Industries."

He sat silent. "Well, tell me!" she shouted at him.

In a soft, raspy voice, he uttered, "I couldn't..., I wouldn't let the Sanchezes destroy you. I acceded to their demands."

Jane stared straight ahead.

"I'm sorry, Jane. I never meant to say any of those things. Please forgive me. I'm exhausted. I'm going to bed." He got up from the chair and walked wearily to his bedroom, his left shoulder brushing the wall of the hallway.

Jane sat alone, her mind in turmoil. Instinct told her to run, to run as far away as she could from the Ochoas and their dying financial empire, yet an equally strong voice asked, *what more can you ask of this man who has sacrificed himself for you in so many ways?* She realized this was her last chance at life. The instinct to run beat fiercely within her, but what good had come from running, nothing but loneliness, misery, and a near death. The Ochoas wanted and needed her. They had made that clear. This was her rightful place. The instinct to run retreated. She realized a new importance in life. She walked to his room. He was stretched out on his stomach too exhausted to take off his tux. She slipped into bed beside him.

He felt her presence. "Is that you, Jane?" he asked in a barely audible voice.

"Yes," she whispered.

He reached out and put his arm on her shoulder. Fighting exhaustion, he whispered in the dark, "Don't leave me, Jane. Please don't ever leave me."

"I won't," she whispered back. He rested his head against her shoulder. She felt him let go. His tears on her bare shoulder were like life giving rain to a withering plant, for she too let go, their tears wiping away the years of tension between them, making way for a rebirth of life, a life of togetherness.

CHAPTER 33

Jane heard Little Solanch talking to himself. When she opened her eyes, he was standing next to the bed looking intently as a child does when it sees something it's never seen before, in this case, Jane in bed next to his father. "Mama, Mama, me hungry," he said, his voice filled with anticipation when he saw she was awake.

She put her extended index finger to her lips and whispered, "Shhh." She marveled at how much progress he had made in such a short time. He was no longer a baby. He was a normal walking, talking two-year-old boy.

"Mama, get you food," she whispered still holding her finger to her lips. He laughed and clapped his hands at the word food.

Little Solanch followed her into the kitchen and played with his blocks on the floor while Jane slipped into her bedroom to change from the expensive gown into shorts and a blouse. She prepared hot cereal for Little Solcanch and coffee for her and Solanch. As she went about her morning tasks, she conceived a three-pronged plan.

First, she would no longer call Solanch he, him, or his. She would call him Solanch on formal occasions, but her private name she would borrow from Mamita, *querido*. She glanced at the clock. Seven thirty-nine. The moment had arrived for her to complete the second part of her plan, to destroy the one thing that had meant so much to her for so many years. She picked up her cell.

"Good morning," she said when she heard a voice. "This is Jane Jones calling. May I please speak with Dr. Schmidt?" The wait for Dr. Schmidt seemed endless. Finally she heard her voice. "Hello? Dr. Schmidt? Jane Jones calling. Yes, I'm fine. And you? Glad to hear you are too. I'll come to the point, Dr. Schmidt. I'm calling to resign my position.

"Yes, I know it's late in the summer to resign, but I didn't know until twenty minutes ago myself so you see I've called you as soon as I could. No, I'm not ill. Something has come up. Yes, it's good. At least I hope it is. As soon as I know for certain you'll be one of the first to know," Jane said cheerfully. "You're very kind Dr. Schmidt, but I'm sure you'll find someone much better than I to fill the position. Give my best to everyone. Thank you and bye for now."

Jane flipped the cell shut, poured a cup of coffee, tied a bib around Little Solanch's neck as he sat on the floor playing with his blocks, and taught him how to feed himself with a spoon. As she did so, her mind conceived courses of action against a woman she had never met, Juanita Sanchez, against an organization, Sanchez Securities, she knew nothing about, but she was resolved to do whatever it would take to right the wrongs the Sanchezes had done to the Ochoas.

Jane realized the third part of her plan would be the most crucial. She feared the financial crisis might cause her *querido* to sink into severe depression if not another full-blown nervous breakdown. She could not and would not allow this to happen. She resolved to remain in high spirits, not be judgmental, and most of all, to tear down the walls between them so their love could flourish. Solanch had been right. They had hurt each other enough.

A few minutes after nine, Jane heard Solanch's cell chiming. She decided not to answer, but after many chimes, she worried it might be important. She found it in the pocket of his tux. "Hello?"

"Jane? It's Mamita."

"*Buenos días* and a very good morning to you, Mamita," Jane said cheerfully.

"*Buenos días*, Jane." Hearing Spanish come from Jane's lips heartened her. "And a very good morning to you." As Jane had hoped, her cheerfulness had radiated to Mamita. "I wanted to tell you Papito and I are going to stay a few days here at The Big House. How are things there?" Mamita asked, sounding more like her old self.

"Little Solanch learned how to eat hot cereal with a spoon this morning, and just a little while ago he learned how to run. He ran into me in the kitchen and nearly knocked me down. That kid's got some power behind him."

Mamita laughed with joy. "Eating and running? Oh Jane, that's fantastico, just fantastico." The joy in her voice cheered Jane. "I can't believe how much he's learned in such a short time. He's a smart one, that Little Solanch, but he's got a good teacher. No wonder he's doing so good."

"I didn't teach him how to run, that much I can promise you. He figured that one out on his own," Jane said laughing.

"How's Solanch?"

"He's sleeping."

"Good. He hasn't slept well for months. He's exhausted. Papito's doing the same here."

"Mamita, would you do me a favor? I need your help since you know everyone and how everything works. I have some ideas that might be of use."

"Tell me what you want me to do."

"Would you arrange a meeting in a few days at The Big House with Sandi, Pedro, Alejandro, Pepe, and Jack Burton and one more thing, ask them not to tell anyone about this meeting, no one. That means Papito, Mamita."

"Oh, top secret stuff. How exciting. I tell no one and I make sure the others no tell either. I have no idea what you're up to, but

I think maybe something big. I like your list of names. I call them and tell them not to tell single soul."

"Eight o'clock sharp, *tiempo americano*."

Mamita laughed. "Ok, Jane. *Tiempo americano* it is."

"One other thing. Tell them the meeting will last all day and as many days as it takes to accomplish what we must accomplish."

"*Díos mío*. These plans of yours sound very big and very interesting. I will tell them everything you said and promise they will be in The Big House at eight in two days."

"Make it five, Mamita. I want to be here for Solanch. I don't want to leave him alone for a few days yet."

Mamita gave a scream of joy. "So it's Solanch now?"

"Yes, Mamita. I resigned my teaching position. I'm staying. If Solanch wants to marry me when his divorce is final, I'll marry him. If not, I'll stay until he asks me to leave."

Mamita cried with joy. "*Gracias a Díos*. Thank you God. I feel so much better already. The heaviness is off my heart. I'll tell Papito when he wakes. He'll be as thrilled as I am. You and Solanch married is a dream of Papito and me for many years. You'll have your meeting in five days."

"Oh, by the way, Mamita. I left one name off the list."

"Who else you want? Tell me and I be sure they're there."

"You. We'll need your experience, guidance, and knowledge to bring us together."

"I will be mucho honored."

"Good. Then it's settled. We'll meet in five days at eight."

They hung up. Their spirits renewed. Each had renewed the other.

Solanch slept in his tux well after the sun had set. Jane sat in a chair next to the bed waiting for him to awaken. When he did, the first thing he saw was her. She smiled and said, "*Bienvenido, Querido*."

He yawned and stretched. "What time is it?" he asked too groggy to realize the significance of the word *querido*.

"It's a little after ten, at night. You've slept almost a full day. Hungry?"

"Hmm," he said struggling to regain his senses.

"Pepe brought over some nice things to eat. Let me get something for you. I'll give you a late night supper in bed. How's does that sound?" she said cheerfully.

"Sounds good to me, but give me a few minutes to change out of this tux. I think I've worn it long enough. A shower is in order."

"That would be nice too," she said as she bent down and kissed him on the cheek. "You take your shower. I'll heat up the food."

Pleased with the kiss, he asked, "When do I get more of those?"

"After you've showered and eaten."

"Three nice things to look forward to." He smiled at the thought. He struggled to his feet. Jane rushed to his side, took his arm, and helped steady him. "Thanks. I am a bit wobbly. Don't worry. I'm okay, now that you're here." Then he looked at her and said softly, "Thanks for being here when I need you."

Jane went into the kitchen and looked at what Pepe had sent. She could see the great care and love he had put into each prepared dish that not only looked wonderful but smelled just as good. She had no doubt about their taste.

She put on Mamita's faded blue half-apron. As she bustled about the kitchen, she heard Little Solanch's footsteps running toward her. He ran as fast as he could into her and threw his arms around her legs.

"Hey buster," Jane laughed. "You're getting too big for your britches. Do you know that?" He laughed, pleased he had made his mama laugh and pleased with himself he could get out of his bed and run.

He heard noise coming from the bedroom. He looked at Jane and asked excitedly, "Papi? Papi?" She nodded her head. He ran down the hallway yelling, "Papi? Papi?"

"She heard Solanch say, "Whoa, not so hard!" and Little Solanch laugh. Jane went back to the bedroom.

When Little Solanch saw her, he looked up and said "Mama. Mama." Then he looked up to Solanch. "Papi. Papi." He looked at Jane. "Me love Mama." Then he looked at Solanch. "Me love Papi." He reached out a hand to each of them and looked up. The three of them put their arms around each other and held tight.

As they embraced, Jane whispered in his ear, "I resigned, *mi querido*. I'm staying." He leaned down and kissed her on the lips. That was the moment the three of them became a family, a loving, inseparable family.

CHAPTER 34

In the days that followed, Jane devoted her energies to fulfilling the needs of Little Solanch and her *querido*. The next morning, she taught Little Solanch colors, letters, and numbers. In the afternoon, she read him stories, stories he devoured. Within two days, Little Solanch knew all his colors, the letters of the alphabet, and the numbers from one to twenty. Late in the afternoon on the second day, he demanded he read to Mama and Papi. He put the upside down book in his hands and told them the story, occasionally turning a page and pointing to a picture as they had done.

On the third morning, Jane taught him how to read the first three words in his favorite story. Little Solanch looked at them carefully. Then he did what she hoped he would do. He looked through the book finding the words in other parts of the story. These discoveries thrilled him. He screamed the word and ran to her if she was the closest or Papi if he was the closest. "Look, me read," he said proudly pointing to the word.

"I read," she corrected him.

"I read," he repeated after her. Every so often, Solanch or Jane added new words. Little Solanch pushed his blocks aside and sat on the floor, studying his book hour after hour, learning his new words, and looking for them in the stories.

On the fourth day when Mamita and Papito came to visit, Little Solanch ran to them with a book in his hands. "See Mamita?

I read," he said, pleased with himself he had remembered Jane's correction. Papito reached down and put him in his lap, kissing him on the cheek.

Mamita put her hands over her eyes and cried. "*No lo creo*," she said over and over through tears. When she had recovered, she turned to Jane and said, "I no believe. You a miracle worker," to which Papito agreed.

By day, Jane was a mother and teacher. By night, she was a wife. She and Solanch sat for hours on the sofa as he told her all the dirty tricks Sanchez Securities had used to ruin Ochoa Industries. He explained how they had made extravagant promises to governments, if they cancelled their contracts with Ochoa Industries and permitted Sanchez companies to seize Ochoa assets, the governments would profit handsomely. Governments, looking for fast profits, had taken Sanchez Securities' advice and canceled their contracts. Those Ochoa companies not involved in government contracts became the objects of hostile takeovers by Sanchez Securities who bought the financially distressed Ochoa owned companies for pennies on the dollar.

Night after night, Solanch tried to explain the financial collapse of Ochoa Industries to Jane, but there was no rational explanation. Each night's discussion ended with him saying, "I don't understand it. Our companies were successful. We were good citizens. We cheated no one. We made the best products, we had the best workers, we had the best managers, and we paid the best wages. It was Sanchez greed, lies, blackmail, and corrupt government officials that bankrupted Ochoa Industries."

Each night, after he had exhausted himself, he and Jane walked hand in hand to the bedroom where they lay side by side, enjoying the quiet closeness in the dark of the night. What they had dreamed of for years was now a reality. They slept the sleep of fulfillment and peace, content with their newfound life.

On the morning of the fifth day, Jane arrived at the meeting at seven thirty so she could get her ideas properly organized, as if they weren't already, but it was the teacher in her that drove her to be overly prepared. She was surprised to see every member of the invited group seated around a large, highly polished table. The smell of hot coffee along with pastries, eggs, and sausage filled the air. Pepe had prepared breakfast in his usual excellent way, making even a simple egg into something incredibly delicious. Jane sat down and enjoyed a cup of coffee along with a hot cheese Danish and one of Pepe's egg creations as well as delightful conversation with people she hadn't seen in years, but promptly at eight, she began the meeting.

"Thank you all for coming this morning," she began. "I'm sure it was the prospect of Pepe's good cooking that brought you in so early." Everyone seated around the table smiled. "I've asked each of you to be here because I know you, I know you are all highly qualified people, and I owe each of you a personal debt of gratitude. The first person I met when I crashed landed at El Satélite all those many years ago was Sandi. Sandi saved my life. She called for help before my car rolled over me, and then she looked over me like a beloved sister. Sandi, thank you so much for everything you did. I have never forgotten you!" She walked around the table to where Sandi was sitting, embraced her, and kissed her on the cheek. "And Sandi, you did one other most wonderful thing. You introduced me to New Mexican steaks Pepe's way."

She stood beside Pepe. "That brings me to the second person I met at El Satélite, the man sitting beside me, Pepe. It may not sound like a very important thing he did, but to me, many years ago, it was something very important. He brought my luggage to the room so I would have the personal things I needed. What girl doesn't want to brush her hair every once in a while!" Everybody laughed. "Then he prepared the most excellent dinner I had ever eaten. Pepe, your New Mexican steak revived my body and spirits, but even more than your excellent food, I appreciated your thoughtfulness and kindness." She leaned down and kissed him on the cheek. He blushed a deep reddish-brown blush.

Jane moved around the table to where Jack Burton was seated. "Jack, you're a lawyer, and lawyers are supposed to be feared, not loved, but in your case I make an exception. I can't tell you how much I appreciated how you tried your darndest to protect me from the state police in hearings that were more like the Spanish Inquisition than the Spanish Inquisition. I can't thank you enough for the hope and strength you gave me through those difficult hours. Even though you're a lawyer, you're going to get a kiss." She put her hand on his shoulder and kissed his cheek.

He placed his hand over hers. "Just because I'm a lawyer doesn't mean I'm not a man."

"Next is a woman who needs no introduction. You all know and love her."

Jane motioned toward Mamita. "I first met Mamita at the little house. She wore a faded yellow dress and a blue half-apron, an apron that said welcome to my home or in Spanish, *mi casa es tu casa*, my house is your house. I was so caught up in my New York ways I missed her simple, honest message, more than once, much to my peril. It nearly cost me my life. She has taught me selflessness, caring for others, family devotion, faith in God, and unrestrained love. It has taken me many years to learn her lessons, but thanks to her perseverance, I think I've got a pretty good handle on all of them, except one. I still can't cook."

"Don't worry. We fix. You see."

Jane looked at Mamita through misty eyes. "I owe you so much. You are truly *mi* Mamita. I love you with all my heart." She bent down and kissed Mamita's cheek.

"Next on my gratitude list are Pedro and Alejandro. These two men not only are master builders, they are creators, innovators, and talented artists as well. With their hands and some tools, they can take the rudest of elements and make them into things of beauty, a process I will never understand, but these two men do. They put their hearts and souls into everything they build, and by the way, Little Solanch thanks you for the beautiful bed you made him. Now if we could only keep him in it." Everyone laughed. "Not only do you gentlemen build, but you understand cost analysis. Without your skills, the projects I have in mind will never be realized." She reached down, took their hands, and kissed them on the cheek.

"Each one of you and your skills are needed. Jack, here is where I need your legal counsel. If I get too far out of bounds, you've got to reel me in. I don't mean to sound bossy, but from what I gather, we're facing a difficult challenge. If these ideas aren't any good, we'll toss them and get some better ones, but for now, they seem to be the only ones we have. Ladies and gentleman, let's get to work."

CHAPTER 35

Jane outlined her plans to the group in less than an hour. Much to her surprise, they liked her ideas, added a few of their own, and set to work to make them happen. Time was of the essence. In less than a day, the Ochoa fortune had fallen from forty billion dollars to less than thirty-three with bankruptcy a real possibility.

Faced with such an unthinkable deadline, the group rolled up their sleeves. They worked all day and into the night, sometimes separately, sometimes together. They solved problems that normally would have taken days if not weeks in a matter of hours. As the projects began to gel after a week's work, the group felt tremendous satisfaction in the progress they were making, yet they knew they were fighting father time as the Ochoa fortunes sank lower each day.

Eight days into the project, Jane and the group received crushing news. Through loopholes and fraudulent manipulation of various legal systems, Sanchez Securities had seized nearly all the remaining Ochoa assets, sending the price of its stock on the New York Stock Exchange into what is known in financial circles as the death spiral, a stock that falls so fast it can't recover. The once proud Ochoa Industry stock that had traded at an all time high of $273.48 just a year earlier had become a penny stock, worth less than a nickel.

Mamita's cell chimed. She answered. The terror in her eyes told everyone in the room their worst fears had been realized. Moments later, Arthur Meachim, Ochoa Industry's Chief Financial Officer, entered the room. In a matter-of-fact voice said, "Dow Jones has taken down the Ochoa Industries trading symbol from the big board. We are officially bankrupt." The group sat in stunned silence.

After a long period of anguished silence, Jack, in an emotional voice, said, "Mr. Ochoa pledged me to secrecy many years ago. I never would have betrayed his confidence, but under the present circumstances, I think it's time to reveal it."

He sat quietly, collecting his thoughts before he continued. "When I was a senior in high school, I had no hope of going to college, let alone law school. My family had no money. My father had trouble holding a job for more than a few months. He was an abusive alcoholic. He hit my mother. He hit me when I tried to protect her. He didn't want me to go to college. He refused to help me fill out applications for scholarships. He threatened to beat my mother if she helped me. My poor, frightened Mother worked two and three menial jobs so we would have food on the table. I've never known how Mr. Ochoa found out about me, but one day, I received a letter that contained an offer for a full paid scholarship, not only for my college expenses, but for law school as well. The most astounding part of the letter was he promised me a job after graduation. Without Mr. Ochoa's help, I wouldn't be sitting here today. He has made me a wealthy man. I will do anything for him, give him my last dime if I have to because I love—" Jack stopped mid-sentence, blinded by tears.

A long silence followed. Regaining his composure, he continued. "I'm not the only one he's helped. He's helped many others. Men and women he's not only educated but employed. They've contacted me, and they're willing to contribute whatever is necessary to help the man who helped them."

No one spoke until Mrs. Ochoa, reaching into her pocket and taking out a handkerchief from her pocket to wipe away tears, said, "I never know these things. He never told me."

In a soft voice, Jane said, "Thanks, Jack, for sharing a side of Mr. Ochoa none of us knew existed. Mr. Ochoa is indeed a great man. On that we can all agree. We all love him and want to help him. The offers of money are generous, but we'll have to refuse them because he would not approve. He doesn't want payment for what he's done for you or anyone else. However," she said forcefully, "he still owes me a debt, one I've never collected. Mamita! Can the Sanchezes steal my five million?"

"No, Jane, it yours. They no can touch."

"Then I have five million dollars?"

"No, Miss Jones, you don't have five million dollars," Arthur corrected her.

"I don't?" Jane's heart fell.

"No. By my calculations, you have twelve million three hundred sixty-five thousand eight hundred forty-two dollars and fourteen cents thanks to compound interest and good investments, investments that I personally selected and managed I might add," Arthur extolled proudly, breaking into a smile when he saw the joy his words brought to the others in the room. Without another word, the group went back to work working faster and harder than they had before.

Several days later, Jane and the group had completed plans for two businesses. Jane looked at those seated around the table and said, "Mamita? You have the final word. What think you?"

"I am so impressed with all your plans. Yes, I'm very excited. I want to see all these things happen. Thank you, all of you. Words have no meaning as how I feel at this moment."

"Thanks, Mamita. Your approval means everything to us." Jane sat down, emotionally spent. She sat looking at the group and said, "Each of you has contributed so much in so little time. I've never experienced anything like this in my life. This is what working together truly means. This is what I wish I could have taught my students."

She looked at each one of them. "I love you all." She held out her hands to those seated next to her and they held out their hands to the person next to them until they held hands forming a bond of mutual admiration for each other's hard work, creativity, and professionalism. None of them would ever forget the thirteen days they had spent together to save the man they loved and respected.

After many moments in which each reveled in the accomplishments of the group, Jack spoke. "There is one little detail we kept from you, Jane," breaking the circle of hands, his eyes full of mischief. "We hope you aren't angry, but we've been supplying details of both projects to Ben Spencer in computers since the third day of these proceedings, hoping this day would come. He's been working on a power point presentation. With your permission, we, the group, would like to invite both Mr. Ochoas to a presentation so they can see what we've been up to these last thirteen days."

"That's a super idea, Jack," Jane exclaimed.

"You heard the lady everybody. We'll reconvene at five this afternoon so we can go over the presentation and meet with both Mr. Ochoas at six. Class dismissed!" Jack said with an impish smile and a wink in Jane's direction.

When everyone had filed out of the meeting room, Mamita put her arm around Jane's waist and said, "Let's have a nice sauna bath, a massage, an excellent Pepe lunch, get some rest, then get all dressed up nice, and we'll knock our men out with our presentation. Welcome to our family, Jane, for better or worse."

CHAPTER 36

Jane arrived at the meeting room a few minutes before four thirty. Everybody was there. "I should have known you'd all be here." She glanced around the room. "Wow! I don't recognize the ole place. What have you people been up to? I see you've been working overtime."

"We decided last week if we could get everything together, we'd put this little show on not just for both Mr. Ochoas, but for you as well," Sandi said proudly. "It's a little something we whipped up this afternoon to surprise you, and by the look on your face, I think we've accomplished our goal."

"That and then some. It's a fairyland come true."

Hundreds of white LED lights twinkled between elegant floral arrangements and product line that graced display tables and racks. As Jane moved about the room, she saw mock-ups of the interiors and exteriors of the stores she intended to build along with examples of advertisements for print, broadcast, and billboard media. "I can't believe you've done all this in such a short period of time."

"We had a little bit of help. Pedro, Alejandro, their crews, and lots of others worked most of the miracles with the lighting, building the models, making the various products, and working on the advertising. Mamita and I worked on the floral arrangements."

"Mamita? You've known about this all along?"

"*Sí*, I keep secret good, no?"

"Well, I never." Jane had to sit. The shock of all the things that had been done without her knowing was too much. "You're all nothing but a bunch of schemers. I didn't know I was working with such a dangerous lot."

"You got that right. You can't trust a one of us."

"Ahem," came a coughing sound from the far end of the meeting room. A bespectacled, red-haired head, and a waving hand popped out from behind a white screen. "Hi, Miss Jones. I'm Ben Spencer from computers? You don't know me, but don't worry about that. Everything's all set for the power point. I've got it all arranged on storyboard so talk about anything you want. I can follow you with pictures, charts, graphs, statistics, and even music if you want. Gotcha covered."

"Thanks," was all a startled Jane could think to say.

Promptly at six the Ochoas arrived. Mamita took her husband's arm with one hand and her son's arm with the other as they walked toward the group. "See, Jane," Mamita exclaimed proudly. "*Tiempo americano.*"

As Mamita approached the assembled group, Jane was stunned by her radiance and poise. Her hair beautifully styled, her makeup and elegant dress brought out her muted beauty as she walked with the poise of a queen.

In contrast to Mamita's radiance, the Ochoa men looked depressed. Jane saw etched in their faces the full extent of the collapse of their business empire.

The group embraced the Ochoas. Amongst the chaos, Solanch found a moment to lean down and whisper in Jane's ear, "Little Solanch misses you, and so do I." He kissed her on the lips.

After many minutes of joyful reunion, Mr. Ochoa looked about the room and asked in amazement, "What is all this?"

"These fantastico people have been working for you, Papito."

"They have?" a bewildered Mr. Ochoa asked, not understanding the meaning of Mamita's words.

"Yes. That's why me and Jane have not been home so much."

The group moved aside so Mr. Ochoa and his son could see what they had done.

"I don't know what to say."

"Don't say, Papito. Let them say to you."

CHAPTER 37

Jane outlined the two businesses that she and the group had planned, one a computerized restaurant named 2Dayz and the other a computerized woman's shoe store called La Zapata Barata, The Cheap Shoe. As Jane explained the business models, the Ochoas and the group sampled Pepe's entrees and desserts to be served at 2Dayz. After they had finished eating, Sandi showed the Ochoas the various shoe styles to be sold at La Zapata Barata and the interior and exterior designs for both stores.

When Sandi had finished, Jane looked at each person seated around the table and said, "I take special pride in the group's creation of La Zapata Barata. We have created a new type of shoe store that we hope will run Zapato Barato out of business now that it's owned by Sanchez Securities. Pardon the bad pun, but we feel that would be just desserts for Sanchez Securities.

"Our religious instruction and our personal values have taught us to forgive those who have sinned against us, that we should turn the other cheek, but I've run out of cheeks as far as Sanchez Securities is concerned. As for Juanita Sanchez, please forgive me, but I can find no forgiveness in my heart for a woman who has mistreated a family," Jane's voice shook with emotion, "I have come, to love, so very much." A long pause ensued as Jane wiped away tears that filled her eyes. Once they had been dispatched, she smiled and added, "Believe it or not, I've run out of things to say." Everyone laughed.

Mr. Ochoa rose to his feet, stunned by all he had seen and heard. "All this is quite grand, but I haven't the money to do any of these things."

"Oh yes you do," Arthur said confidently. "Thanks to the five million you gave Jane years ago and my expert investment strategies, Jane has over twelve million, three hundred thousand, money she is investing in these two projects. It's enough to get us started. It's going to be close. We'll be down to our last penny, but if just one of the business models succeeds, we'll make it." He smiled, basking in the smiles of approval from those seated around the table.

Then his cold, analytical accountant side took control of him. "Mr. Ochoa," his smile replaced by a look of concern. "I wouldn't be worth my salt as an accountant if I didn't caution you that these ventures are a tremendous risk with less than a fifty-fifty chance of success. This risk is further compounded by the fact that there is only enough capital to sustain each business for two months at most. In normal circumstances, I would strongly recommend you disaffiliate yourself from these enterprises. I recognize these are not normal times, but if both businesses fail, you will have lost Miss Jones' entire investment, and she'll be penniless."

Arthur's frank assessment stunned the group. Mr. Ochoa looked at those seated before him. He spoke in a soft, matter-of-fact voice. "As always, Arthur, you are the voice of reason. I have no right to risk Miss Jones' money in this way. Her money is her money."

Jane stood. "You're right, Mr. Ochoa. My money is my money." She emphasized the word *is*. "And these are two risks I'm willing to take, but I'm not the only one willing to take a risk. I want you to know the kinds of friends you have. Jack Burton and others have offered to invest as much money as needed to get these projects into operation."

"Jack? You would do that?" a shocked Mr. Ochoa asked.

"I would!"

"So would I," Sandi interjected. "Between Pepe, Arthur, Pedro, Alejandro, and me, we can each come up with a hundred thousand which is another five hundred thousand dollars if you'll accept our offer to buy into the projects."

"I have a thousand I can spare," Ben said sheepishly.

Mr. Ochoa remained standing, his eyes glistening. "What friends I have. What magnificent friends I have." The magical glint returned to his eyes. "If you're willing to take the risk, so am I. When do we get started?"

"After a good night's sleep," Jane fired back.

CHAPTER 38

Jane was at The Big House promptly at eight a.m. as were Jack, Arthur, Pedro, and Ben. The meeting wasn't a surprise to any of them. Jane had asked them to meet with her at the conclusion of the previous night's presentation.

She began the meeting with, "The question before us this morning is what's to be done with this place, The Big House? Pardon the mixed metaphor, but is it a white elephant, an albatross around Mr. Ochoa's neck? He thinks so. He's dismissing the entire staff and plans to lock the doors forever this afternoon. Solanch tells me he wants to auction off the contents as soon as possible or try to sell it as is. Arthur, does Mr. Ochoa have to close this place this afternoon?"

Arthur alternately thumped his thumb and fingers on the polished table for a long time considering all sides of Jane's question. "No," he said drawing out the word *no*. "As far as the building and surrounding grounds are concerned, all obligations have been met until the fourteenth of next month. The major problem is we have no money for payroll."

"Is that the only major obstacle confronting us until the fourteenth of next month?" Arthur thought long and hard before he nodded his head.

"That's good," Jane said much to the surprise of the group. "Pedro, how long will it take to have this place ready to receive guests?"

"We're ready now."

"I hoped you'd say that. Here's my plan. First, we're going to change the name of this place. Even for the Ochoas, the name The Big House meant cold and impersonal because it reminded them of Sing Sing Prison in upstate New York or Alcatraz in San Francisco Bay. I've been studying my Spanish and with Pepe's unknowing help, I've come up with the name, El Gran Lugar, The Great Place, a name that describes the most exclusive facility in the world for companies and their employees to hold meetings, conventions, and to take their vacations. Ben."

"Yes, Miss Jones."

"I want you to contact every employee and ask him or her to report to work as soon as possible. Stress the fact they must arrive before Mr. Ochoa locks this place up, and tell them we're not sure if we can pay them, that there is a strong possibility they will never be paid for their services. We must be honest with them. Remember that. We must be honest with each and every person. I imagine many of them, especially those with families, won't come under these circumstances, but we'll try to manage with the few who do. Jack, will you help Ben draft the message so there are no legal misunderstandings that might get us sued for breach of payment in the future?"

"Will do. Come on, Ben. Let's hit it." He and Ben got up from the table and left the room.

"Excuse me, Miss Jane," Pedro said. "I've got lots to do if El Gran Lugar is to be as *gran* as you want it to be." Jane smiled as Pedro left the room.

"Well, Arthur. That leaves the two of us. Let's find out what Pepe has for breakfast."

CHAPTER 39

The Big House seemed a more appropriate name than El Gran Lugar as Jane and Arthur left the meeting room and started down the dimly lit corridor. Without its gleaming lights and its numerous employees going about their daily duties, the building looked sad and eerie. The sadness of its darkened bigness darkened Jane's inner soul, making her feel frightened and insecure as she contemplated the many decisions she had made. Who had given her the authority to take the risks she had taken? Had she bitten off more than she could chew? Her spirits dropped lower and lower with each step as she and Arthur made their way to the kitchen. For the first time in fourteen days, uncertainty held sway in Jane's mind. She hoped she was doing the right thing.

She dreaded meeting Mr. Ochoa even though he had supported her business plans a few hours earlier. Her business plans were one thing. That was her money she was gambling with, but The Big House. That was a different matter altogether. This was his. He had built it with his own money. Who was she to countermand his order? She feared he might consider her a meddling, New Yawk, know-it-all woman. Her consoling thoughts were that Jack hadn't stopped her, hadn't even suggested she had overstepped her authority. No one had. They had agreed with her. These thoughts fought to brighten her mood, but an overriding fear of what she had done darkened the bright thoughts.

"*Buenos días*," Pepe greeted them as Jane and Arthur entered the kitchen. I theenk maybe ju both need café."

"Thanks but no thanks, Pepe. I've got work to do," Arthur said dryly as he walked through the kitchen and out its front door.

"Ju no haf to say Señorita Hones. Pepe know what ju want." He filled a cup with hot coffee, put in a level teaspoon of sugar, stirred gently, and placed it in front of Jane who had seated herself at a small table in a corner of the kitchen. "Now I *preparo* ju a leetel sumtheen to eat." He went about his breakfast preparations, content to be in his own private world, the kitchen.

Jane had just swallowed the last bite of breakfast when Sean McCarthy walked into the kitchen. "What ju do here?" asked a surprised Pepe when he saw him. "Ju no work here no more. Nobody work here no more. No even me."

"That's where you're wrong, Pepe. I got a twitter telling me to come to work, and here I am, ready to work."

"Ju did? I taught Señor Ochoa close theez place today."

"He must have changed his mind."

"Good morning, Pepe, Sean."

"Ju too, Señora Kravitz?" He looked at Sandi in amazement.

"Me too, Pepe. And a lot more me toos are coming back to work because the parking lot is filling up."

"No." Pepe drew out the word low and slow. "It no can be. Señor Ochoa said…"

"No matter what Señor Ochoa said," Sandi interrupted him. "Today is a new day." She saw Jane. "Good morning, Jane. Mind if I join you?"

As Sandi and Jane sipped their coffee, The Big House filled with people going about their daily tasks. From the looks on their faces, it was obvious they were glad to be back working even without pay. Long before the clock struck twelve, everyone had returned.

A few minutes before noon, Jane heard Pepe's cell ring. He spoke in Spanish. When he had finished, he turned to Jane. "Dat was Señora Ochoa. She and el Señor come to haf last lunch wit me here in keetchen."

Jane's moment of truth had arrived. A look of fear swept over her face. "Sandi, twitter Jack, Arthur, Pedro, and Ben and tell them to report to the meeting room. Immediately! I want you there too for moral support."

Sandi took out her cell and twittered the others while Jane asked Pepe to direct Mr. Ochoa and Mamita to the meeting room and to serve luncheon as soon as possible. She grabbed Sandi's hand. "We gotta get out of here." She pulled Sandi toward the kitchen's rear door and not a moment too soon because no sooner had the door closed behind them than the Ochoas entered through the kitchen's front door.

A few minutes later Mr. and Mrs. Ochoa entered the meeting room. Both had worried expressions on their faces. When Mr. Ochoa saw Jane standing by the table along with the others, he asked, "What's going on? Why is everyone working? I dismissed them all yesterday. They must leave immediately before they sue me for breach of payment." The look on Mr. Ochoa's face matched Jane's feelings, only for different reasons.

The doors of the meeting room opened. The wait staff entered smartly dressed in their crisp culinary whites. Jane motioned for everyone to be seated as she took her position next to Mr. Ochoa while the wait staff went about the business of preparing the table for luncheon. "Jane," Mr. Ochoa whispered. "What is going on? Mamita and I came here to have a last luncheon with our dear friend, Pepe."

Jane placed a finger to her mouth, a gesture meant to quiet him. The moment she did it, she hated what she had done, treating

Mr. Ochoa as if he was an errant schoolboy, but what was done was done. He accepted the gentle rebuke, turned to Mamita, and said something to her in Spanish.

Jane had hoped to discuss her plans for The Big House after luncheon, but the tension around the table mounted. She realized she had to say something. "Mr. Ochoa." She stood. "I want you to know that I take full responsibility for what I'm about to tell you. I consulted with everyone seated here earlier this morning, everyone except Sandi who I let sleep in." Her humor lessened the tension in those seated around the table. "But what I'm going to tell you is solely my doing. I hope you don't think badly of me. I have only the greatest respect for you."

Mr. Ochoa looked up at her and smiled. "Whatever it is you have to tell me, I'm sure it's not as serious as you think it is."

The wait staff returned with bottles of wine and appetizers they served to those seated around the table while Jane remained standing. When they had left the room, she explained her plans for The Big House.

It took her a few minutes to outline the plans, including changing the name from The Big House to El Gran Lugar. When she had finished, she waited for a reaction from either of the Ochoas. They sat quietly. After what seemed a forever wait, Mr. Ochoa looked up at Jane and said quietly, "During the last few months, I have watched everything I have worked for so many years slide into the financial abyss. My world has been out of control. I saw only negatives. I must admit the thought never occurred to me, this place you have so aptly renamed El Gran Lugar, could be an asset. I saw it only as a huge liability, costing huge sums of money, money I no longer have. I wanted to be rid of it as soon as I could because it represented a past, a past I wanted to forget."

He looked at Jane. "To resolve a problem, it takes someone who can think pragmatically, someone who has the courage of their convictions. That someone has been you, Jane. You have shown tremendous courage to seek not only solutions but also the courage to enact them. My family owes you tremendous debts of gratitude, debts we will never be able to repay."

He rose from his chair and stood next to her. He put his arms around her shoulders and kissed her on the cheek. "Thank you for being you," he whispered in her ear.

CHAPTER 40

Several days later, Ben and his staff had formulated a sophisticated advertising campaign that appealed to those who had sufficient funds to afford the high-class amenities El Gran Lugar offered. They sent expertly designed brochures printed on the finest high gloss paper available to reputable CEO's of corporations, boards of directors, and top ranking executives around the world and designed a website that focused not only on the hotel's many amenities but also its beauty and charm.

Jack went to New York City to do battle with the various city agencies to get the necessary building and occupancy permits for 2Dayz and La Zapata Barata while his law associates met with bureaucrats in Santa Fe to get the proper residency permits to convert The Big House from a convention center to a full service hotel and vacation destination under the new name, El Gran Lugar.

The nation's economy had fallen on hard times. Bureaucrats in New York and New Mexico were as anxious to grant permits as Jack and his associates were to get them. What normally would have taken months if not years for various permits to be granted were granted in weeks enabling Pedro, Alejandro, and their building crews to spruce up El Gran Lugar to meet and exceed the demanding demands of the world's most sophisticated clientele and to remodel run-down buildings in the Bronx and

Manhattan's financial district into new and exciting places of businesses.

In the midst of these events, Jack called Solanch late one afternoon with news of a different sort. That night after dinner had been eaten, Little Solanch had been put to bed, and Papito and Mamita had retired for the night, Solanch made margaritas for Jane and himself. He handed her a filled glass and sat next to her on the sofa. As they sipped their drinks, he said casually, "Jack Burton called today."

"Great!" was Jane's immediate reply. She thought a moment and said less enthusiastically, "Has Jack run into legal snafus? I was afraid he would just at the last moment. That'll throw all our time tables off."

"No. No legal snafus. Not this time," Solanch said coyly. "He's untangled one for a change."

"Well?" Jane asked impatiently. "Are you going to let me hang in suspense? What did Jack have to say?"

"Not much. At least not anything of any real importance."

"Then why bring it up?"

"I thought you might be interested. That's all."

"Interested in what," she said, tiring of his coyness.

"Just that since Juanita has squeezed every last penny out of me and Ochoa Industries she can…"

"I might have known," Jane interrupted him. She could feel anger race through her body at the mention of that woman's name.

"She's decided to finalize the divorce."

Jane sat stunned. Before she could recover her senses, he slipped off the sofa and onto his bended right knee. He took her hand. "Jane, will you marry me?"

She said nothing. He asked again. "Will you marry me?"

Finally she came to her senses enough to mumble, "Yes."

He got up and bent over her. His lips almost against hers asked, "May I kiss the bride to be?"

They kissed a kiss filled with years of unrequited love. When their lips parted, he sat on the sofa next to her, took her hand, and said, "I'm sorry about one thing. Jack called late this afternoon. I didn't have a chance to get a ring, but I couldn't keep it a secret another moment. I was ready to burst with excitement during dinner."

"It's not the ring I want. It's the man."

Solanch roared with laughter and kissed Jane over and over. When he had finished, he yelled, "Okay Mamita, Papito. You can come in now. And wake up Little Solanch. We're going to have a pre-wedding party."

Papito came running into the living room hugging and kissing them both and wishing them well. Mamita along with Little Solanch joined the hugging and kissing. Solanch made margaritas for everyone except Little Solanch who got a warm glass of milk.

After the celebration and everyone had gone to bed, Jane and Solanch did the same. This night would be a night like no other, a night neither would forget, for they shared their bodies for the first time in their lives with the only person they could, each other.

Chapter 41

With great fanfare, El Gran Lugar reopened and celebrated its first client, a Chinese company that rented the hotel's facilities for two full weeks. Even with the world's economy in shambles, corporations along with the world's wealthiest entrepreneurs filled the hotel to capacity week after week. Guests had nothing but words of praise for Mr. Solanch Ochoa, his beautiful hotel, his talented staff, and his chef, affectionately known to all as Señor Pepe.

Weeks later, 2Dayz and La Zapata Barata opened for business, but unlike the hotel, both were dismal failures as the economy slipped from recession into the depths of Depression. Jane couldn't be certain whether it was the economy or the business models that had caused the businesses to fail, but one thing was clear. Neither had come close to being successful.

Amidst the worry and confusion of two business failures, Jane and Solanch married in a small Catholic church in Albuquerque, a wedding that included immediate family members along with close business and personal friends that numbered fewer than forty. The small number of wedding guests was Solanch's idea since he realized Jane had no family with few if any friends who would be able to attend a wedding so far from New York.

The morning wedding was a far cry from the opulent one that had been staged on an island in the Bahamas for Juanita and Solanch. This wedding focused not on opulence but on love, togetherness, and simplicity. Jane wore a simple white dress with white shoes from the defunct La Zapata Barata. Solanch wore a dark blue suit with white shirt and a muted blue tie. After the wedding, they returned to El Gran Lugar where they hosted a reception in the conference hall that began at noon and ended at midnight so all employees at the hotel plus hundreds of business associates and friends could attend.

When the reception had concluded and Jane and Solanch found themselves alone in the back seat of the Suburban, he put his arm around her shoulder and whispered, "Hello Mrs. Jane Solanch Jones Ochoa." She smiled. "But to me, you'll always be my Naschita, my wise little owl." He kissed her softly on the lips as she snuggled against his arm.

CHAPTER 42

Papito and Mamita decided the best wedding present they could give Jane and Solanch was to move into The Big House and take Little Solanch with them. The newlyweds should have been deliriously happy, together and alone in a house they both loved, but reality refused to let them enjoy even a few weeks of wedded bliss for outside the little house, the winds of economic chaos swirled about them, threatening not just their happiness, but their way of life.

Jane railed at the idiots', her name for the president and his corrupt Hayverd cronies, who, it seemed to her, were bent on ruining her first real happiness. "Is that all these idiots can think of is raise taxes? Do they think we're made of money?" she fumed when she saw the news on TV. She as well as Solanch knew if anything were to happen to the hotel, they, as well as the entire Ochoa family, would face an uncaring world without a penny to their name.

CHAPTER 43

Depressions are a man-made phenomenon born from the greed of a few high placed individuals in the business, banking, and government communities who create tremendous amounts of wealth for themselves while destroying the financial lives of millions of others. These are the glory days for those who engage in corruption, intimidation, and even murder because the doors of insanity are swung wide-open and the criminals set free to unleash their reign of terror upon the unsuspecting populations of the world. With twisted, illegal manipulations of the world's political, legal, and financial institutions, these well-dressed, soft-spoken criminals accuse anyone who fights for the rule of law and constitutional government, anyone who dares challenge their criminal activities, of the very crimes they, the criminals, are guilty of committing.

These corrupt rich, who hide their wealth from the suffering masses, cast a long, dark shadow on honest, wealthy individuals who struggle to keep their stores and factories open during such difficult economic times so people will have jobs, but the people don't see it that way. In their eyes, every rich person is a blood sucking capitalist who is to be despised, who must suffer, and who must be destroyed. Such ideas please the corrupt rich who encourage socialistic class warfare. The people's blind hatred of all wealthy people serves to hide the corrupt riches' daily despicable acts against millions of suffering individuals whom they pretend they are helping, yet stashed away in the dark recesses of their corrupted brains, they know one fearful fact. When the millions of people they have destroyed discover what they have done, they will have to answer for their crimes with their fortunes, maybe their lives, a risk they are more than willing to take, for they believe the day of reckoning will never come.

Sanchez Securities thrived in this culture of corruption, building a worldwide financial empire that earned them the wealth and power they desired. As for Juanita Sanchez, she had gotten her wish. She married the world's wealthiest man, Ming Wu, making her the richest woman in the world.

One afternoon Jane returned to the little house. She liked to refer to it as the little house in the desert. A gentle snow coated the desert sand. She was happier than she had been in months. She waited for her *querido* to return home, and when he did, she went to the liquor trolley, mixed a margarita for him, and poured a glass of milk for herself. She set the margarita in front of him, sat down on the sofa beside him, and held the glass of milk in plain view for him to see. He looked exhausted.

"Have a sip of your margarita. Let me know if I make them half as good as you?" she asked playfully.

He didn't move. "Go ahead! Have a sip!"

He sighed and said, "I'm too tired to reach that far."

She laughed as she reached with her other hand for the margarita glass. "Don't, Jane. I'm not in the mood for margaritas tonight."

"Then how about a sip of milk?" She put the glass to his lips. He brushed it aside. "I'm too depressed to eat or drink." He tried to manage a smile that failed to materialize. "I know you mean well, but my heart isn't in it."

"Anything happen I should know about?"

"I don't want to depress you."

Jane put the glass of milk on the table. "Solanch Ochoa, you tell me this minute what's happened. You know I'll worry myself to death not knowing."

"Yes, I know," he said softly. He was quiet for a few moments before speaking. "Tim Wheatly, my roommate at Hayverd?"

"Yes," Jane said cautiously.

"He committed suicide this afternoon, jumped from the top floor of the Prudential Center Building in Boston. I heard about it less than an hour ago. This recession, Depression, whatever the uneducated Hayverd nincompoops want to call it. I'm sick of it!" he lashed out angrily. "I'm sorry, Jane. I need to be alone. I'm going to lie down."

Each day Solanch came home more depressed than the day before as the grip of the Depression tightened its hold on everyone and everything around them. One morning at breakfast he noticed Jane didn't have her usual cup of coffee. He stood and said, "Let me get you a cup of coffee, *Querida*?"

"No, *Querido*. No coffee for me."

"What? No coffee? Are you ill?"

"*Well*"—Jane dragged out the word *well*—"you might say I am," she said playfully.

"Oh no!" He sank back down. Jane could see fear sweep across his face. "I'll call Dr. Martinez in Albuquerque." He picked up his cell.

"Hey, put that down. I've been to the doctor. He says I'm pregnant."

"You're what?"

"Pregnant. Too early to tell if it's a boy or girl, but I have a feeling it's a boy if any of my grandmother's old wives' tales are even half true."

Solanch jumped up from his chair, bent down, and kissed her on the lips. "Why didn't you tell me this before?"

"I tried, but…"

He hugged and kissed her. "This is the happiest I've been since we got married. I've got to call Mamita and share the good news with her." He thought for a moment, "Or have you done that already."

Jane blushed. "Sorry, *Querido*. Everybody knows but you."

He laughed heartily. "It figures. The father is usually the last to know, but I don't care. I'm going to be a father, a father. I don't care if it's a boy or a girl. I'm going to be a father." He couldn't stop kissing Jane.

With the news of a baby on the way, Mamita and Papita along with Little Solanch moved back into the little house, glad to be back with those they loved and those who loved them.

CHAPTER 44

Papito called a family meeting. Mamita, Jane, and Solanch joined him around the kitchen table. After the usual family chitchat, Papito began.

"I want to get your input on some ideas I've had for some time. I haven't been certain they were any good, but now I think their time has come. First, we must change our business model. No more Ochoa Industries. Instead, we'll be known as Group Ochoa or GO. Second, we will issue no stock. We will own our businesses free from the influences of outside sources. This will limit growth. We'll never be as big or as powerful as we once were, but it ensures never again will a hostile takeover such as the one mounted by Sanchez Securities be possible. I'm convinced it means financial security in these uncertain times. I've learned from my mistakes, and believe me, being too big to fail does not ensure financial stability. Everything fails sooner or later, even the United States of America."

Solanch looked at Jane and Mamita who nodded their heads in agreement. "We agree with the changes, Papito."

"Third, this terrible Depression is causing tremendous suffering in New York City. People are starving. We own two closed stores. We must put them to good use. I've talked to Pepe. He suggests we give away oatmeal, bread, coffee and tea twenty-four hours a day. He assures me he can buy oatmeal for next to nothing, he can get government surplus milk, and we can buy in bulk flour, sugar, butter, coffee and tea. That will help keep the price down, but whatever the price, we must take care of the people who are suffering."

"We all agree, Papito. This is something we must do," Mamita said.

"One last thing we must consider. This plan is risky. It will take up all the profits from El Gran Lugar. We will be cutting it close to the edge. If for any reason the hotel should fail, we'll be penniless."

"I can always go back to teaching."

Papito smiled, put his hand over Jane's, and gave it a squeeze. "I knew I could count on you." He looked at the others as they smiled in agreement. "This is the right thing to do. We can't turn our backs with so much suffering going on."

"As always, Papito, you're right," Solanch said softly. "We must and we will do these things."

CHAPTER 45

2Dayz and La Zapata Barata fed the hungry. Shivering Manhattanites, who in good times would have stuck their noses up at such fare, waited in line for hours to receive a portion of oatmeal, a thick slice of buttered bread, coffee or tea. Many were skeptical. They thought the oatmeal would be poorly prepared with skimpy portions. They were surprised to find it delicious and satisfying. Many broke down in tears saying, "God bless you," to those who served them.

Dreadful years passed as the Depression worsened. Banks failed. Storefronts boarded up. Even schools closed. Cities that had once been prosperous fell into disrepair. Desperation filled the people, and desperate people do desperate things. Food riots broke out in big cities and small towns alike. People were hungry.

La Barata Zapata and 2Dayz continued to feed the hungry, and by the huge lines that extended for miles at both locations, it seemed as if everyone in the city needed to be fed. Police were on duty at both places to maintain order, but the waiting, huddled masses were so exhausted and hungry no one thought to create a disturbance. All were grateful for a place where they could get something to eat.

Cable and broadcast TV stations documented how La Zapata Barata and 2Dayz, two failed businesses, had become havens for the hungry in the two boroughs of New York City. They documented Mr. Ochoa's life, the collapse of his business empire, and his generosity to the thousands of hungry New Yorkers who lined up at his stores day and night.

Mr. Ochoa's kind, handsome face, his tousled white hair, and especially the glint in his eyes gave starving people hope for a better future. The Mayor of New York City issued a special proclamation to honor Mr. Solanch Ochoa for his efforts to stem the hunger of thousands of New Yorkers. Seven months later the president awarded him the Medal of Freedom, the highest honor a president can give to a private citizen for his service to the country.

The president asked him to make numerous public service announcements for radio and television that offered hope to those who had none. Mr. Ochoa did them willingly. He became a symbol along with La Zapata Barata and 2Dayz to the nation's starving millions, symbols of hope and change, a hope the Depression would end soon. Few Americans wanted charity. They wanted a change, for the better. They wanted jobs, and none were too proud to do whatever dirty work the job might entail.

Despite the nation's economic woes, these same years were happy years for Jane and Solanch. Jane gave birth to a seven-pound boy whom she insisted naming Solanch the Fourth to maintain the succession of the family's first name, a name she had become fond of once she heard the story of how it had come to be.

When she had been in her sixth month of pregnancy, she asked her father-in-law to tell her about the origin of his unusual first name. Papito had to admit he couldn't be certain if what he was about to tell her was a collection of thinly veiled truths or nothing more than myths and wishful thinking.

As far as he knew, the name had originated in the peasant ranks as a last name in northern Spain where the Solanches had lived peaceably tilling the soil and tending their sheep sometime after the fall of the Roman Empire in the fifth century. In the eighth century, when the Muslim Moors invaded Spain and threatened all of European Christendom, the peasant Solanches joined the fighting ranks of the Spanish Gothic King Roderic. They fought bravely by his side in a battle against the Moors in 711 AD in north central Spain, a battle that Roderic won, but several months later, the Moors counterattacked, forcing Roderic and the Solanches to retreat from Spain and seek refuge in central France as the Moors took control of Spain and southern France. The exiled Solanches lived for centuries in France learning the French language and customs, yet they never abandoned their Spanish language, their Spanish heritage, or their Christian religion.

Over the next seven centuries, the Solanches fought bravely for the Christian cause until the Muslim Moors had been driven out of France and then Spain. For their loyalty and distinguished service to Spain, King Ferdinand and Queen Isabella in 1484 elevated them from the peasant class to that of honored noblemen, a status that brought them wealth and power. A number of peasant families throughout Spain adopted the Solanch name not as a last name, for that would have brought the wrath of the law upon them, but as a first name to honor the proud Solanch family.

As with so many family fortunes, it takes but one bad decision to lose them. In 1585, the Solanches invested heavily in King Phillip's Spanish Armada. He had promised them huge tracts of the richest farmland in England once Spanish troops had landed on English soil and killed the English Queen, Elizabeth. Unfortunately for the Solanches and the Spanish Armada, the English navy inflicted heavy losses on the Armada in 1588 sending many of its proud warships and soldiers to the bottom of the English Channel. With the loss of the Armada, the Solanches lost their wealth and the once proud name of Solanch disappeared from the ranks of the wealthy Spanish noble families but lived on as a peasant first name.

As Papito told Jane the origin of his family namesake, he did so with that wonderful, mischievous glint in his eyes. Jane couldn't be certain what part or parts of the story were true or just wishful thinking, but it made no difference. She wanted her first male child to be named Solanch as a tribute to his grandfather and father.

During these same years, Little Solanch was no longer little. He grew so fast Jane and Mamita had to keep buying him new clothes, a task they both reveled in. Jane decided she could no longer spend the proper amount of time teaching him. A full time teacher was hired to teach him subject material that was well beyond his years but not his mental capabilities. He had become what Jane and Mamita considered a genius.

Two years after the birth of her son, Jane was pregnant once again. She and Solanch were thrilled. Jane knew this child was going to be a girl based on her grandmother's old wives' tales that had predicted a male child the first time round. During a family meeting, they agreed to add a fourth and a fifth bedroom and two new bathrooms so each child would have a bedroom and bathroom of their own. Jane quipped if they kept adding rooms, soon the little house would be as big as The Big House. Then she informed the family this was to be her last child. One stepchild and two of her own were more than enough for her to handle. Besides, she admitted, "I'm not getting any younger." Mamita, Papito, and Solanch laughed at Jane's honesty and agreed. Enough was enough, especially in such difficult financial times.

Mamita and Papito had their own surprise for Jane and Solanch. "As you both know," Mamita began, "this little house has been Papito's and my world for over forty years. This is where you, my dear son, were born. This is where our happiness has been, this is where our memories are, but children grow up. They have families of their own. Papito built this house with love for a family. Papito and I want to share with you the love and happiness we have had in this little house. We want you to raise your family here. Papito and I will live at The Big House." Seeing the distress on Jane's face, she added, "Don't worry. We intend to visit you mucho."

Jane hugged and kissed them both. "You better be here mucho. If you're not, we'll miss you terribly."

Mamita and Papito smiled the smile of love at their ever-growing family and the continuation of joy and happiness in their little house.

CHAPTER 46

Months passed. Many events occurred, some good, some bad. One of the good things that happened was Jane learned Mamita's last lesson, how to cook. With Mamita no longer living in the little house, Jane wanted to be the one to prepare and serve the meals that would not only sustain her family but show her love for them. Even though Jane was well into her second pregnancy, Mamita came to the house on a daily basis, teaching her, her vast repertoire of dishes. Jane was an apt student, learning the basic art of cooking in a few weeks with Mamita on call to help with the more complicated recipes. After a few months of cooking lessons, she had mastered Mamita's loving touch in preparing and serving the flavorful yet nutritious meals her family needed and would enjoy in the years to come.

Jane had her baby, a little girl, just as her grandmother's old wives' tales had predicted, making Jane a true believer in her seemingly foolish tales. At Jane's insistence, the new arrival was named Solancha in honor of the proud Solanch name. The bedrooms and bathrooms had been completed and each child had his or her own bedroom. Laughter and the homey smells of food cooking on the stove filled the little house.

Little Solanch, now called Solanch the Third and shortened to T by Jane, had outgrown not only his clothes but his children's books. They, as he himself proclaimed, 'were too babyish.' He wanted to read books and novels about business, culture, finance, economic theories, history, mathematics, politics, and religion, subjects a normal eight-year-old would never find interesting much less understand, yet he devoured them all. Not only did he devour them, he wanted to discuss them in great detail with Jane. Exhausted by the needs of two small children plus cooking for a family of five, Jane did her best to read a few of the books so she could have an intelligent conversation with him. The teacher they had hired could no longer help him. He had outgrown her knowledge. He had become his own teacher.

When the State Board of Education questioned why Solanch the Third wasn't enrolled in any public or private school, Jane asked them to test him at any grade level they wished. The educators began at the third grade, a test T found quite amusing, pointing out two errors. He also found errors on some of the other tests he was given, tests that covered advanced concepts taught at the high school level and beyond. He answered all questions with accuracy and fluency in both English and Spanish. By the end of the day, the educators agreed he should continue with his own educational program since it was far superior to anything he would receive at any public or private school.

It was a typical New Mexico summer's day with a cloudless sky and a red-hot fireball centered high above the desert that burnt the landscape brown and created little wind devils that swirled the dust in all directions, when one of the bad things happened. Jane had been inside the little house all day taking care of the children and discussing several key points on Keynesian theories of finance with T. Unexpectedly, the door opened, letting the hot, dry wind sweep dust and heat into the house. Solanch walked through the kitchen and sat on the sofa. He looked beaten, not tired or exhausted in the usual way, but beaten. Jane recognized the symptoms and dropped everything she was doing to be by his side. T seeing his father home at an unexpected hour knew something bad had happened. He went to his room where he spent the rest of the afternoon. Solanch the Fourth and Solancha slept their childish dreams unaware of an ugly world that came ever closer to their beds.

"What is it *mi querido*?" Jane asked, her heartbeat increasing by the second.

"Did you have the TV on this afternoon?"

"No. I've been cooking and discussing Keynesian theories of how to get out of a Depression with T." She tried to make her words sound like a joke, but she knew he would find no humor in them.

"Too bad our fearless leader the president has been reading the same books as our son."

"What's happened?"

"My socialist Hayverd comrades have figured out how to kill this economy and us at the same time."

"What do you mean?"

"The president." He stopped to collect his jumbled thoughts because he couldn't believe what he had heard. "Said." He paused again to be certain to recall the words as accurately as he could. "That in these days of economic crisis and deprivation of the masses, the rich should not take advantage of this nation's economic crisis, that they must pay their fair share in taxes." He paused to collect his thoughts. "But that's only the half of what he said. He named names. He said places like Vegas and El Gran Lugar should not profit at the people's expense."

"He said what?" Jane exploded. A wave of anger surged through her. "What does he mean 'should not profit at the people's expense'? He of all people should know we don't profit. We employ over two hundred people. We feed thousands every day." She fell silent, embarrassed by her sudden spurt of anger. Once it had subsided, she asked in a subdued voice, "He singled El Gran Lugar out? He didn't mention anyone else by name?"

"Just Vegas, but he's attacked them for years. Now it's our turn." Solanch sat quietly on the sofa as did Jane, both lost in thought.

"That isn't the worst of it. Beginning tomorrow, he's going to enact a luxury tax of twenty-five percent on anyone who stays in Vegas or with us." He ran his fingers through his hair. "Why is he trying to break us? Why? We've taken our profits and fed tens of thousands. Why is he doing this to Papito, a man he awarded the Medal of Freedom, a man who made public announcements, a man who has become a symbol of hope and change? I don't get it. I just don't get it."

Jane reflected some moments in silence before she said, "Me neither, *mi querido*, but me thinks there's something rotten in the city of Washington." She reflected many moments before she continued. "The president didn't single us out for no reason, that's certain. He has his reasons. I haven't the slightest idea what they might be but whatever they are, you can be sure they're no good."

In an effort to change the subject, she reached over, kissed him on the cheek, and said as cheerfully as she could, "Let me prepare a little something to eat and a little something alcoholic to drink. Maybe that'll stimulate our brain cells so we can figure this thing out."

He smiled weakly. That was all Jane needed. She headed for the kitchen. Humming softly, she went about the tasks she knew would please him. She knew her man and how to make him happy.

CHAPTER 47

The president's twenty-five percent luxury tax had its desired effect. Guests canceled their reservations and left the hotel. Mr. Ochoa sat at his desk, desolated, that a hotel he had once considered to be *The Big House* and a *white elephant* was to close forever. He had come to love his hotel and his distinguished guests whom he had greeted in their native language, a little touch of home that brought smiles to those he greeted in this way. His guests had come to know him as a kind, charming man, as well as a great man for helping those who so badly needed help during desperate times. To show their respect for him, they had become anonymous contributors to his feeding the suffering people in New York City, but that was in the past.

Hearing of the hotel's closing, Jane asked Mamita and Papito to move back to the little house, a proposal Mamita gladly accepted because any hotel without guests is a lonely place.

For Jane and the Ochoas, their worst nightmare had been realized. They were penniless with three children in the middle of the desert.

CHAPTER 48

Jane should have wished to be any place on Earth but the little house, yet she wouldn't have traded a single minute to be anywhere else. The Ochoas were her family. They meant more to her than her real family had. She loved them with more intensity than she ever imagined herself capable. She had been certain after so many years of listless living she had lost the ability to love, but the intensity of her love even in the face of adversity grew stronger. She realized that love's never lost no matter how hard one might try to suppress or deny its existence. She was thankful she had the opportunity to experience the joy of fulfilled love, a love that made all else seem inconsequential. The children, Solanch, Mamita and Papito were all that mattered to her.

Something else changed in Jane's life, her religious views. She had been a life-long Catholic but in name only. As a child, she never went to church. Even in her darkest days of depression, she never asked God to give her guidance or to deliver her from the hands of evil because the thought had never occurred to her. She had seen no use for prayer, but Mamita through her actions and the cure of Little Solanch had given her a faith that had never existed before. She prayed, not for herself, Solanch, Mamita, or Papito but for the deliverance of the children, quiet prayers to an unseen God she wasn't sure existed, but she prayed He did.

CHAPTER 49

Jane was at the kitchen sink washing lunch dishes when she noticed a cloud of dust in the distance, something she hadn't seen since the closing of the hotel. She watched as it came closer. A car appeared over the rise in the tire-rutted sandy lane leading to the little house. "Solanch," she yelled. "Come quick! A car's coming." Solanch came running. No one but a few trusted employees at the hotel knew the little house existed, and they had been sworn to secrecy.

Two men got out of the car. "Do you recognize them?" Jane asked.

"No!" came the tacit reply.

"Don't let them in, not until we find out what they want," Jane commanded. She gripped Solanch's hand.

Both men dressed in business suits knocked at the kitchen door. "Whatchuwant?" Solanch asked in a gruff voice.

"We've come to see Solanch Ochoa."

"I'm Solanch Ochoa and I don't know either of you."

"Are you Solanch Ochoa Senior?"

'No, Junior."

"Then it's your father we've come to see. Is he here?"

Papito hearing the commotion had entered the kitchen, standing far away from the door, but when he heard his name mentioned, he went closer, straining to look through one of the door's glass panes.

"Ignacio," he burst out. He rushed to open the door. "Ignacio Valdez. *Bienvenido a mi casita, Señor*." He embraced the man as Jane and Solanch looked on in bewilderment.

"*Díos mío*, Solanch. Is it really you? Miles and I had a devil of a time finding you." He paused a moment before he added, "Promise you won't get angry when I tell you how we found you."

Solanch smiled and said, "How could I ever be angry with you, my dearest friend, Ignacio. How did you find us? Almost nobody knows we're here."

"It wasn't easy, my friend. Believe me. It wasn't easy. Miles and I searched everywhere for you. Albuquerque, Santa Fe, the hotel. It was as if you had dropped off the face of the Earth. Then I remembered your chef. Miles did the Internet search. We found him in Santa Fe living with his wife and five children. When I asked him where you lived, he ran to another room, locked the door, and refused to talk to me. It was only after I talked to him through a closed door and convinced him my intentions were honorable that he let me in. After much mental arm-twisting, he gave us directions, but even with his directions, Miles and I have been driving around in circles for hours. We were about to give up when Miles spotted what looked like a tire-rut to nowhere. He said we'd tried everything else we might as well have a go at this. I agreed, and here we are."

"How do you two know each other?" Jane asked with intense interest.

"Ignacio and I go back a long way, don't we Ignacio." Ignacio nodded his head. "Ay, so many, many years ago, to the Texas oilfields where he and I unloaded pipe from the trucks for four dollars a day. We thought that was big money back then, didn't we." They laughed.

"What we didn't know in those days. As the gringos would say, 'two dumb Mecs' and they were right." Ignacio turned to Jane. "We had no idea the Americans made five times more'n us. We were satisfied with our four dollars. I've often thought about it," he said turning to Solanch. "Maybe it was better we didn't know. At least we were happy. Had we known we were being cheated, it would have made us angry, and we might have said and done things that would have changed our lives, maybe even ended them." He turned to Jane. "The foreman made it clear he wasn't against shooting men he thought were stealing. Solanch and I knew what he meant."

"That we did, Ignacio. That we did. Those were the bad old days. Thank God they're behind us. I wouldn't have the strength to work as hard as we did back then. How did we do it, Ignacio? How did we do it?" he reflected, emphasizing the word *did*.

Misty-eyed, the two men fell silent. They saw the hardships of the past in each other's eyes. Many moments later Papito turned to Jane and continued. "Once we got out of the oil fields, we went our separate ways. I went into business and he became a politician, but we've remained good friends all these years. Don't you recognize Ignacio, Jane? He's our state senator."

"Ex-state senator, Solanch. The socialists pushed me out a while back. They didn't like my extremist capitalistic ideas of hard work, low taxes, reduced spending, balanced budgets." A sad smile crossed his face.

"I'm sorry to hear that, Nacho. I know how much it meant to you to represent the people of New Mexico."

"It did, once. Not any more. They're just a bunch of unprincipled thieves in Santa Fe. I'm glad to be rid of them, and obviously the feeling is mutual."

"Why didn't I hear or read anything about this?"

"For a very good reason, my friend. The gang of thieves controls all the media outlets. The president himself has personally

waged war on the First Amendment. He's shut down radio and
TV stations and Internet sites that are the least bit critical of him.
We have lost our freedom of speech. We have lost our economic
system. We have lost our beloved country to socialist thugs. This
is why I have searched for you."

"Me? What have I got to do with anything?"

"You don't know it, but you are the most popular man in
America. Your radio and TV public service announcements
connected with the people. Millions of starving, suffering people
have been shouting your name from coast to coast and border
to border. Representatives of Congress, senators, governors of
every state in the union have been demanding the president's
resignation. Many of those same politicians have openly stated
they want to draft you for president. They want you so badly they
have passed a one-time amendment to the Constitution that
allows you, a Mexican national, to serve as president.

"You're too popular for your own good, Solanch. The president
had to isolate you. That's why he enacted the twenty-five percent
tax on your hotel, knowing full well no one would remain at such
a ruinous rate. He ruined you financially and isolated you out
here in the desert so neither you nor any member of your family
could or would challenge his presidency. The presidency is yours
for the asking. All you have to do is say yes."

Papito and Ignacio discussed the ramifications of a
constitutional amendment that enabled a foreign born citizen to
become president of the United States while Jane made coffee
and sandwiches, followed by several rounds of margaritas, and
finally dinner. Once dinner had been eaten and given some time
to digest, Ignacio thanked Jane for a fine dinner, then with a
tear in his eye, hugged his dear friend Solanch, and said it was
time he and Miles left while they could still find their way home
in daylight.

Jane took Ignacio's hand in hers and said, "We're thankful you came." She smiled a contented smile, contented because she believed her prayers had been answered, that God existed. That was something worth knowing.

CHAPTER 50

The president rescinded the twenty-five percent hotel tax, citing the need to create more jobs in the hotel industry, but it was one of many last ditch efforts to save his presidency. El Gran Lugar reopened. The Ochoas breathed a sigh of relief as reservations poured in from all parts of the world. Although business returned to normal, it took many months before the lives of the Ochoas returned to any semblance of normalcy. "The experience", as Jane referred to it, had changed their lives, especially those of the children, who had heard hushed conversations and seen fear on the faces of their parents and grandparents for many months. They sensed something was wrong. They noticed the adults seldom left the house. They noticed tenseness in those they loved and trusted. It frightened them. In their young minds, they were certain somebody wanted to hurt them or take them away from the little house and those they loved.

At night they were afraid to be alone in their beds and demanded they sleep with their parents, but that wasn't enough to stop the frequent nightmares. Scarcely a night passed that one of them didn't wake up screaming. By day, they clung to the adults afraid to let go of them. Jane knew she and Solanch had to be patient, that no amount of reassuring words and no amount of loving would make the children's worries go away any time soon. An unseen force had more power over their imaginations than parental reassurances could overcome. Only time would stop the nightmares and slay the boogeymen who lurked within the recesses of their young minds.

T was the first to settle back into his normal routine. Maybe it was easier for him because he was the oldest, or maybe it was because he had an outgoing personality along with his father's good looks that made him popular with the guests and staff members at the hotel. No matter the reason, Jane was pleased to see him return to his studies and organize games with the young people who stayed at the hotel. His favorite was baseball. He called it a game for the brain because of the strategy involved. He likened it to chess with ball, bats, and gloves instead of rooks, knights, kings, and queens.

Solanch the Fourth called C and his sister Solancha took much longer than T to believe Jane and Solanch that the bad men had gone away. Even under this cloud of doubt, both grew rapidly in mind and body under Jane's watchful eye with good eating habits, plenty of exercise, and lots of home study that included English and Spanish in their daily conversations along with reading good literature and religious instruction. Jane could tell both C and Solancha were intelligent but not super intelligent like T. She considered that a good thing since she could barely keep up with his voracious appetite for knowledge.

Solanch played a major roll in the education of his children as well. He discussed cultural, financial, and political theories with T, read and discussed stories with C and Solancha in both English and Spanish, but once the studies were done, it was time to play games. T's favorite was chess. Solanch tried to beat him but he never could. C and Solancha's favorite was horsey. They loved seeing their father on all fours, climbing on his back, gently kicking him in the side with their heels, listening to him whinny like a horse, yelling "Giddyup", and feeling the rocking motion of his body as he crawled through the various rooms in the house.

They could have played horsy forever if it hadn't been for the fact that Solanch's back and knees could only take so much of this type of fun.

Many weeks later, Solancha returned to her bedroom. She became the happy little girl she had been before "the experience". Months later, C returned to his own bed, but he seemed different. Jane was certain there was nothing to worry about, believing he hadn't totally recovered from "the experience". She did her best to make him happy, but with each passing year, he became increasingly withdrawn. She could never be certain whether "the experience" had caused his withdrawal or was a natural part of his personality.

C wasn't the only one who had a dark shadow hanging over his head. Jane had one as well as she watched her babies grow into childhood. She tried to dismiss her fear as silly, a thing of the past, yet it weighed heavily on her mind. As babies, she had been keenly aware that C and Solancha weren't pretty babies. She regarded them as ugly. Further heightening her fear was the way other people reacted when they saw them. They didn't say, "My, what beautiful babies they are. I'm sure you're very proud of them." Instead, they said, "What nice babies you have. You must take very good care of them." She realized she was parsing words, yet the words fueled her fear.

As C and Solancha grew older, Jane realized her fear hadn't been unfounded. She could see neither child would be attractive. They would be plain, like her. Both had her broad forehead, hawkish nose, and small mouth. The old hurts from plain Jane jokes, the numerous male rejections had left their scars, deep scars time would never heal. These deep scars forced her to question herself. Who had given her, a plain if not ugly woman, a nobody from the Bronx, New Yawk, the right to marry such a handsome Spanish-Mexican man as Solanch Ochoa?

She worried the unattractiveness of her children might cause a breach between her and Solanch as well as the children. Solanch never mentioned the topic except when someone noted the children had their father's eyes. He would smile and say, "I'm glad I contributed something," but for Jane, these were painful moments.

Solanch was aware of her unhappiness, and after careful consideration, he decided he must say something to alleviate her fears for her sake and the sake of their marriage. "Jane, you've been unhappy for a long time, and I know why. We've discussed this topic as much as I care to, so I won't bring it up again. I want you to know you've made me very happy. I hope I've made you happy too. I've never lost my love for you and I never will. You, the children, and my parents are all that mean anything to me. Always remember this, *mi querida*. You're stuck with me for the rest of your life."

He placed his right index finger under her chin and kissed her on the lips. In a soft, sexy voice said, "I'm going to make us both a margarita, and when we've finished, I'm going to make mad, passionate love to you." His words and actions reassured her that looks meant nothing to him, that he loved his children and her just as they were. It was she who couldn't accept the plainness of herself and her children. She regretted beauty was something Juanita could give and she couldn't.

CHAPTER 51

"President Dead" flashed on the TV screen. The news shocked Jane as it did the nation. Her eyes filled with tears as she listened to the reports. She hadn't agreed with any of the president's policies. She blamed him for the economic chaos based on European theories of socialism that had choked the financial life out of the country she loved. She knew he didn't deserve her tears, yet she mourned the loss of a human life. Her newfound faith in God enabled her to forgive him for all the terrible things he had done to the country, its people, and her beloved family. The time had come, as she knew it would, that even presidents have to pay their debt to society for the millions of lives destroyed because of ruinous economic policies. Rather than face impeachment and the wrath of the American people, he shot himself in the basement of the White House. She considered his act of suicide an ungodly, cowardly one, but in death, he became nothing more for her than a closed chapter in the book of history.

CHAPTER 52

The president's death had no effect on ending the Depression. The nation struggled to regain its economic equilibrium with little success, for once prosperity is lost, it's next to impossible to regain. Jane was thankful the hotel was open and profitable so the economic lives of the Ochoa family could return to normalcy, and just as important so they could feed the hungry people in New York City as well as other cities and towns since Mr. Ochoa had joined forces with many charities to alleviate the nation's hunger.

As Jane sat drinking coffee at the kitchen table, she smiled as she reflected on the nickname thankful people all over the country had given her father-in-law, Oatmeal Ochoa, and at his reaction when he had first heard it. He had laughed and said, "I am greatly honored. It's a name I shall treasure for the rest of my life."

In the chaotic days after the president's suicide, true to Ignacio's word, various politicians had wanted Mr. Ochoa to become president. He was a nationally known, charismatic, generous man with tousled white hair and a magical glint in his eyes. He told those same politicians without hesitation, "This magnificent country must never change its constitution for the exclusive benefit of one of its citizens. To be president, one must be extraordinary. I am not that man. Like oatmeal, I am ordinary. Besides,"—he paused for effect,—"being president is too much work. I'm looking forward to spending as much time as I can with my beloved wife, my family, and my hotel." Papito's words pleased Mamita, because she, like him, wanted the remaining years of her life to be dedicated to her husband, her family, and the family business.

Much to the Ochoa's surprise, the American public wasn't going to let Mr. Ochoa off the hook so easily, not a man who had given so much of himself to them during the dark days of the Depression. Although he sought a quiet, unassuming life, the American public demanded to see and hear him on various radio and TV programs. The sight of his calm countenance and the soft, lyrical sound of his voice gave the nation hope for a new, prosperous future.

No matter how much Mr. Ochoa protested he didn't want a public life, the American people considered him to be their unelected elder statesman. He was a man they could trust, a rare commodity in those uncertain days. The people didn't bestow their trust on just anyone. They had been lied to and financially ruined for over a century by people they thought they could trust. Mr. and Mrs. Ochoa, because of their honesty, integrity, and work ethic, became the second family of the United States after the newly elected president and his wife.

For all the hoopla surrounding them, the Ochoas lived like everyone else during this long period of recovery, simply and economically, but they were happy beyond all measure, for it was the children who made the little house in the desert a home. They brought love and joy to their parents and grandparents each day just as the parents and grandparents brought joy, love, and trust to the children.

CHAPTER 53

Since time immemorial, parents and grandparents have marveled at how fast their children grow. The Ochoas were no exception to the rule of marvel. "*Ay, caramba*! You're growing faster than a little morning glory after a gentle rain," Mamita exclaimed every time she bought a new outfit for one of the children, but the biggest marker for the passage of time arrived one day when it came time for T to go to university.

T and his father seldom disagreed on anything, but when it came time for the selection of a university, they had a hearty disagreement. T wanted to go to Hayverd where his father had gone. His father wanted him to attend any other university but his old alma mater. He blamed Hayverd for the Depression and Tim Wheatley's suicide. He feared his son might succumb to the same fate as Tim, especially since he was just twelve years old.

T's rationality overcame his father's reluctance, but only with his father's one stipulation. "Not for nuttin if you ever come home spoutin' socialist rhetoric, I'll yank yah out of dat university so fast it'll make yah 'ed spin. So fuhgeddaboudit," comments that gave Jane a hearty laugh.

"Now yah tawkin' like me," she chided her husband whereupon he answered with, "Whatchatawkinbout. We tawk da same tawk." They laughed and put their arms around each other's waists.

Seeing his parents happy made T feel happy and loved. He reassured his father not only would he not put up with any professor's socialist rhetoric, but he would stand and defend democratic capitalism no matter what grade the professor might give him. He too had seen the damage socialism had done not just to his family but to the country he loved.

The Depression continued. Lines for food at La Zapata Barata, 2Dayz, and all the other locations Mr. Ochoa helped fund remained as long as ever. Amidst so much economic misery, T settled into his new life at Hayverd. The university experience gave him the opportunity to hear a variety of ideas. He enjoyed listening to the campus hot shots spout their communist and socialist rhetoric about government-sponsored womb to tomb care. They considered themselves original thinkers, the smartest people on campus until T, through logical argumentation, shredded their shoddy arguments to pieces. Whenever the hot shots saw him in the crowd, they concluded their comments and fled. Single-handedly he stopped socialist and communist rhetoric on campus. He became the most popular and influential student at Hayverd.

CHAPTER 54

When Lady Luck turns her back on an enterprise, all things that had once been deemed good crumble into all things bad in a matter of moments. Those individuals who had profited through years of corruption and bloody crimes now had to pay the price for their years of misdoings. Sanchez Securities felt the people's wrath. Jane felt no pity for the Sanchez family when she heard various governments had canceled their contracts with Sanchez Securities and had prosecuted the executives of their corrupt companies.

While Sanchez Securities suffered setback after setback, at the same time in China, Ming Wu, Juanita Sanchez's billionaire husband, was convicted of selling defective parts to China's aircraft and automobile industries that had killed thousands of Chinese citizens as well as hundreds of others around the world. He alone had given Chinese manufacturing a bad reputation, and for his crime, the government seized all his assets. He was left with nothing but the clothes on his back. A few hours after the seizure, he hanged himself in the basement of an abandoned building in downtown Shanghai.

Fearing reprisals, Juanita fled China and returned to her father's home in Mexico City, a home that was being foreclosed on by a number of banks. Her father, Hugo, owed huge amounts of money. The Sanchezes experienced the same economic pressures the Ochoas had felt years earlier when Sanchez Securities had squeezed the life out of their financial empire. These pressures were too much for Hugo, who escaped the bankers' wrath by slitting his wrists in the bathroom of his foreclosed house.

Although no longer a wealthy woman, Juanita still believed in the strategy that a strong offense is a good defense. She perused the newspapers looking for wealthy bachelors or widowers she might marry. She set her sights on a wealthy lawyer, Jaime Gutierrez, whose wife had died of cancer. Dressed in a black suit, veiled hat, and six inch black stiletto heels, she attended Mrs. Gutierrez's wake at a funeral home in Albuquerque.

After having spent a considerable amount of time trying to garner Mr. Gutierrez's attention without success, she left the viewing room and started down a long corridor to exit the building. Halfway down the corridor, she recognized Solanch in the distance opening the door for Jane. She stopped. She knew no escape was possible. She turned her back to the wall so as to ward off any frontal assault her ex-husband might launch against her. She relied on her best offense is a good defense strategy to carry her through this difficult situation.

She waited for Jane to be within easy talking distance before she fired her first salvo. "If it isn't the frumpy, dumpy Mrs. Ochoa along with her not so humpy husband," Juanita said as sarcastically as she could.

"Hello, Juanita," Jane said in an exaggerated friendly tone as she approached her. She stopped in front of Juanita and turned so they were face to face, a move that so surprised Juanita she took a step backward. She had expected a confrontation with her ex, but most certainly not from "the mousy little school teacher who was afraid of her own shadow" as she referred to Jane.

"Surprised I recognize you?" Jane continued, noting Juanita's step backward. "Yes, I know who you are. I recognize you from your pictures on the society page of the *Albuquerque Journal.*" She frowned. "But," she said slowly for dramatic effect, "I must say I am disappointed. You look so much older in person than you do in the newspaper. Isn't it amazing what editors of newspapers can do these days with an airbrush and Photoshop?" Her voice dripped with sarcasm.

She leaned forward, looked intently at Juanita's face, and in a surprised voice said, "I never would have believed it if I hadn't seen it with my very own eyes. From your pictures, I never would have guessed you wore so much makeup and powder. I thought you had more style than that, you ole powder-keg you." She poked Juanita in the stomach with her elbow to emphasize the joke she had made. "Who da thunk it, but as we all know, seein' is believin'."

She lowered her voice and in a conspiratorial tone added, "You really must buy more expensive cosmetics to cover those crow's feet of yours. The cheap stuff you're usin' ain't doin' the job."

She paused. "Oh dear, I almost forgot." She drew back in mock distress and put her hand to her mouth. "You might not have the money for expensive cosmetics." She tsked her tongue several times and said, "Too bad your daddy never taught yah crime don't pay but then he was a crook too, wasn't he." In her best bronx accent added, "Whatsadahmattah, Juanitie. Lost all yah dough?" She looked at Juanita from head to toe. "Still, it doesn't seem to have lessened your appetite any. I see you've made eating a national sport.

"Solanch and I must be leaving you to pay our last respects to a fine, Christian woman, Mrs. Adela Gutierrez, two things you wouldn't know anything about. Solanch," she turned to him, "I think we've wasted enough of our time talking to this money whore. I can't tell you how un-de-lighted I have been to meet you. We really shouldn't have lunch any time at all because we don't intend to see you, evah, ah-gah-in." Solanch gently took Jane's arm and without so much as a glance in Juanita's direction escorted her into the viewing room.

CHAPTER 55

"Hallelujah! Hallelujah! Hallelujah!" Jane shouted. "It's been a long time coming, but it's finally here. It's finally here!" C came running into the living room. "What happened? Something good?"

"Yes! It's something good! The Depression is over." She took C's hands and the two of them danced around the room shouting, "The Depression is over." Mamita and Solancha joined in, all of them shouting in unison, "The Depression is over," and dancing with wild abandon.

When they had run out of breath from the singing and dancing, Mamita turned to Jane and asked, "How you know the Depression is over, Jane?"

"It's on the news, Mamita. People are going back to work all over the country." She looked heavenward and said with reverence, "Thank you, dear Lord!" The others along with Jane crossed themselves and said, "Amen," softly after her.

Jane, like all other Americans, could breathe free and easy, knowing the Depression was over. There was work to be had and along with work came prosperity. The *New York Daily News* ran the headline "Welcome back normal times." The food lines at La Zapata Barata and 2Dayz disappeared, a sign that the recession-Depression-recession was really over.

One late fall evening, the newly elected president telephoned Mr. Ochoa Senior. The president asked him to be his business ambassador, a position that would require him and Mamita to travel the world meeting with CEO's of companies and heads of state spreading the word of democracy and capitalism. When Mr. Ochoa protested, the president interrupted him. "Let me assure you. This is not a good-will ambassadorship. This is serious business and you're the right man for the position. Our nation's financial security depends on your negotiating skills, skills few if any other individuals have at this moment. The country needs you, Mr. Ochoa." The President, in a quiet, emotional voice added, "The truth is, I need you, Solanch."

A period of silence followed, broken by Mr. Ochoa. "I am at your service, Mr. President."

"Good. I hoped you'd say that without too much arm-twisting. What did I say that made you change your mind?"

"You called me, Solanch. I knew you wouldn't use my first name unless you really wanted me."

"That I do, Solanch. That I do."

They wished each other a good night, heaving huge sighs, the president, a sigh of relief, and Mr. Ochoa, a sigh of worry and responsibility.

T graduated from Hayverd and The London School of Business summa cum laude at both schools in record time, a task he accomplished as easily as if he had been born with the knowledge. When asked what his hurry was to graduate, he explained he wanted to be home in New Mexico with his family, a family he loved and missed. As his father had done before him, he managed El Satélite, gaining valuable business experience as his knowledge and skills would be needed elsewhere and soon.

C had become a laid back, increasingly sullen, below average student who enjoyed hangin' more with his family and friends than schoolbooks. If truth were known, he enjoyed hangin' more with his friends than family. When Jane asked him what his plans for the future were, he told her, "Like hazy, ya know, but I think when I, like, graduate high school, I'll probably go to, like, Hayverd like Papito and T, if they, like, accept me, ya know? If they don't, then I'll go someplace else, ya know? I haven't, like, decided, ya know?"

He shrugged his shoulders, took a carton of milk out of the refrigerator, gulped down the remainder of its contents, and threw the carton with a right hook into the trashcan. "Yes, sports fans," he hissed. "Two points for the C." He looked blankly at Jane and said, "Lots of time for stuff like that, ya know? Don't sweat it, mumsey."

"Somebody's gotta sweat it," Jane fired back.

He walked out of the kitchen, muttering in a bored tone, "Whatevah."

Jane smiled a small, tragic smile. After having taught so many slackers over the years, now she knew what it meant to be the mother of one. The one thing she regretted was his casual attitude toward education and life that drove a wedge between them. She was not as close to him as she was with T and Solancha. A regret she hoped time would heal.

Even though Solancha was years away from going to university, she knew she wanted nothing to do with Hayverd. She'd heard enough about it to know it wasn't for her, too male dominated, too cliquey, too old-fashioned, and too stuffy. She wanted to breathe free and not be bound by lots of silly, old boy rules. She was her mother's daughter, plain, not only in looks but in thinking. She didn't want any fancy smancy, highfalutin university. "Why should I travel halfway round the world to get the same education I can get at The University of New Mexico," was her reasoning. "Besides," she argued, "didn't mother attend a state school in New York and look at all the things she's accomplished, teacher, businesswoman, and mother? What more could I possibly want out of life than that?"

Now that Papito was the nation's business ambassador, Solanch took over his father's position as head of the hotel while Jane and T took control of the fledgling GO enterprise that owned two stores, La Zapata Barata and 2Dayz. Now that the Depression had ended, the two of them discussed the pros and cons of either maintaining or changing the business models for both stores.

Jane wanted change. T disagreed with his mother's wanting to change the model of either business, arguing neither store had been given sufficient time to establish a client base so that customer complaints could be analyzed and then if necessary, appropriate modifications could be made to each model. "Don't fix it until you know it's broken," he admonished his mother. He drove home the point that a concept shouldn't be modified or abandoned unless proved unworkable by empirical data. Lovingly, he looked at his mother, kissed her on the cheek, and cautioned her, "Don't give up the ship too soon."

The time had come, a time Jane and Solanch thought would never come and a time T never knew existed, to reopen La Zapata Barata and 2Dayz for business. Two weeks before both stores stopped serving oatmeal, the employees hung huge signs in the windows declaring "Depression Over! Back To Business!"

As the two stores were being readied, Jane realized T might be right about not giving up the ship too soon, but the thought of failure after all they had been through as a family worried her. She felt responsible for these business models. She had been their architect. Years ago, she had been certain they would be runaway successes, but with the passage of time and a crippling Depression, the certainty had vanished, replaced by skepticism and uncertainty.

Two comforting thoughts helped allay her fears. With the hotel a proven success, the family's financial future no longer depended on the success or failure of either store as it had years ago. The family's future was secure with or without the businesses, but the most comforting thought of all was T was going to New York to take charge of both operations. She would miss him, but she knew both stores couldn't be in better hands. She smiled at the thought he was the only thing in life Juanita had gotten right.

CHAPTER 56

Jane needn't have worried about the viability of her business models. Both stores opened to long lines of eager customers excited to see both stores up and running after having served as oatmeal kitchens for so many years. At the close of the first business day, the stores had sales that would please any business owner.

To Jane's surprise, she and T faced a success problem as hundreds of investors demanded to buy GO stock. This sudden surge of investor cash frightened Jane. She wanted to retain the no investor business model envisioned by Papito, but T wanted to allow outsiders to invest so the stores could be franchised to all parts of the country as soon as possible.

Jane argued that neither she nor T knew if the stores' business models would be successful in the long run, and if the models failed, GO would face a financial crisis it could not survive. It would be overexpanded with investors selling off their shares of stock as quickly as they could, leaving GO with stores it could no longer afford to service and a huge debt it would be unable to pay. GO would be bankrupt, and they, the Ochoa family, would be in worse financial difficulty than during the Depression.

T had to heed his own advice not to abandon the ship too soon and to agree with his grandfather's assessment that investors do more harm than good. Jane tried to comfort him with, "Don't worry, sweetheart. Even smart people make bad decisions," a comment that did little to heal his well-educated male pride.

Several years passed before Jane decided to open a second chain of shoe stores for women, La Chica Nueva, The New Girl, a store using the same business model as La Zapata Barata but one that sold more upscale shoes and apparel than La Zapata Barata. She decided to open a shoe store for men using the same model as La Zapata Barata called El Hombre, The Man. Business boomed at all three stores. They became known as *the shop for people who hate to shop*.

CHAPTER 57

One afternoon T called to tell Jane he was coming home and asked if he could bring a friend. "Bring whomever you want. We have lots of room," Jane said enthusiastically. Mothers have a sixth sense when it comes to a son's friends, and Jane was no exception. Thanks to the lessons she had learned from Mamita, she would be ready.

The next day she heard a car pull up in front of the house. Wearing a loose-fitting, yellow dress and a faded blue half-apron, she waited until the dust had settled before she opened the kitchen door and stepped out into the heat. She saw T appear from the back of the Suburban followed by a young woman wearing a straw hat with black hair sticking out around the edges. Jane rushed to T, kissed him on the cheek and said, "Welcome home, son." Then she extended her arms to the young woman who was standing nearby and said, "*Bienvenida! Bienvenida!*" She embraced her before T had a chance to say a word.

"Would you like a hot cup of coffee to wash down some of this dust?"

The young lady smiled and said, "Yes, Mrs. Ochoa. A cup of coffee would be nice."

Jane laughed and said, "Please call me, Jane."

"Oh, I couldn't. I haven't met you. At least not formally."

"I had this exact same conversation with T's grandmother too many years ago. I know how you feel, but this isn't New York. Now, we'll start over again. I'm Jane. What's your first name?"

"Justine. Justine Galasso."

"Justine," Jane said lovingly. "What a wonderful name. Starts with J, just like mine." She paused and added, "Reminds me of justice. A good thing to…"

"She's from da Bronx," T interjected.

"Oh?" Jane stopped short. "Da Bronx. What part?"

"Woodlawn."

Jane and Justine regaled each other with their Bronx accents and chatted about the places they knew in da Bronx while T poured the coffee. Jane interrupted her chat for a few moments to take things out of the oven and the refrigerator and place them on the kitchen table. When all was ready, she said a short prayer and crossed herself. They had a lovely lunch with lots of lively conversation. When they had finished, T reached over and took Justine's hand. "I have a confession to make to both of you."

"Uh-oh, Justine. This sounds dangerous," Jane teased.

"It isn't dangerous at all, Mother," T said gently. "I want you both to know that I have always wanted a girl from da Bronx, a girl just like my mom. It took me years to find her, but I finally have." He looked lovingly at Justine. "And she's sitting next to me right now." He put his index finger under her chin and kissed her softly on the lips.

CHAPTER 58

The last piece of Jane's original business plan was finally realized with the opening of two stores called La Mujer Elegante, The Elegant Woman, one on Manhattan's Fifth Avenue and the other on Rodeo Drive in Beverly Hills. The business model for this store was reminiscent of the small store Jane had visited so many years ago when she had bought the tight-fitting, black dress for the Trump-Tower-Twelve fiasco.

La Mujer Elegante, as its name suggested, was an elegant shopping experience that did not adhere to La Zapata Barata's formula of fast shopping. It was designed for the rich, elegant woman of leisure. When she entered the store, by appointment only, she was greeted by a uniformed doorman and taken to her own personal associate who escorted her to an exquisitely decorated, private showroom where she could view modeled garments or try them on if she wished. Each associate was properly trained so she could suggest for each client the appropriate matching garments, shoes, proper accessories, and cosmetics. Thus, the client could achieve the most glamorous fashion statement possible. In addition to showing garments, shoes, accessories, and cosmetics, the associate served each client wine, assorted fruits and cheeses along with exorbitant prices.

T married Justine, and they had a little girl they named Jessica. They lived happily in a fancy section of Manhattan in an un-fancy third floor walk up. Like Jane, Justine had a flair for business. She recognized a business opportunity when she saw one, and like T, wasn't afraid to take risks, a situation that brought concern to Jane until she realized she had done the same when she had come to New Mexico. She knew she had to remain silent as Justine and T outlined their latest business plan that sounded more than risky to her.

T and Justine reasoned if people watched business and sports on twenty-four-hour news channels, then they would watch traffic from cities around the world along with global weather accompanied with music and no on air talking heads to keep costs to a minimum. They planned to team up with a global weather service and use traffic cameras already in place from various cable and TV stations around the world. Justine explained it was always rush hour someplace in the world as well as bad weather so they'd have plenty of material to choose from twenty-four hours a day. "We're going to call it World-Wide Weather and Traffic. It'll be available on TV and the Internet with apps for cell phones. What do you think, Mama?" Justine had come to think of Jane as much her mother as her actual mother.

Jane laughed. "It all sounds terribly risky to me, but who am I to tell you about risky?" She lowered her head in thought. *World-Wide Weather and Traffic*, she repeated several times to herself. Then she raised her head and smiled. "Make it work, you two." She hugged them both. T and Justine hugged and kissed her.

"That's all we needed to hear. We'll do our best to make it a success for little Jessica and us," T said as he put his arm around Justine's waist and kissed her on the cheek.

C graduated from high school due more to the irresponsible educational policy of social promotion than a diploma based on knowledge and skills. A few months before he had been given the unearned diploma, he had applied to Hayverd where he knew he would be accepted. His parents warned him Hayverd might not accept him with such a poor high school record, but he assured them he would be accepted. He was right. Hayverd did accept him not because of his academic record but because of his family name with the stipulation that he had to maintain at least a C average to continue to the next semester. His parents warned him that it might not be an easy task since he had no study skills or work ethic not to mention knowledge, but he assured them it was "a piece of cake" he never ate because he failed every course the first semester and returned home.

Failure made him angry and bitter. "Hayverd is a stupid university," he fumed. "The professors are stupid. None of them understood me. I'm smarter than all of them put together. The students are stupid. They hated me. Everybody was against me. Now you know why I failed. It wasn't me. It was Hayverd." He slammed his hand down on the countertop and shouted, "I don't need no stupid university. I'll show 'em. Some day I'll be president of that pile of bricks. That'll show 'em they made a mistake, one huge mistake. I'll make 'em pay, every last one of 'em." He stomped out of the house and sped away but not before spraying it with sand and loose gravel from spinning tires.

To Jane's delight, La Mujer Elegante was a tremendous success. She opened additional boutiques in London, Paris, Rome, Hong Kong, Tokyo, San Francisco, Chicago, Miami Beach, and Rio.

Each became a travel destination for the rich and famous. Much to her surprise, T and Justine's World-Wide Weather and Traffic network became an international success. *Who would have thought watching traffic and weather could become an addiction*, Jane thought to herself, but in her case, it had happened as it had with millions of other people.

Jane had always thought global warming was a lot of hot air, but the more she watched World-Wide Weather the more she realized the mere thought we humans could change the temperature of the planet by driving a car or flicking a light switch was beyond stupidity. *Another example of man's arrogance and Hayverd nincompoops trying to steal our money with huge tax increases in the guise of saving the planet,"* she mused.

One afternoon while Jane was analyzing buying trends and sales figures for La Mujer Elegante on her laptop at the kitchen table, she heard a truck pull up outside the house. The kitchen door banged open. C slammed it shut behind him. He paced the floor for a few moments and exploded. "Do you know what those greedy capitalist bankers have done to me, me?" he screamed. Jane sat quietly, staring at the computer screen.

"Do you?" he repeated over and over to get Jane's attention.

She hoped her tranquility would settle him, but when it became obvious he wasn't going to stop until she answered, she looked up at him, took off her glasses, rubbed her eyes, and asked in a tired voice, "What's happened, my dearest son, to make you so upset?"

"They denied me a loan. Me! I only asked for a measly million. They wouldn't listen to reason. I can't get over how stupid and greedy all bankers are. They suck the blood out..."

"They're not stupid and they're not greedy," Jane interrupted him in a tired voice. She turned back to the laptop and resumed her work, hoping this would calm him.

"That's right. Take their side. I should've expected that from you because you're just like them, a greedy, bloodsucking capitalist. In fact, you're a whole lot worse. Whatchadoin' on that laptop? Countin' all the fifties and hundreds you've sucked out of working people's pocketbooks. That makes you a bigger bloodsucker than any banker. I wish my father had never married you. I wish Juanita Sanchez had been my mother and not you, you ugly bitch."

Even though her back was to him, he saw her flinch. He knew he'd hit a nerve. "That's right. An ugly bitch. You shoulda stayed in da Bronx where you belonged. Wanna know somethin' else? I wish I'd never been born into this family of hypocrites. I don't dare tell my friends my real last name. They'd laugh me out of existence. I tell 'em my name is Sanchez. That name has street cred. That's a name people respect because its power, real power, power to the people to overturn greedy capitalists like you and the bankers, power so that people can live without fear knowing a compassionate government will take care of them.

"If my friends knew my grandfather, the biggest, filthiest capitalist of them all, was the one shootin' his mouth off about capitalism and democracy all over the world they'd blackball me for sure. They would…"

Jane shoved back her chair. She turned and faced him. Her voice shook with anger. "You can say what you want about bankers and me, but don't you ever use that foul mouth of yours to besmirch your grandfather and all he's done not just for this family but for millions of people all over the world. That I won't tolerate for one New York minute. Apologize this minute."

"I won't apologize for saying the truth. The Ochoas are nothing but a gang of greedy, filthy capitalists sucking the blood out of other people so they can live…"

"This is your last chance to apologize. It's now or never," Jane screamed at him.

"I'll never apologize to the likes of you, him, or anyone else," he screamed back at her.

"Then you are no longer welcome in this house until you apologize to every member of this family. What you have said is intolerable and inexcusable. Now get out and stay out until you apologize."

C slammed his fist down on the table next to her laptop. She heard him sob, and watched him run to the kitchen door, open it, and slam it so hard the glass shattered.

Jane knew this was one wound time would never heal.

CHAPTER 59

Both Papito and Mamita were well passed their eightieth year. They had visited every country in the world more than once, met with every dictator, king, queen, prime minister, and president the world had to offer. They had eaten exotic foods and danced to various rhythms hundreds of nights. Now they were tired. They wanted to come back to the little house, to be with those they loved, and to lead a quiet life until their end time came. Papito announced his retirement as business ambassador to the president who reluctantly accepted his letter of resignation.

Jane was sitting at the kitchen table analyzing production costs for 2Dayz when the phone rang. She hoped each time the phone rang it would be C asking for permission to come home. She missed him, her first born. Oh, how she missed him. She had many regrets in life, but this was the most painful. *I shouldn't have angered him. I should've been gentler. I shouldn't have lost my temper. I shouldn't have asked him to leave.* She blamed herself a thousand times for the breach between them. Oh how she wished he would call. She would set things right.

She picked up the phone in hopes of hearing his familiar voice. It was a female voice, dashing her hopes. "Hello?"

"Yes," Jane said in a bored voice.

"Mrs. Ochoa?"

"Yes, yes, it is I," she continued in the same bored tone.

"This is Heather Thompson calling."

"Yes, Miss Thompson. What can I do for you?" Jane heard laughter.

"This is Heather Thompson, President of the United States."

"Okay, Sandi, you've had your little joke! I've got lots to do so what's up?"

"No kidding, Mrs. Ochoa, this is the President of the United States."

"And I'm Margaret Thatcher."

"Mrs. Ochoa, this really is the President."

"Sandi, this is my private cell number. I hardly think the President of the United States would have my private number."

"She would if I gave it to her."

Jane jumped out of the chair. "Solanch, is that you?" she asked in disbelief.

"Yes. I'm standing in the Oval Office next to President Thompson."

"Oh, no! You must be kidding!" Jane ran her fingers through her hair. "She must think I'm a total idiot."

"I think no such thing, Mrs. Ochoa. I've asked your husband to be my business ambassador to continue his father's work. As you already know, this will mean lots of travel."

"Yes, of course, Madame President."

"I must tell you he has accepted the position, but only on the proviso that you serve with him."

"I…I…" Jane stammered.

"Just say yes, *Querida*."

"Yes, Madame President. I will be proud to serve you and the country."

"But there's something else I want you to do that's equally as important. I want you to consult on a regular basis with the Secretary of Education, Ed Myerson. We've got to get this education mess under control, and I think you're the right person to do it. Before you answer, let me warn you. These two positions mean a lot of responsibility. With this in mind, are you willing to serve in these capacities?"

"Yes," Jane said breathlessly. She realized this was her second chance to have an impact on a profession she respected and the people she loved, students and teachers. She wasn't going to let this opportunity slip away, not by a long shot.

Solancha accomplished all she had set out to do. She graduated from high school with a B plus average along with being an excellent field hockey forward. She had been popular with the other students because she had a wonderful zest for life. She almost always had a smile on her face that brought smiles to others. She regaled her friends with funny stories and impersonations. When they encouraged her to make comedy her career, she told them she had much more important work to do than to be a comedienne.

Because of the many hours spent playing field hockey, she had a *killer body* as many a young man could attest. She wasn't ravishingly beautiful. She didn't have to be. Her kindred spirit and her killer body won her friends easily and stole the hearts of many young men whose sole desire was to possess her, but she was much too busy studying and playing field hockey to pay them any attention.

After high school, she attended The University of New Mexico and repeated her high school successes in both academics and athletics. She graduated fifth in her class, went on to the Fuego School of Global Management in Albuquerque where she studied global finance. She knew the fate and future of GO rested entirely on her shoulders since C had never returned home and T had his own business interests. She was determined to be prepared.

CHAPTER 60

"I don't know what all the fuss is about, fancy hairdo, fancy dress. You've got me dressed to the nines. It's only my birthday. You'd think with all this pampering I was meeting every king and queen in the world tonight."

"You're only sixty-five once, Mrs. Ochoa. It's another one of those little milestones in life that must be celebrated. It's like graduation from kindergarten."

"Now you are talking ancient history." Jane sighed. "I wish I didn't have to attend this dinner. I'd much rather celebrate at the little house with my husband, Solancha, and…" She stopped mid-sentence. A sudden, uncontrollable sob welled up in her throat. Her eyes misted.

"Are you all right, Mrs. Ochoa?"

"Yes, Anne. I'm sorry. I didn't mean to frighten you. I just had a thought that upset me, that's all." Once Jane had regained her composure, she said, "I don't want my mascara to run now, do I. No more bad thoughts." She smiled at Anne and squeezed her hand to reassure her everything was all right, but everything wasn't all right. She thought her intense love for C would have diminished over time. It hadn't. He was her firstborn. Nothing could change that. Nothing he could say or do would change her love for him. A mother's love is never lost. His anger, his sob remained fresh in her mind and went with her wherever she went.

She knew she mustn't dwell on C tonight of all nights because this was to be a happy night. She thought about the dictators, kings, queens, prime ministers, and presidents of the various nations she had met. She had been to every country in the world at least once and many more than once. *Who da thunk it? Me, Jane Jones from da Bronx, New Yawk, the President's Assistant Business Ambassador to the world. Me, Consultant to the Secretary of Education. Me, plain Jane Jones. A nobody.* She shook her head in disbelief that not only had she met world leaders, but she'd dined, danced, and talked with them on any number of sensitive topics. *The ironies of life*, she mused, yet for Jane, the biggest irony of them all was that she, the most "unfashionista" of the "unfashionistas", had become the leading fashion guru for celebrities, politicians, and women of wealth the world over. *Yes, who da thunk it, plain Jane Jones from Bronx, New York, a nobody, had become Jane Jones Ochoa, a somebody.*

Jane never realized and no one ever told her the reason for her success was her plainness. Dictators, kings, prime ministers, and presidents felt comfortable in her presence because she didn't intimidate them with dazzling beauty that so often makes men's heads swim in circles and render them babbling idiots or cause queens to be jealous of her physical beauty. Instead, she had affable qualities of charm and sincerity that won the friendship and respect of all who met her, but the most important aspects of her personality were her intelligence and wit. She was able to discuss in depth and at length economic, political, and religious issues that caused concern to those who engaged her in such conversations. Her wonderful sense of humor smoothed over many delicate situations and paved the way for agreements that would never have been possible otherwise. For these reasons, she was a favorite with heads of state who demanded she sit to their immediate right at important state dinners.

"I wish I could be at home tonight with my family, huddled together on the sofa watching one of T's cable channels," she said more to herself than Anne. Her thoughts focused on the sofa, that raggedy ole sofa that had seen so much history, her six nights of stimulating talks with Solanch, her argument with Mamita when she had nearly left, Solanch proposing to her, plus all the other wonderful nights shared together talking and watching TV. "So much history."

As Anne placed the tiara on Jane's head, she protested. "Now really, Anne. A tiara? Don't you think that's a little over the top. It's just a birthday party."

"You see queens all the time, Miss Jane. Now it's your turn to be a queen, if only for a night."

Jane smiled. "Oh, all right. You win. I'll wear the tiara and not fuss, but I still say it's over the top."

There was a knock at the door. Anne opened it. Jane couldn't see who it was but heard a male voice say softly, "They're ready for Mrs. Ochoa."

Jane entered the conference hall that had been decorated to within an inch of its life with all types of birthday paraphernalia celebrating her sixty-fifth birthday. She had to admit it was a tremendous sight to see so many people in front of her standing at the many beautifully decorated tables as she strode to her place on the dais to thunderous applause. Once she was seated, everyone in the room sat down. The orchestra struck up a tune that had been popular during one of Jane's sixty-five years. A smartly dressed cadre of wait staff served dinner, a sumptuous meal that could only have been created by Pepe and his talented staff.

When everyone had finished their dinners and the last dish had been removed from the tables, Solanch strode to the podium.

He looked lovingly at Jane, then at the audience in front of him, and began. "Good evening, ladies and gentlemen. We have gathered this evening to celebrate the birthday of one of the most extraordinary, magnificent women I have ever had the pleasure to meet in my life, my wife. I want you all to know that it took me many years to win her over, the most difficult years of my life, and it nearly cost me my life, but after many twists and turns, I was lucky enough for her to finally accept my proposal of marriage. I have never been happier than to share my life with this woman I secretly call my Iron Lady" he paused, "along with other names I have for her." The crowd giggled as Jane faked a frown.

"I call her my Iron Lady because she is a lady with a thousand ideas and the cast iron conviction, courage, and willpower to carry them out. She's the lady who has created jobs for thousands of people throughout the nation and the world. Some of her ideas, I must admit, sounded pretty crazy at the time such as creating a computerized restaurant that served only one entrée for lunch and another for dinner with no substitutions, puh-leeze," he drew out the word "puh-leeze", "or not allowing women to try on shoes in a computerized shoe store. Now those ideas take courage, yet she had the conviction that her business models were the right ones.

"Yes, she's a lady of courage who faces problems like these and resolves them in a most efficacious manner. This wonderful willpower of hers has given me the strength and courage to face life's many tempests. Without her, and I do not exaggerate when I say this Ladies and Gentlemen, I would have been a ship without a rudder lost in those tempests. She is a lady whom I'm not only proud to call my wife, the mother of my children, my best friend, confidant, and business advisor, but." He stopped, looked intently at podium in front of him, then in a quavering voice added, "She means much more to me than all those wonderful things. She is..." He struggled to form the words. "She is my heart." Tears filled his eyes. "My soul. She is..." He stood silent for many moments before he was able to whisper, "my everything." Tears filled the eyes of many in the audience as Solanch unabashedly wiped tears from his eyes with a handkerchief.

Once he had regained his composure, he added, "Good thing my wife insists I carry a handkerchief," a comment that brought laughter and applause from the audience. He continued his tribute, finishing with "since it isn't polite to mention a lady's age, I promise I won't, except to say, Happy Birthday, *mi querida*, and to tell you, you'll always be my Naschita, my wise, little owl, whom I love with all my heart." He walked to where Jane was seated and kissed her on the lips to the sound of "ah's" and soft applause.

Once Solanch had finished his tribute, the orchestra struck up a tune that sounded familiar to Jane. She knew she'd heard it before but couldn't think where. The people seated at the tables moved to the side of the room while the wait staff with military precision moved the tables and chairs to provide a wide avenue down the middle of the room. A spotlight flooded the rear door of the conference hall. The doors opened. Men and women dressed in tuxedos and formal gowns walked down the broad avenue forming two rows on either side of it. When the last person had entered the hall, the doors closed. A standing microphone was placed on the floor in front of the dais. A portly, middle-aged man walked to the microphone while others lined up behind him.

"Good evening Miss J. I'm Waddell Stamford and standing before you is every student you ever taught at Pheasant Valley Middle School. We are all alive and one hundred twenty-three strong." He faded back into the line along the avenue as the next person came to the microphone.

"I'm Ashley Parsons. We know and understand how hard you worked for us, and although we all hate to admit it, in those our middle school days, not many of us worked very hard for you or ourselves."

"I'm Chris Whittaker. So we thought we'd take this opportunity on your sixty-fifth birthday to let you know how your efforts turned out."

"I'm Ramón Miraflores. Mi English is mucho, much better theez days. I work very hard to make it better, thanks to you Miss J. You helped me, and everyone standing behind me and beside me."

"I'm Timmy Randall. It's like Waddell said. We are one hundred twenty-three, and just in case you ever wondered, here's what we've become. Forty-three of us are moms doing all the stuff moms do. Eight of us are househusbands doing the same stuff as the moms. Two of us are doctors. One of us is a lawyer. One of us is mayor of a town. Six of us are teachers from kindergarten through high school. Eight of us are teacher aides. One of us is a university professor. Four of us are nurses. Nine of us are paramedics. Thirteen of us own our businesses. Six of us are plumbers. Eight of us are electricians. Twelve of us have military careers. None of us is a general. Sorry about that Miss J." Everyone laughed. "And finally one of us is a millionaire, but we won't tell you which one of us it is. It's our little secret." He looked at Jane and smiled that same wicked little smile he'd had in middle school. "I hope all that adds up to one hundred twenty-three, but you know as well as I do Miss J, I wasn't so good at math, even though I am a math teacher at Pheasant Valley High School." Laughter filled the room.

"I'm Marcia Henley. The Depression affected all of us deeply, Miss J. We have talked amongst us, and we all agree. Thanks to you, your great teaching, your patience, and your no-nonsense approach to life taught us what we needed to survive those difficult days."

"I'm Maria LaCosta. You did more than teach us English and Math. You taught us responsibility to ourselves, to our families, and to our country. Lessons none of us ever forgot. All of us owe you a tremendous debt of gratitude."

A tall, bald man came to the microphone. "I'm Lamont Jackson and," he stopped for a moment and was joined by a woman, "and this is my wife, Wanda. I want you to know she still hasn't forgiven me for calling her a retard."

"No I haven't, and don't you ever call me that again." Wanda flashed an angry face at him. Everyone laughed.

"Well, as they say, Miss J, what goes round comes round. Wanda and I have three sons, and they're all worse than I ever was. They drive Wanda and me nuts, but we sure do love 'em just as you loved us. Oh, by the way, before I forget, I'm the one who's the mayor, Mayor of Port City, California."

Jane clasped her hands to her mouth and laughed between the tears as yet another speaker came to the microphone.

"I'm José Garcia Lopez. You may not remember the day I stood on a desk and said I was the Statue of Liberty, Miss J, but I remember it well."

Jane nodded her head she remembered.

He smiled a bright, broad smile, pleased she remembered. "That one day made a big difference in my life. That was the day I decided when I was old enough I would join the Marines. When I graduated high school, I joined the Marine Corps and became a Captain. I am very proud of this country and the Marines Corps. Thank you, Miss J. You made a huge difference in my life."

Quiet descended upon the huge conference hall in honor of a man who had given service to the country and everyone stood at attention until he returned to his place in line. When he had done so, another speaker came to the microphone.

"I'm Alex Rodriguez. Remember how I loved the sound of the pencil sharpener, and how I smeared my face and shirt with the lead filings? Well, after high school, I got to thinking about that day in your class, and I decided to do something about it.

THE IRONIES OF LIFE

I became an inventor and invented not only the silent pencil sharpener but also a pencil sharpener that has no shavings so no student will ever bother a teacher again with noise or dirty shavings. Maybe you've heard of my company, No Fuss No Muss pencil sharpeners. I'm sure you've guessed by now. I'm the millionaire." Everyone laughed and applauded.

"I'm Chris Perkins. You have always lived in our hearts, Miss J. We are proud of you, and we hope you are proud of us. You are our most beloved Queen. And on this your sixty-fifth birthday, we all want to say," there was a pause as trumpets sounded a royal tribute, then everyone shouted, "Long live our Queen!" The orchestra struck up the tune that Jane had vaguely remembered. Then it came to her as her former students sang the Pheasant Valley High School alma mater.

Drums rolled. Lights dimmed. The spotlight focused on the rear door. The doors opened. The orchestra struck up "Happy Birthday". A huge cake the shape of a black stiletto pump that stood six feet tall with "La Mujer Elegante" emblazoned along the sides and "Happy Birthday, Miss J" across the toe festooned with sixty five blazing candles appeared on a motorized cart with Pepe at the controls.

After the singing of "Happy Birthday", Jane came down from the dais. She asked those gathered around her to help blow out the candles, which they willingly did. Someone announced coffee and cake would be served in the next room. Once the cake had disappeared, Jane's students surrounded her. She held their hands and kissed their cheeks. The party lasted well into the wee hours of the morning for no one wanted to leave this most memorable of nights. They wanted to be with their Queen, and she with them.

CHAPTER 61

"Mrs. Ochoa?" the voice on the phone sounded somber.

"Yes, this is she," Jane answered.

"This is John Hamilton, Ambassador to Bolivia. I believe we met several years ago at a conference in Miami."

"Yes, Ambassador Hamilton. Your name is familiar to me." Jane was used to these types of calls. She received several each day from various parts of the world concerning any number of topics.

"Good. That makes my task a bit easier."

Jane waited a few moments and asked, "What is your task, Mister Ambassador?"

"I'm sorry, Mrs. Ochoa. I have bad news for you."

"Yes," Jane said nonchalantly, rearranging papers on the kitchen table wondering what kind of bad news he had to tell her. As the president's assistant business ambassador, she was used to hearing bad news.

The ambassador hesitated and said, "Unfortunately, Mrs. Ochoa, there's no easy way to tell you this, so I'll tell you straight out."

"Yes, Mister Ambassador. I would appreciate that very much."

"As the American Ambassador to Bolivia, it is my official duty to inform you that your son, Solanch the Fourth Ochoa, died this morning."

Jane gasped for breath. A sudden pain squeezed her heart. She grasped the side of the kitchen table to steady herself.

Ambassador Hamilton heard her gasp. He waited what seemed like an interminable amount of time before he spoke. "I'm terribly sorry I had to be the one to inform you, Mrs. Ochoa." He paused. "I know this is a terrible shock." He paused again. "My deepest condolences to you and your family."

Jane didn't say a word. Finally she was able to utter, "Thank you, Ambassador Hamilton. I apologize for what just happened."

"No apologies needed, Mrs. Ochoa. I understand."

"What happened?"

"Maybe we should discuss this in a few days after you've had time…"

"Thank you, Ambassador Hamilton," Jane interrupted, "but I want to know how my son died."

"He was alone driving his truck on a road the Bolivians call the Death Road. Are you certain you want me to continue?"

"Yes, Mister Ambassador. I'm certain. I need to know as much as you can tell me."

"The Death Road is one of the most treacherous roads in the world with many blind curves. It's an unpaved, one lane road in the Andes. This morning was foggy. Visibility was zero and the mud road slippery." He stopped to give Jane a chance to digest what he had told her. When she didn't answer, he continued.

"Your son rounded a curve, slid off the road and into a deep chasm."

"How deep of a chasm?"

"I don't think that's important for you to know, Mrs. Ochoa."

"How deep is the chasm?"

"The Bolivian Police inform me the accident occurred in one of the remotest areas of Andes. They doubt if they can retrieve the body."

Jane gripped the edge of the table as hard as she could. With great effort said, "I know this hasn't been easy for you, Ambassador Hamilton. Please call if you have any additional information."

"Yes, I will, Mrs. Ochoa."

"Good-bye, Mister Ambassador." She flipped the cell shut, put her head down on the table and sobbed uncontrollably. She couldn't believe she would never see her beloved son again, that she would never have the chance to heal the breach between them, and that death would separate them forever. This, the worst of all regrets, she would take to her end time.

CHAPTER 62

After a long period of sadness, Jane said, "We have mourned C long enough. We must celebrate life," and so the Ochoas did. Laughter returned to the little house, and they lived happily for many wonderful, successful years.

Mamita celebrated her one hundredth birthday with a huge party in the conference hall reminiscent of Jane's sixty-fifth. A few months later, they held a second party when Papito turned one hundred. These were the glorious, happy days, but glorious, happy days like all good things must come to an end, and so they did for the Ochoas. Mamita was the first to leave at one hundred three. Jane and Solanch knew Papito wouldn't be far behind. They were right. Several months later he joined his beloved Mamita.

Jane and Solanch retired from their government as well as business responsibilities. They enjoyed their retirement in the little house. They entertained their twelve grandchildren, eight great grandchildren, and three great, great grandchildren at The Big House as often as they could.

Jane marveled at Justine who not only managed to have ten children but along with T managed a number of highly successful cable networks. Solancha had managed GO just as successfully and found time to have two sons.

The years slipped away, and so did Solanch at the age of one hundred fourteen. Although surrounded by loving family members and adoring employees who took excellent care of her, Jane found herself alone once again. At night, her bed was cold and empty. Oh, how she missed her *querido*.

She was one hundred seventeen. She knew she wouldn't see her one hundred eighteenth birthday. She didn't mind. She knew it was time to go. She was ready to join her maker.

She sat in the rocking chair, the same one she and Mamita had rocked Little Solanch back to health in. With the little strength she had left, she managed to push the chair back enough to make it creak. She smiled at the sound. It brought back so many memories. She closed her eyes. She looked as if she was asleep with her head bowed on her chest, but she was anything but asleep. Her active mind like a short-circuited electric wire flashed scenes reminiscent of events long since past. Occasionally she would jerk back in the chair and raise her head a little as if she was waking, but she wasn't waking. She was laughing, an invisible, internal laugh, when the images amused her, and when the images brought back sad or unpleasant memories, an expression of sadness lay upon her face.

She sat quietly in the chair as she recalled her sixty-fifth birthday party. She could hear Solanch's tribute to her, one that had moved her to tears. She could hear the orchestra playing some indistinct tune. She could see the spotlight focused on the rear conference door and all her students streaming through it. She could see their shining faces clearly as if the party had been yesterday. She could feel their warm hands in hers. What a glorious night that had been. A night she would never forget. The chair moved back and forth several times as she laughed at all the humorous stories they had told her.

The chair didn't move for a long time, but when it did, it jerked with two creaks as Jane's fading brain flashed a picture of a bloated Juanita Sanchez trying to look thin and sexy in a dress that was much too short and tight. The world's wealthiest woman had ended up in a mental institution where she died a penniless, raving maniac. *Serves her right,* Jane thought, unrepentant at such an uncharitable thought.

The chair stopped creaking as she thought of all the changes she had brought to the once broken educational system, a system no longer built on the psycho babbles of self-esteem, self-glorification, and meaningless activities of past decades that had passed for education, but based on strict academic principles that demanded students become scholars instead of boorish, out-of-control ruffians. She was proud she had been a part in restoring the American educational system to its position as the preeminent educational system in the world, yet she saw signs of backsliding as various interest groups rebelled against this policy or that, striving with all their might to break a well-organized, successful educational system. She knew in time all her work would be undone by secular, socialist nitwits.

The chair remained still as the image of C's body at the bottom of the chasm, broken and bloodied, took hold of her mind. She tried to reach out to hold him in her arms, to tousle his hair and kiss him as she had done so many times when he was a little boy. Oh how she loved him as she tried to reach out across the depths of time, but just when she thought she had found him, he slipped away into nothingness. Her faith they would be reunited in heaven comforted her.

The chair remained still as the word *hope* for some reason stuck in her brain and wouldn't let go. For nearly eighty years, her life had been based on hope. Hope her children would be born healthy, hope her business ventures would succeed, hope the Depression would end, hope the future rebuilt on democracy and capitalism would be better than the past, but that's all she had for the future was hope. She saw the same forces building that had once before destroyed all she held dear.

She had seen its beginnings with C. *Young people,* she sighed to herself, *are always certain they have all the answers. Well, they'll have to learn the hard way. Socialism isn't the answer.*

She could understand the temptations of socialism. She too had once wanted a protected, uncomplicated, risk free life. She had had it for nearly forty years, and it had bored the daylights out of her. She had had no interests, no zest for life. She had welcomed death at an early age to put her out of her misery. She had nearly wasted her life as she trudged through one meaningless day after another, but the complicated life, a life full of risks, and unforeseen twists and turns that capitalism offered had evaporated in an instant any desire for an early death, replaced by a desire to live as long as she could, to see if her hopes and dreams came to fruition, and to see her children, grandchildren, great grandchildren, and great, great grandchildren grow and succeed as she had.

Yes. The signs were all there, arrogance, complacency, run-away prosperity all of which allowed cultures of corruption to develop. Yes. Bad times most certainly were ahead. She knew there was nothing she could do about it. She had fought the good fight to preserve all she held dear, but she knew the socialists, the communists, or some other "ist" or "ism" would in time try to destroy all the things that meant so much to her. Her only hope was her grandchildren would be strong enough to stand up against these forces and defeat them. Yes. It was time for her to go.

She felt a soft hand on her shoulder. Someone placed a blanket over her. She heard a noise by her ear and felt a kiss on her cheek. Inwardly she smiled. She heard the voices of children playing. She heard a, "Shhhh," and the children quieted. Oh, how she wished the children hadn't quieted. She wanted to hear them laugh and squeal their childish squeals as they ran about the house. She wanted to hear their sweet, innocent voices, voices that gave her so much joy, for they were the voices of the future. She wanted to hear them one last time.

The chair remained still as images of C's broken body flashed before her eyes along with the sights and sounds of Solanch walking across the parking lot in his tight fitting jeans, his high heeled boots clicking on the pavement, his hat tucked down over his eyes, and that sexy walk of his flashed through her brain. *Oh, that sexy walk of his.* Flashing images of C and Solanch appeared and faded at a dizzying rate. The chair creaked. She grasped its arms to steady herself. The flashes stopped. One image became clear. Her dearly beloved Solanch with his hat pulled down rakishly over his forehead. The chair stopped. Her hands slipped off its arms. She sighed one last sigh and saw no more.